WHAT THE WALLS KNOW

WHAT THE WALLS KNOW

A Lizzie Crane Mystery

Skye Alexander

First published by Level Best Books/Historia 2022

This novel is entirely a work of fiction. The names, characters and incidents portrayed in it are the work of the author's imagination. Any resemblance to actual persons, living or dead, events or localities is entirely coincidental.

Skye Alexander asserts the moral right to be identified as the author of this work.

Author Photo Credit: Anne Schneider

First edition

ISBN: 978-1-68512-186-0

This book was professionally typeset on Reedsy.
Find out more at reedsy.com

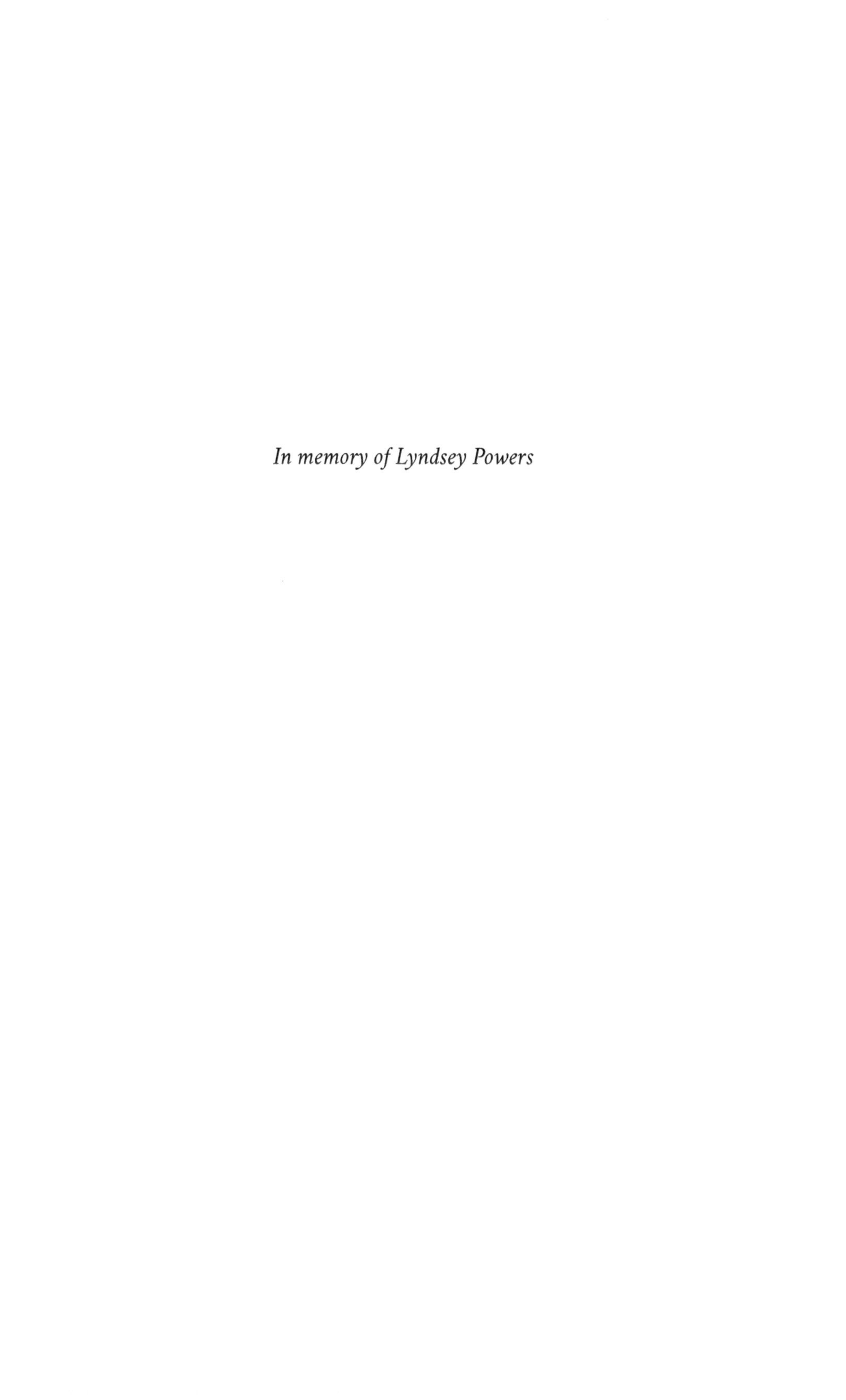

In memory of Lyndsey Powers

Praise for the Lizzie Crane Mysteries

"Set in the Prohibition era…it's filled with plot twists, intriguing characters, and snappy dialogue…Rich with juicy historical details—especially the motorcars!—and surprising turns, this book should appeal to fans of Agatha Christie and Dorothy Sayers."—The Historical Novel Society's Historical Novels Review

"Lizzie Crane and the New York City-based Troubadours are back on the road in Massachusetts, this time hired to provide entertainment for the fiftieth birthday celebration of Duncan Fox, the owner of a creepy rockpile called Halcyon Castle. Of course, the musicians are no sooner settled into their rooms when a murder is discovered, drawing the self-styled amateur detective Lizzie into an unofficial investigation that brings her and her band mates into a world of séances, fortune-telling, secret passages, disembodied voices, ancient animosities, and, for Lizzie, a re-connection with an old heartthrob. In *What the Walls Know*, author Skye Alexander takes her readers on an exhilarating ride that will keep them turning the pages all the way to the exciting and altogether unexpected climax. This is a great read, filled from beginning to end with accurate historical references, and unforgettable characters."—Gregory Stout, author of *Lost Little Girl* and *Gideon's Ghost*

"The Golden Age of Mystery is alive and well in *What the Walls Know*, the second of Skye Alexander's clever and charming Lizzie Crane novels. Set in 1925, in the ironically named Halcyon Castle, the author brings together an eclectic group of characters in the tradition of great British mysteries. Bootleg alcohol, illegal drugs, and period-perfect details about that era's craze for all things occult are seamlessly woven into the story. Agatha

Christie fans: You've found your next great read."—Lori Robbins, author of the On Pointe and Master Class mystery series

"A delightful mix of mystery, romance, and the Roaring Twenties set against the background of coastal New England during Prohibition. In actress and singer Lizzie Crane, Alexander has created a refreshing heroine, whose charm and keen understanding of human nature make her an amateur sleuth to watch. Highly recommended."—Paula Munier, USA Today bestselling author of the Mercy Carr series

"Skye Alexander … vividly recreates the Roarin' 20s through her depiction of the architecture, fashion, literature, and language. She's also created a smart and sassy heroine in Lizzie Crane with a supporting cast that's the 'bee's knees'."—Kevin Kleusner, author of *The Killer Sermon*

"Alexander brings the period to life with a twisting tale of murder and mayhem that will satisfy any fan of historical mystery."—Edith Maxwell, Agatha-winning author of the Quaker Midwife Mysteries

"Alexander's protagonist, Lizzie Crane, is a ball of fire. You'll love her talent, her courage, and her clothes."—Kate Flora, award-winning author of *A World of Deceit*

"A castle set on a peninsula with guests gathered to celebrate the host's birthday is the perfect setting for murder and performances by jazz singer Lizzie Crane and her band. Alexander makes good use of the fads and fashions of the 1920s while giving the reader an intimate look into a real castle with Gothic furniture, stone halls, and secret passages in this richly imaged and well-paced mystery."—Susan Oleksiw, author of *Below the Tree Line*

Chapter One

October 1925, Gloucester, Massachusetts

"Seek patiently, slowly, perseveringly, the truth that may be concealed in the night."

— *W. Somerset Maugham, The Magician*

"Are you sure Dracula doesn't live here?" Melody asked as they approached Halcyon Castle. The pretty blond musician peered nervously out the window of Sidney's Buick, like a child watching a horror movie through her fingers.

"Don't be a silly goose," Lizzie chided her nineteen-year-old friend. "That's just stuff and nonsense, designed to keep you awake all night. Bram Stoker has made a bundle scaring girls like you with his wicked tales."

But she had to admit the Gothic Revival castle, perched on a rocky bluff overlooking the ocean, exuded doom and gloom. The estate sat on an isolated promontory that jutted into the north Atlantic, with only a single, winding driveway leading in and out. Two ferocious-looking metal dragons guarded the entry gate. The chilly drizzle and drifting fog made the place seem even more eerie. Lizzie stared up at the castle's turrets with their slit-like windows, while thoughts of Anne Boleyn and other imprisoned ladies rose in her mind.

"I think it's exciting," said Bert, the young horn player who'd joined their group only a month ago, after the death of their previous saxophonist.

Melody hugged her arms across her chest and scrunched down in the backseat. "I think it's creepy."

"Well, I think it's quite dramatic and theatrical, don't you, Sidney?" Lizzie asked her longtime friend, who sat beside her, gripping the steering wheel as he assessed the situation.

"It's a job, and a high-paying one at that," he said flatly.

The dragon-guarded gate swung open to admit them. No sooner had they crossed through than it shut behind them with a loud clang. *How could the gate operate on its own like that?* Lizzie wondered. Despite her appreciation of drama, she felt apprehension rise in her chest. As Sidney shifted his prized 1925 Buick convertible into second gear, she realized they were cut off now from the mainland, trapped on the peninsula.

Beneath them, waves broke on the rocky neck. Sidney drove another fifty yards until he came to a moat of foaming seawater spanned by a narrow wooden bridge. Fog slithered around them, veiling the way. Cautiously, he inched across the wet planks into the castle's granite-paved parking area, where gas lamps struggled to cut through the thick evening mist.

Waving her hand dismissively, Lizzie said with more confidence than she felt, "Anyway, Stoker wrote all that Dracula stuff more than twenty-five years ago, and no one's produced a vampire yet. There's nothing to worry about, Mel."

"Well, I hope the weather improves soon," Bert said. "This is my first time in New England, and I want to see the scenery while I'm here."

Leaving the motorcar's engine running, Sidney grabbed his umbrella and stepped out into the drizzle. "Wait here while I find out what's what."

"I'm coming with you," Lizzie said. She pulled her cloche hat tight over her bobbed hair and turned up the collar of her rubber slicker.

They picked their way carefully across the slippery paving stones to a portico lit by a dim yellow lamp. Sidney grabbed a doorknocker shaped like a gargoyle and banged on an oak door studded with hand-cut iron nails, a sign of affluence in a long-ago day. After waiting a minute or so, he knocked again. This time a panel the size of a sheet of writing paper slid open behind a metal grate, and someone eyed them from within.

"Good evening. I'm Sidney Somerset, and this is Elizabeth Crane. We're with The Troubadours from New York City."

When the person behind the grate didn't respond, he said, "We're entertainers. Mr. Duncan Fox invited us here to perform for his guests this week."

The panel slammed shut.

They waited a bit longer, then Sidney hammered on the door again.

"Do you think we're in the wrong place?" Lizzie asked.

"There couldn't possibly be two places like this in Gloucester, Massachusetts. But it *is* rather odd. I telephoned Mr. Fox yesterday to let him know when to expect us."

"Well, no sense standing out here in the damp." She brushed at the wet sleeves of her raincoat and turned to go back to the auto.

Just then, the door creaked open on its iron hinges. A man with frazzled gray hair, a cardigan sweater buttoned haphazardly over his ample belly, stood staring out at them with intense dark eyes. A crimson scarf circled his neck, and wire-rimmed spectacles perched on his nose. As he stepped back to let them enter, a broad smile lit up his face.

"*Entrez-vous,*" he said heartily and held out his hand. "I'm Duncan Fox, your delighted host. So good of you to come. You must forgive my sister's manners. Frances is the skeptical sort. Doesn't trust anyone, not even me."

The only illumination in the shadowy entrance hall came from lanterns mounted on tall, black posts, like streetlamps out of a Dickens novel. High-backed oak choir stalls lined the stone walls on both sides of the hallway. The floor and vaulted ceiling were made of stone too. Lizzie felt as though she'd entered a crypt, and a chill ran up her spine.

Sidney grasped Fox's soft, fleshy hand, then introduced himself and Lizzie. "Good of you to invite us."

Their host turned to Lizzie and bowed from the waist with an air of gallantry, one hand held behind his back and the other across his protuberant stomach. "Welcome, dear lady."

She smiled at the formality. "Thank you, Mr. Fox."

"Please call me Duncan. We're all on a first-name basis here. Despite my home's Old World ambiance, we're very modern. Now, what about your mates? Have you left them outside in the rain?"

"They're waiting in my motorcar," Sidney said. "We wanted to make certain we'd come to the right place."

"Well, you must bring them in straight away. We'll have a spot of tea to chase the cold." He pressed a button on the wall. "Now, Sidney, be a good chap and go fetch the rest of your troupe while I introduce this lovely lady to my friends."

Duncan helped Lizzie slip off her raincoat and hung it on a wooden hall tree while she removed her damp hat and shook out her coffee-colored hair. Then he crooked his elbow and offered her his arm. After guiding her down the dimly lit hallway, he steered her into a spacious parlor furnished with several sofas upholstered in dark red velvet and a dozen or so leather armchairs. The wallpaper depicted pastoral scenes. Floral broadloom carpets lay on a wooden floor. A welcome fire crackled in the fireplace.

Men and women sat at tables, playing cards. Duncan clapped his hands twice. The men and women looked up from their games and turned their attention toward him.

"Dear ones," he said, "please welcome Lizzie Crane. She and her colleagues are musicians who've driven all the way from New York City in this dreadful weather. They're going to entertain us this week and celebrate my fiftieth birthday."

A woman with long, unnaturally blue-black hair and unnaturally red lips called out, "Halloo, there!" A flowered caftan covered her zoftig figure like a colorful tent. Around her neck hung a beaded pouch festooned with feathers that reminded Lizzie of Indian fetishes she'd seen in the Museum of Natural History. "I'm Ophelia Wraith, Duncan's oldest and dearest friend. We've known each other since we were children. Whoops, there I go, revealing my age. Forget I said that." She laughed heartily, her plump cheeks flushing beneath her face paint. As she eyed Lizzie, her expression suddenly grew serious. "You've been through a difficult time lately. Did someone close to you die recently?"

Startled, Lizzie nodded. "Yes, the former saxophonist in our group. He was killed two months ago."

"He wants you to know that he's fine—and he thinks the young man you've chosen is a splendid replacement."

"Well, that's good to know," Lizzie said, trying to make light of the woman's odd revelation. *How could she possibly know about Henry's death?*

Ophelia slapped her palm to her ample chest and rolled her eyes. "Oh, dear me, I shouldn't have said that. I have a bad habit of blurting out things I pick up from the Other Side. I keep forgetting that not everyone hears what I hear. I didn't mean to scare you. Can you ever forgive me?"

Before Lizzie could answer, Duncan Fox turned to greet a woman about his own age wearing tortoiseshell spectacles and a tweed suit. A tall, thin man who seemed almost pale enough to see through, accompanied her.

"Natalie, Greg," Duncan said. "How did you sneak in without me seeing you?"

"We made ourselves invisible and slipped through the walls," the pale man said, and for a moment, Lizzie thought he might be serious.

"Lizzie, may I introduce Natalie Talbot, my sister's longtime friend, and Natalie's husband, Gregory?"

As they exchanged greetings, footsteps clattered down the hall. Duncan turned toward the parlor's entrance, where a housemaid stood with Melody, Bert, and Sidney in tow.

"Oh, good, Inge, you've rounded everyone up," Duncan said, a cheery grin baring his large, crooked teeth. "Would you please bring more tea and another bottle of port for my guests? You know what Benjamin Franklin said, don't you? 'Wine is constant proof that God loves us and loves to see us happy.'" He waved in Lizzie's three companions. "Come, join us."

After a round of introductions—most of which Lizzie forgot—The Troubadours seated themselves on the red velvet sofas. The young serving girl, whose broad pink cheeks and blond braids echoed her German heritage, set a tray of sweets, a pot of tea, and a bottle of port complete with cellar dust on one of the room's many tables.

"May I?" Duncan asked Lizzie, holding the bottle poised over a crystal glass.

"Ab-so-lute-ly."

"Melody, my dear, may I serve you a splash of port?"

"Thank you, sir, but I'd rather have tea instead, if that's all right."

"A teetotaler, eh? Of course, you may have tea instead." He set down the bottle and poured tea into a dainty porcelain cup for her. "How about you, gentlemen?"

"Port for me," Sidney said enthusiastically, and Bert nodded in agreement.

While Lizzie sipped her port—very good port, too, she noted—she studied two women seated at a table near the fireplace. One, perhaps a decade older than Lizzie's twenty-six years, had finger-waved brown hair and wore a stylish plum-colored frock with a rope of pearls. She dealt cards for the other, whose close-cropped hair and square-shouldered suit—complete with trousers—gave her a mannish appearance.

"What game are those ladies playing?" she asked Duncan.

"It's not a game. Cora, the lady with the pearls, is doing a tarot reading for Helen."

"A tarot reading? What's that?"

"The tarot is an oracle rooted in the Renaissance. It can foretell the future or provide advice about the present."

Curious, Lizzie said, "How does it work?"

Duncan smiled. "I don't think anyone really knows, but a reading often reveals information a person wouldn't necessarily be privy to otherwise."

Lizzie stood and edged closer, trying to get a better look at the cards. Unlike an ordinary poker deck, the cards the woman named Cora had laid on the table were illustrated with colorful scenarios. "Do the pictures on the cards mean something, or are they just for decoration?"

"The symbolism is both universal and personal," Duncan said, maneuvering her away from the two women. "Come, it's intrusive to witness another person's reading. If you're interested, I'm sure Cora would be glad to do a reading for you while you're here."

A young male servant, hardly more than a boy, stirred the coals in the fireplace, sparking bright flames. At another table, the flamboyant Ophelia sat across from a petite chestnut-haired young woman whom Duncan had introduced as his daughter, Sabine. A wooden board decorated with the letters of the alphabet lay on the table between them. The two women placed their fingertips lightly on a heart-shaped planchette and sat very still. After a few moments, it began gliding effortlessly around the lettered board.

"What are they doing?" Lizzie asked.

"They're consulting a talking board. They ask questions, and the board spells out answers."

She watched as the planchette skated smoothly across the board's surface. "But surely, they're moving that little thingamajig to make it do what they want."

Before he could reply, however, the heart-shaped device homed in on the letter M and hovered there, quivering beneath the women's fingertips for several moments. Then, as if it had a mind of its own, the planchette spun around three times and whipped away, landing upside-down in the fireplace.

Duncan's daughter uttered a startled yelp.

"What in the world?" Ophelia said, clapping both hands to her chest.

Cora and Helen looked up from their card reading. Everyone stared at Ophelia, and then followed her gaze to the fireplace, where the flames consumed the planchette.

"It just flew out of my hands," Ophelia explained to her gawking companions.

The square-shouldered Helen frowned. "What did the board spell right before it went haywire?"

"I'd asked what we might expect to transpire while we're all gathered here for Duncan's birthday," Ophelia answered. "It spelled 'tonight' and then sat for a moment on the letter 'M.'"

"I bet it meant to spell magic," Helen said.

The others laughed—nervously, Lizzie thought—and nodded in agreement.

"Of course," Cora said, twisting her pearls. "That makes perfect sense."

"But now that Father's talking board is defunct, we'll never know," his daughter Sabine said.

"Don't worry, dear, I brought one with me." Ophelia reached across the table to pat the younger woman's hand. "Shall I fetch it from my luggage?"

Sabine shook her head. "No, I've had enough for one night."

"I think I'll turn in too. It's getting late," Natalie said.

Apparently, the talking board incident had disrupted the group's amiable mood, for the other guests decided unanimously to call it a night. After mouthing a few pleasantries, they retired to their bedchambers. Lizzie's three friends, who heretofore had watched the goings on without comment, now stood together nervously awaiting direction.

Jeepers creepers, what must Melody be thinking now? Lizzie wondered. "I gather it doesn't usually do that," she said to Duncan.

He shook his head. "You probably think us an odd bunch."

"Yes, a bit. But musicians can be pretty odd too," she said. "Duncan, my friends and I have had a long day, and we'd be grateful for a good night's sleep."

"Of course. I'll have Inge show you to your bedchambers. I believe your luggage has already been carried upstairs. We'll talk in the morning." He steepled his hands in front of his chest. "May you enjoy a peaceful repose. If there's anything you require, you need only pull the velvet cord beside your bed, and one of my staff will respond posthaste."

"Good night, Duncan. Sleep well. And thank you."

"*Bon soir.*"

* * *

An insistent rapping woke Lizzie. Opening her eyes a slit, she saw the sky outside was still pitch black. The fire in the marble fireplace had died, and a damp chill hung about the elegant bedchamber with its four-poster bed and graceful Queen Anne furnishings. She dragged herself out from beneath a down comforter, snapped on a bedside electric lamp, and pulled on a silk robe with a Chinese dragon embroidered on the back.

She opened the door and saw Melody standing there, her face nearly as white as her flannel nightgown.

"Mel, what's wrong?"

"I heard men's voices in my bedroom, but I couldn't see anyone there."

Shivering, Lizzie stepped back to let her enter. "Sure you weren't dreaming?"

Melody shook her head. "I'm sure."

"What did they say?"

"I couldn't understand them. Do you think they were ghosts?"

Trying to calm her anxious friend, Lizzie said, "I doubt it. Poor little bunny, it's probably just your imagination. This place is a bit overwhelming, I admit."

"I'm scared. Can I stay here with you tonight?" Melody asked, twisting her nightgown in her fist.

"All right." Lizzie shoved the door's heavy iron bolt into place. "Don't worry. Everything will look better in the morning, you'll see."

Melody crawled into the oversized bed and pulled the covers up to her chin. "I hope so."

Lizzie slid in beside her friend and turned off the lamp. For a long time, she lay awake in the dark, listening to Melody's deep breathing. Having grown up in the Bronx amidst flesh-and-blood villains and omnipresent evils, Lizzie didn't fear the shadowy threats that troubled her younger and more sheltered colleague. She didn't believe in ghosts or demons or supernatural occurrences. Still, she couldn't ignore the eerie ambiance that pervaded this gloomy place. Maybe when the sun came out, the castle would shake off its foreboding aura and blossom with laughter and celebration. She crossed her fingers under the eiderdown.

Chapter Two

"Death is nothing at all.

It does not count.

I have only slipped away into the next room.

Nothing has happened."

— Henry Scott Holland

A woman's scream jolted Lizzie from her slumber. She jumped out of bed, tied her silk robe over her nightgown, and flung open her bedchamber's door.

"Who screamed?" Melody asked, clutching the comforter to her chest.

"That's what I'm going to find out," Lizzie said. "Stay here."

The door to the guest room next to Lizzie's gaped open. Peeking inside, she saw the German maid Inge standing beside a canopied bed with velvet drapes similar to the one in Lizzie's own room. On the bed lay a motionless form, covered by a floral-patterned quilt.

The servant clapped her hands over her mouth, as if she feared she might scream again. Lizzie approached the girl slowly and gently touched her arm.

"What's happened here, Inge?"

The young housemaid turned to Lizzie, a horrified expression on her face.

"She's dead, ma'am. I brought the lady her breakfast tray—yesterday she told me she wanted to take breakfast in her room this morning. I found her like this."

Tentatively, Lizzie lifted the woman's wrist and felt for a pulse. Nothing. Her skin was cold and lifeless, and her arm had already stiffened with rigor mortis. Lizzie forced herself not to recoil, not to upset the frightened maid even further.

"We must notify the police," she said. "Is there a telephone nearby?"

"Downstairs, in the foyer."

Behind them, Ophelia Wraith's corpulent form, draped in a red flannel nightgown and plaid robe, filled the doorway. "What's going on?"

"It appears this lady is dead," Lizzie said.

Ophelia took a few hesitant steps into the room, but stopped several feet from the deceased's bed. "Are you certain?"

"I'm no doctor, but it sure looks that way to me."

"Natalie?" Ophelia said as she inched toward the bed. "Natalie?"

"Go find the housekeeper," Lizzie told the wide-eyed maid. "Tell her to telephone the police and alert Mr. Fox."

"Yes, ma'am," the girl said, relieved to be able to escape from the room.

Cora Delaney, wrapped in a chenille robe, appeared next in the bedchamber's doorway. "I heard a scream. Is everything all right?"

"I'm afraid not," Lizzie said. "Sadly, it seems Mrs. Talbot is dead."

"Natalie? Dead?" The card reader crossed to the bed and bent over the woman's lifeless form to see for herself.

"Someone better tell Gregory," Ophelia said.

"Tell Gregory what?" Helen asked. She clutched a woolen bathrobe over her blue pajamas. Her short hair was flattened on one side, and her left cheek bore the imprint of her pillow.

"Natalie's dead," Cora said.

"You can't be serious. How did she die?"

Lizzie shrugged. "Haven't the foggiest. Do you think we should call for a doctor?"

"Better a coroner," Ophelia said.

* * *

"Oh, Lizzie, how awful!" Melody said when she heard the news. "Whatever are we going to do?"

"Wait to hear what Duncan has to say. Looks like the lady simply died in her sleep."

"But she wasn't very old. What if somebody killed her?"

"Good heavens, Mel. Why would you think that?"

The flutist shook her blond curls as if trying to cast out the idea. "I guess it's this scary castle and all these strange people."

"Get dressed, and we'll go downstairs for some breakfast. I'll feel better after I've had a cup of coffee," Lizzie said.

"I wonder if Sidney and Bert know yet?"

"If they don't, they will soon. Bad news travels fast. I'd better tell Sid before he hears about it from someone else." *Yet another death at another one of our stints—in only two months' time,* she groaned inwardly. *Sid will have kittens.*

Lizzie considered the possibility that Duncan might cancel his birthday celebration due to the circumstances. *Rats,* she thought. What had promised to be an interesting and financially lucrative engagement was now in danger of going bust. Any minute the police would arrive. Even though she had no reason to be afraid and Natalie Talbot most likely died from natural causes, Lizzie cringed at the thought of dealing with cops. She'd had enough of that at the last place where they'd performed.

She knocked on the door to Sidney's bedchamber. "It's Lizzie, open up."

After a few moments, the heavy oak door eased open. He peered at her with sleepy eyes, obviously displeased at having been rousted from his warm bed at such an early hour.

"What's up, Bearcat?"

Lizzie pushed into the room without waiting for an invitation. "One of Duncan's friends has turned up dead."

"What? Who?"

She never liked surprising Sid with a problem. His careful, orderly approach to life made it hard for him to stay cool when faced with unexpected crises and complications. Lizzie took a seat in a tapestry-covered armchair near the fireplace to deliver the bad news. During the night, the coals had diminished to barely glowing embers, yet they still gave off a welcome bit of warmth. Sid tugged his paisley robe tighter over his pajamas and paced back and forth the length of his bedchamber.

"Natalie Talbot," she said. "We met her and her husband Gregory last night."

Sidney ran his hand through his dark, thinning hair. "Which ones were they again? We met so many people I can't remember them all."

"Not a very memorable pair," she said. "Rather dowdy, actually. About Duncan's age, I'd guess. The man was tall and thin and white as a sheet. The woman looked like a schoolmarm, spectacles, clunky shoes, the whole bit. She's the deceased."

"What happened? I mean, why did she die?"

"Too soon to call it."

"Damn it all," Sidney swore as he fit a cigarette into an ornate silver holder and lit it. "What are the chances that someone would die on us *again*, just when we're at the start of our stint? Do you think we're jinxed, Bearcat?"

Lizzie drummed her fingers on the arms of the chair. Confusion, anxiety, and a host of other emotions swirled through her. Even though this situation bore none of the nefarious notes of The Troubadours' previous traumatic engagement, unwanted visions of that last venue still troubled her.

"Most likely, the woman just died in her sleep. She looked peaceful enough, lying there in her bed. No sign of struggle or mayhem," she said. "I told Melody, but I don't know if Bert's heard the news yet. I think we need to meet with them and try to defuse things. They're both young, and I don't want them getting all grumpy over this. Melody's spooked enough already. She was afraid to stay alone in her bedroom last night."

"You're right," he agreed.

"Melody and I are going down to breakfast in a few minutes. I'm guessing at least some of Duncan's friends will be there. Maybe I can learn more from them. How about you tell Bert, and we'll all meet in the foyer in, say, an hour?"

Sid nodded and exhaled a lungful of smoke. "Okay."

Fifteen minutes later, Lizzie and Melody descended the stone staircase that led to the castle's ground floor. They followed the seductive aromas of bacon and coffee to a dining hall with a heavy-beamed ceiling. Renaissance tapestries depicting hunting scenes hung on the walls. A massive oak table, darkened almost black with age, and high-backed chairs dominated the somber space. A crackling fire in an enormous fireplace warmed the room.

Two of the women who'd appeared earlier in Natalie's bedchamber—Ophelia and Cora—plus an older woman wrapped in a gray shawl with a long gray braid hanging down her back, clustered together at one end of the dining table. Lizzie and Melody sat far enough away to give them space, yet close enough that they could hear what the other women said.

No sooner had a freckled serving girl poured coffee for the two New York musicians than Ophelia said, "Don't be strangers. Come join us."

Lizzie picked up her cup. "It's okay, Mel," she told her young friend. "They won't turn you into a toad."

After introducing the entertainers to Yvonne, the woman in the gray shawl, Cora said, "Gregory didn't seem very distraught when he heard Natalie was dead."

"Well, why would he?" Ophelia asked. "It's obvious there's no love between them."

The older, gray-haired woman stirred sugar into her tea. "Still, she is—*was*—his wife for many years."

Ophelia raised a dark-penciled eyebrow and toyed with the feathered pouch that hung on a beaded cord around her neck. "And an unfaithful one at that."

Lizzie's ears perked up, but the others cast their eyes down at their food in uncomfortable silence, as if they wished Ophelia hadn't broached the subject.

"You do know that Natalie's been having an affair with Roger Young for ages," Ophelia said. "Why in the world Duncan invited *him* to this gathering, I don't know. It was sure to cause trouble."

Lizzie flipped through her mental catalog of the people she'd met last night, trying to remember someone named Roger Young, but recalled nobody by that name.

Cora laid her knife and fork together on her plate, signaling that she'd finished eating. "I got the impression he and Duncan were friends. I know Roger is, well, rather coarse and irritating, but Duncan has all sorts of peculiar friends." She glanced at the other women seated at the table and laughed softly. "Including us."

"Did Gregory know about his wife's affair?" Lizzie asked. She wasn't even clear yet who was who in this odd group, let alone their complicated interrelationships. But she tucked away all the information they revealed to consider later.

Ophelia snorted. "He would've had to be blind, deaf, and completely senile *not* to know."

"Or maybe he didn't care," Cora, the tarot card reader, said.

"I'm not sure it's right for us to be talking this way in the wake of our friend's death," the gray-haired woman said, hugging her crocheted shawl tighter around her shoulders.

"She wasn't *my* friend," Ophelia said. "Just because we were both in the same profession doesn't mean we liked one another. Tell the truth, Yvonne, did you consider Natalie a friend?"

The older woman ran her thumb around the rim of her teacup. "No, but I honor her as a kindred soul who's been called home. I hope she's at peace."

"Hmph," Ophelia muttered.

Cora tapped her long, slender fingers on the table and looked at Lizzie and Melody. "I apologize for dragging you two into this catty discussion. I fear we've been quite rude. You don't share in our long, complex history."

"No apology needed," Lizzie said. "This is a shock to all of us. My condolences for your loss. I hope we'll be able to communicate openly in the coming days until we learn what happened to Mrs. Talbot."

Ophelia shook her long inky hair, then patted the errant strands back into place. "Oh, I'm sure we'll be doing a lot of communicating in the coming days."

* * *

As the four musicians walked toward the end of the peninsula on which Halcyon Castle sat, Lizzie thought about King Arthur's fabled Tintagel, protected like this one by the surrounding sea. The isolation that kept outsiders at bay also kept the castle's inhabitants cloistered. Along the way, they passed a saltwater swimming pool that filled and emptied daily, according to the ocean's tides. However, no one deigned to brave the bracing water on this brisk autumn morning, and the lounge chairs around the pool remained empty.

At the end of the estate, Lizzie gazed out over the blue-green ocean. The morning sun peeked through the clouds now and again, glinting off the waves like diamonds sparkling on a velvet background in a jeweler's case. The last vestiges of autumn's red, gold, and orange foliage blazed against the castle's somber gray walls. It was much too pretty a day to be darkened by death.

"Before Henry, I'd never known anyone who died," Melody said.

"My father died in an automobile accident two years ago," Bert said. "He was a musician too."

Melody touched his arm gently. "Oh, Bert, I didn't know. I'm sorry. That must have been hard for you."

"Yeah, but life goes on, right?" he said, shutting down further discussion.

Lizzie knew he didn't want to reveal the rest of the sad story. His mother had taken up with another man soon after his father's passing and turned Bert out of the house to fend for himself.

"Do you think Mr. Fox will send us packing now?" Bert asked.

Sidney dropped his cigarette on the ground and stepped on it. "Guess we'll just have to wait and see."

"Those ladies at breakfast didn't seem sad about Mrs. Talbot's death," Melody said, tugging at one of her blond curls.

"No," Lizzie agreed. "I don't know if that's a good sign or a bad one, though. Maybe if Duncan's friends aren't too broken up, the show will go on. For the time being, let's assume everything's copacetic."

"As copacetic as things can be when you've got a stiff on your hands," Sidney grumbled.

"Until we know more, let's plan on rehearsing this afternoon as usual," Lizzie said. "I'll let you know when and where we'll be performing. Now Mel, Bert, away with you both. Find something to do that will take your mind off the lady's death. It's unfortunate, but it's not our business. We're here to play music."

* * *

Lizzie and Sidney followed a dirt path bordered by sea roses that led past the swimming pool and down to the rocky shoreline.

"Before you get in a lather, why don't we wait and see what our host proposes?" she said, trying to ease Sidney's mood. "We have no idea what happened to Natalie Talbot. People die all the time. The rest of us go on living."

Sidney shoved his hands into the pockets of his wool trousers. "Why can't they have the decency to die when I'm not around?"

Lizzie sat on a flat boulder a few yards from the breaking waves and inhaled the salty air. The water's rhythmic motion calmed her. Its ebb and flow made her feel that no matter how chaotic and uncertain the present seemed, when you aligned yourself with the bigger picture everything fell into place.

Sidney squatted beside her. "Who are these peculiar people anyway?"

"They might be Spiritualists. It's a religious movement that became popular toward the end of the last century," Lizzie explained. "They think they can talk to the dead." Although she didn't believe any of it, she remembered Ophelia's uncanny comments about The Troubadours' recently deceased saxophonist, Henry Ives.

"You're not serious."

Trying to keep her tone casual, she said, "Sir Arthur Conan Doyle wrote books about spirits. Even Queen Victoria and Prince Albert attended séances."

"Bushwa. They're charlatans who part superstitious people from their money."

"Maybe," Lizzie said. "Houdini has offered $10,000 to anyone who can do something using 'supernatural powers' that he can't duplicate onstage with his magic tricks. I don't know if he's met his match yet."

Sidney tossed a few pebbles into the water. Although he hadn't known the deceased woman, he was behaving as if Natalie Talbot's death were a personal matter. "I had such high hopes for this engagement. After our last fiasco…"

"It wasn't a complete fiasco," Lizzie reminded him. "Oddly enough, Henry's murder piqued Duncan Fox's interest. He might never have known we existed otherwise. Ultimately, that sordid event led him to hire us to play for this party."

She studied Sid's handsome face. At thirty-eight, he looked years younger than his true age, due to his devotion to facial creams and hair dyes. Today, however, a morose mask darkened his countenance, and his usual, take-charge personality had receded into the background. For the seven years, they'd been friends and colleagues, Lizzie had always relied on him to carry her through difficult times. Now, it seemed, she'd have to assume that responsibility herself.

"Let's consider the best-case scenario," she said. "Until notified otherwise, I'm assuming we're going to perform tonight for Duncan Fox's guests, and we're going to be a smash. We may need to adjust our repertoire, though, given the present situation."

"You're right, Bearcat. What do you have in mind?"

"Duncan hired us to play jazz, but under the circumstances, I think we should avoid the livelier numbers tonight and keep it cool. No Charlestons or Lindy Hops. More along the line of Al Jolson's 'April Showers' and Gershwin's 'Rhapsody in Blue.' Maybe mix in a Chopin 'Etude' or Debussy's 'Clair de Lune'—we're all familiar with those pieces, and they're soothing without being maudlin."

"Hmm, that might be the ticket."

"And Sid, for the time being at least, let's try to put the rest of it out of our minds. Yes, it's unfortunate. Yes, it brings back bad memories. But we didn't know the lady who died, and we don't know what caused her death. Don't imagine the worst. Duncan hired us to entertain his guests—and right now, they may need a distraction more than ever. What do you say-ski?"

He nodded. "Okay-ski."

* * *

At Duncan's request, The Troubadours and the other guests gathered in the spacious parlor where last night his friends had engaged in their metaphysical activities. Less than an hour ago, a coroner had arrived and, after officially pronouncing Natalie Talbot dead, arranged for her body to be taken away. Now, a mix of curiosity and confusion wafted through the castle like a miasma.

When everyone was seated, their host took his place in front of the fireplace. Low-banked flames crackled, and vermillion coals glowed, yet the room still felt chilly. Duncan shoved his hands in the pockets of his frayed brown sweater and addressed his guests.

"I think I speak for all of us when I say I'm stunned and saddened by the sudden departure of our dear friend Natalie."

Lizzie scanned the faces in the room, but didn't observe much sadness in any of them. Even the dead woman's husband didn't seem particularly upset, although he might simply have been in shock.

"Because of the unexpected and uncertain nature of Natalie's passing, the policeman who came here this morning suggested doing an autopsy to determine a cause." Duncan looked at the deceased's husband, who nodded. "Gregory is as puzzled as the rest of us, but he gave his consent. He and I have discussed what the best course of action might be now."

A short, dark, muscular man whom Lizzie hadn't met yet sat apart from the others, near the parlor's entrance. He gripped the arms of his chair and leaned forward, as if readying himself to stand, defend himself, or perhaps bolt if need be. Was this Roger Young, the man Ophelia claimed was Natalie Talbot's lover? Cora, the tarot card reader, cast her eyes down at her lap;

her hands twisted a lace-edged handkerchief. Ophelia's husband Kevin pensively stroked his pointed Van Dyke beard. Sabine, Duncan's pretty daughter, shifted restlessly in her chair, her head jerking from side to side like a little bird as she studied each member of the group in turn. Only the elder Yvonne, wrapped in her gray shawl, appeared quietly composed.

"This turn of events has really wrecked your birthday celebration, eh Duncan?" Ophelia said.

He waved his hand dismissively. "That's the least of my concerns."

"I suppose we could still have a celebration," Cora said. "I mean, we all believe that a person's soul lives on after the body dies."

Yvonne nodded in agreement. "Natalie's as much with us now as she ever was."

"And Saturday is Samhain, when we honor the dead," Cora continued. "So this would be a fitting time to mark her transition."

"What do you think, Greg?" Duncan asked the pale widower.

"I think she'd like that."

Duncan turned to Lizzie and Sidney. "I'll understand completely if you want to cancel our agreement and go home to New York. But I hope you'll consider staying on this week despite the unanticipated change of events. Talk it over if you like before you decide."

Sidney looked at Lizzie, and she nodded. "We'll stay," he said.

"Good," Duncan said, steepling his palms together in front of his chest. "If anyone prefers to leave, that's your prerogative, of course. Your friends won't think less of you for it."

Sabine rushed to her father's side and tearfully flung herself into his arms. "I wish things hadn't taken this terrible turn."

"There, there," he said, patting her hair as he paraphrased James Whitcomb Riley. "'I will not say that she is dead. She is just away. With a cheery smile and a wave of the hand, she has wandered into an unknown land.'"

Chapter Three

"The true Tarot is symbolism; it speaks no other language and offers no other signs."

— *Arthur Edward Waite, The Pictorial Key to the Tarot*

Lizzie felt the gloomy castle closing in around her. When Duncan's guests dispersed, she grabbed her coat and hurried outside where she could breathe fresh air. The crisp, salt-scented breeze cooled her flushed cheeks. Against the castle's gray stone walls, the orange and yellow leaves that still remained on the trees seemed impossibly brilliant.

Standing at the easternmost tip of the estate, a rocky cliff that jutted some thirty feet above the water at low tide, Lizzie saw a schooner gliding by. It made her think of a handsome young man who'd taken her sailing two months ago, during The Troubadours' last engagement in the nearby town of Ipswich. More than once she'd thought about trying to contact him. But the events of that visit—and now the crisis here at Halcyon Castle—made her shelve the idea.

Several smaller craft cut through the choppy waves as she watched, including a lobster boat that paused periodically, bobbing on the swells, so its captain could haul up traps and collect his catch. She sat on a granite boulder and let the peaceful vista calm her restless mind. For nearly an hour, she observed the boats, the gulls and cormorants, and the endlessly rolling sea until her anxiety ebbed with the tide.

On her way back to the castle, Lizzie crossed the parking area paved with local granite blocks. She'd read that Gloucester's granite was among the hardest in the country; this small community supplied stone for roads as far away as California and Europe. Among the motorcars parked there, she spotted a shiny black Packard, a sedan from the new Chrysler Corporation, a charcoal gray Studebaker, and a Model T Ford.

When she was a child, Lizzie believed Henry Ford had nicknamed his popular "Tin Lizzie" after her, and she'd adored cars ever since. She'd never owned one, but promised herself that someday she would.

She entered the castle and made her way down a shadowy hallway, peeking into various rooms along the way. Each space was crammed with furniture, artifacts, and adornments from different periods in history. In one, a suit of medieval armor, complete with sword and lance, stood guard near the doorway. Shields hung on the walls between banners that displayed colorful family crests. In the next room, a wild boar's head with long, yellow tusks stared down at her from above a fireplace. It appeared to be watching over a herd of exotic deer-like creatures that "grazed" in taxidermied silence on a grass-green carpet.

She turned down another hall and came upon a parlor done up in the Art Nouveau style with floral-patterned silk wallcoverings and gracefully carved mahogany woodwork. A soft, golden glow emanated from gilded sconces mounted on the walls. Upon closer inspection, Lizzie noticed they were fashioned to look like human arms holding tall candles. *Holy moly*, she thought, and yet she had to admit the effect was elegant, if peculiar.

Inside the parlor, Cora and Yvonne sat hunched over a round mahogany table, studying a pattern of cards. A fire warmed the room. *Where are the other guests?* Lizzie wondered. Were they privately grieving the loss of a friend? Gathered together in support? Engaged in their own esoteric explorations into the dead woman's passing?

She hovered in the doorway, not wanting to disturb the two women, until Yvonne glanced up and motioned her in. "Cora's doing a tarot reading to try to figure out what happened to Natalie."

"May I join you?" Lizzie asked.

"Sure, why not?" the card reader said.

Although she couldn't imagine how a deck of cards could shed light on a person's death, Lizzie's curiosity got the better of her. She took a seat and asked, "What have you discovered?"

"First of all, I don't think she died peacefully in her sleep," Cora said, rubbing her temples with her index fingers.

Lizzie's heart sank. *Oh no, not another murder! Sid will have kittens.* "Why do you think that?"

"Take a moment to look at the cards," Cora said. "What do you see?"

"But I don't know anything about all this."

"Just look at the pictures."

Lizzie examined the illustrated cards laid out on the table. Most of them depicted painful and frightening scenes. "Ouch," she said, pointing to one that showed a man lying on the ground with ten swords stuck in his back.

"Each card has a meaning. The positions of the cards tell the story." Cora tapped a long, manicured finger, circled by a handsome jeweled ring, on a card that showed a skeleton riding a horse. "This card is called Death. Here, he describes the situation."

"I guess that's no surprise," Lizzie said.

"This one represents Natalie," Cora continued, pointing to a card that showed the moon beneath which a dog and a coyote bayed. "And this one describes her adversary. It shows the condition, emotion, or *type* of person that brought about her death."

Lizzie stared at the picture of a heart pierced by three swords. Just the sight of it made her uncomfortable. "Are you telling me these cards mean someone killed her?" *If the tarot really can talk, surely the police will want to know about this.*

Lizzie recalled Ophelia's revelation at breakfast yesterday: Natalie was having an affair with a man named Roger Young. Had her infidelity led to her death? Lizzie shivered as she contemplated the possibility that Natalie's jealous husband Gregory might have murdered her. The ashen man seemed so ethereal, detached, and frail. Was he capable of such an act?

"Could the three of swords mean Nat's heart was damaged due to a physical illness, rheumatic fever perhaps?" Yvonne asked, pointing to the image of the punctured heart.

"Maybe," Cora said. "I don't know if she had heart problems, but Greg should. We could ask him."

A loud crack from the fireplace startled them. Yvonne stood up and went to rearrange the logs in the grille with an iron poker. She pumped a bellows a few times until the flames leapt to life, then returned to her seat at the table.

"What about this one?" Lizzie touched a card on which a forlorn-looking figure stood amidst overturned goblets.

"It suggests emotional pain and loss, a sense of hopelessness," Cora answered.

Lizzie's mind whirred. *Another finger points at Gregory Talbot, cuckolded by his wife. Unless, perhaps, Roger Young killed her because Natalie wouldn't leave her husband.* But as she fumbled with these possibilities, she scolded herself for giving in to unfounded suspicions. Wasn't it more likely that the lady died of natural causes, despite Cora's suspicions? Could the card with the three swords describe a heart attack?

The freckled housemaid who'd served them breakfast this morning appeared at the doorway. "Pardon me, but I wondered if you might like a spot of tea and some cake?"

"Yes, please, that sounds wonderful. I could use a pick-me-up," Cora said, rolling her head slowly from side to side. After the girl left, she bent over the cards again. "Now we move into the future."

"You can actually see the future in these cards?" Lizzie asked.

"That's one of the main reasons people consult them," Cora said. "Okay, the five of wands placed here says we're in for some conflict and tension in the immediate future. Again, that's to be expected. Then we come to the 'ouch' card, as you called it, Lizzie."

"Somebody stabbed the poor man in the back multiple times. Looks like he's got a lot of enemies."

Cora nodded. "Yes, treachery is one interpretation. But the ten of swords can also mean exhaustion, feeling overwhelmed by responsibilities, worn down and such."

"Hmm. What about this ugly fella?" Lizzie pointed to an image of a half-man, half-beast. The card's label read "The Devil."

"In this position, he represents the people and circumstances surrounding the future environment."

"The Devil? That can't be good."

Even though she realized many people might think folks like Duncan and his guests were in cahoots with Satan, Lizzie had always considered ideas like that silly superstition. Until now. She stared at the grotesque creature on the card and wondered if maybe she and the rest of The Troubadours were in danger. Who were these odd men and women whom Duncan considered friends? Did they really possess extraordinary powers? What forces were they toying with? And what about Duncan Fox himself? One woman had already died of unknown causes—under suspicious circumstances—if Cora's cards told the truth. Was someone in this eldritch group responsible? And, if the devil controlled the future, shouldn't Lizzie and her friends hurry back to New York right away, before it was too late?

Nervously she raked her fingers through her fashionably bobbed dark hair. She pointed to another card. "What about this man hanging upside down?"

"He suggests looking at things from a different perspective," Cora said. "And here in the ninth position, he also tells us to pay attention both to what we hope for and fear most."

Confused, Lizzie tapped the last card in the spread, which showed a woman wearing a golden crown and a red robe. She held a set of scales in her left hand. "And this one?"

"Justice." Cora circled her fingertip over the card a few times, as if drawing meaning from touching it. A long moment passed before she said, "Justice will prevail."

* * *

Lizzie and her musician friends climbed two flights of stairs—so wide ten people could have mounted them side-by-side—to the castle's ballroom.

"Let me get this straight," Sidney said. "That fat lady says she talked to our dead pal Henry?"

Lizzie nodded. "She said Henry was doing fine, and he's satisfied with Bert as his replacement."

"Glad to hear it," Bert said with a crooked smile, the left corner of his mouth curling up more than the right.

"That's ridiculous," Sidney said.

"You don't think Henry would approve of Bert?" Lizzie asked.

"I meant that some flamboyant floozy would presume to know what Henry thinks." Sid dismissively waved his cigarette in its engraved silver holder. "How can ghosts think anyway?"

"Haven't the foggiest," Lizzie said. "But how did she know Henry even existed and that he died recently and I had a connection to him?"

Sidney gently rapped his knuckles on the top of her head. "Wake up, Bearcat. The story's been in the newspapers the past two months. Either she read about it, or Duncan told her."

That had to be it. "You're right, of course," she said, feeling a bit foolish.

They entered the grand space that had been built as a ballroom, with a parquet floor designed for dancing. However, Lizzie had trouble imagining Duncan Fox and his shy sister Frances hosting fancy balls here. Chandeliers made of wrought iron hung from a beamed ceiling. A stone fireplace large enough to roast a whole calf had been laid for a fire, but no one had lit it yet. Before the hearth stretched a long trestle table made of dark-stained oak, where Lizzie could easily imagine medieval lords and their knights gnawing on hunks of roast boar and swilling mead. Six high-backed chairs were lined up on each side. A thirteenth chair, larger and more decoratively carved than the others, sat at the table's head.

Afternoon light spilled through tall arched windows hung with velvet drapes, illuminating a raised platform that held a Steinway concert grand piano. Immediately, Sidney moved toward it as if drawn by a powerful magnet. He eased onto the bench, flipped open the key lid to reveal the instrument's ivory smile, and began stroking the piano's keyboard as if he were caressing a lover. While Lizzie prowled the ballroom checking its acoustics, he played a few scales before launching into strains from some of his favorite scores.

Fifteen minutes later, apparently satisfied, Sid called out to the other members of the group who'd been wandering about like barn cats. "Rehearsal time!"

Melody and Bert stopped exploring and took up their positions on the stage. Dutifully, they unsnapped their instrument cases and stood waiting for direction from the group's elder members.

"I know things are pretty disconcerting right now," Sidney said, "but we've made a commitment to stay on for the duration of this event, so let's do our best."

"Sid's right," Lizzie said. "We're professionals. We're here to do a job, not to get sidetracked by events that don't involve us, even if they're unfortunate ones. Can you do that? Put the music first? If not, if you think this is too much for you to deal with, let's talk about it. We're in this together."

Bert cracked his knuckles and shrugged. "I didn't know the lady who died. She didn't mean anything to me."

"Melody?"

The young flutist toyed with the amethyst necklace she wore for good luck and scanned the ballroom as if searching for alternatives. Finding none, she nodded.

"Okay then. In addition to our usual jazz numbers, Duncan asked us to play something by Mozart," Lizzie said. "I'd like to sing 'Der Holle Rache Kocht in Meinem Herzen' from *The Magic Flute,* if that's okay with everyone."

"Show off," Sidney razzed her.

"I admit, it's a flashy solo that will showcase my vocal ability, but it also gives Melody an opportunity to shine. We're here to impress so why not pull out all the stops? Especially now, when our audience may be glad for a diversion. What do you think, Mel?"

The pretty blond flutist agreed. "It's a beautiful piece. I think I'm up to it."

"But let's hold that back until after they've finished supper," Sidney said, flicking his cigarette ash into a marble ashtray.

"What about a movement from Bach's *Brandenburg Concerto No. 1?*" Bert suggested. "I do a smashing French horn on that piece. Melody's darb on violin too."

"Another attention seeker?" Sidney glanced at Lizzie, who nodded. "Okay, you're on."

For the next two hours, they rehearsed what, for them, was an unusual schedule. Although the quartet was best known for playing jazz, performing these classics gave them an opportunity to stretch their abilities.

At four o'clock sharp, a wooden door with a glass panel swung open. A robust, red-cheeked kitchen maid bearing a silver platter emerged from an elevator. She set the tray on the long trestle table and uncovered plates of deviled eggs, pickled French artichokes, cream cheese-and-cucumber sandwiches, and apple tarts. While the girl arranged a china pot of tea, a matching cream-and-sugar set, and four cups and saucers, Lizzie approached her.

"I didn't realize this room could be accessed by elevator."

"Yes, ma'am," the girl said. "Would you like me to show you how it works?"

"Ab-so-lute-ly."

Lizzie had ridden in plenty of elevators in New York's residential and commercial buildings, hotels, and department stores, including some still powered by steam. She especially admired the Art Nouveau metal cages designed in the last century. In those early days, uniformed men had to manually haul the platforms up through the shafts with thick ropes. Even her apartment in Greenwich Village had a cranky old lift. But she'd never operated one herself.

"This one's quite simple, really. No ropes or levers. It's electric." The girl pointed to a row of six buttons on a panel just inside the elevator's door. "All you have to do is press the one for the floor you want to go to. The red button at the bottom stops the lift. The green one rings a bell. This lift makes it easier for us to bring food up from the kitchen, but Mr. Fox mainly had it installed so Miss Frances Fox could get around. She can't climb the stairs."

"Oh? Why not?"

"When she was a young lady, Miss Fox was injured in a horseback riding accident. She still has trouble walking."

"How sad," Lizzie said. "Thanks for the tea and for showing me the elevator."

"You're welcome, ma'am. If you want to summon the lift, all you have to do is press the button on the wall there."

The girl stepped inside, closed the door, and the elevator rumbled away.

Chapter Four

"Time will bring to light whatever is hidden."

— Horace

Only nine of the twelve side chairs at the antique oak banquet table were occupied that evening. Lizzie guessed the empty chair next to Gregory Talbot had been meant for his dead wife, Natalie. *Who are the others for?* she wondered. *Deceased loved ones or visitors yet to arrive?*

Duncan Fox, wearing an out-of-date, ill-fitting suit with a flashy blue-and-gold ascot at his throat instead of a tie, presided at the table's head in a heavily carved armchair. His unruly gray hair stuck out every which way as if he'd just come in from a blustery wind; obviously he'd made no attempt to comb it into place. Despite his friend's death, Duncan seemed quite animated as he bantered with his companions. Occasionally, he clapped his hands in childlike glee and laughed unabashedly when someone said something he found funny.

At his right sat his daughter Sabine with her handsome husband Jonathon beside her. Her moss-green gown, adorned with hundreds of seed pearls sewn on by hand, complimented her shell-pink skin and chestnut hair. A red fox stole hugged her shoulders. Her flitting hands, quick movements, and tiny head, which jerked from side to side as she tried to take in everything going on around her, made Lizzie think of a sparrow. *An attractive couple, but it's all for show,* she decided. *They don't seem to have any chemistry between them.*

They reminded her of a Norman Rockwell illustration: perfectly presented, but flat and without passion.

From the stage, Lizzie studied the other guests. At Duncan's left sat Ophelia Wraith, wearing a voluminous tangerine-colored gown that made her look like a pumpkin. She'd twisted her long inky hair into an elaborate updo and fastened it in place with several garish combs and pins. Beside her sat the man with the Van Dyke beard, her husband Kevin, who seemed old enough to be her father. His rumpled tweed jacket would have been more appropriate attire for a day in the country than a proper dinner party.

The card reader, Cora, the only fashionably attired lady in the group other than Sabine, sat beside Kevin. Atop her turquoise crepe de chine gown, elegant in its simplicity, she wore a gorgeous mink wrap. A jeweled clip glittered in her finger-waved brown hair. A muscular man in his early thirties, with coarse features and a dark-shadowed jawline that suggested a naturally heavy beard, fidgeted beside Cora. Lizzie guessed him to be Roger Young. Obviously ill at ease, he gripped his knife and fork upright in his hands while he talked, as if he feared he might need to defend himself with them. Helen Simms at his left, wearing a double-breasted man's suit, cast disparaging glances at him. She scooted her chair a few inches away, as if she worried he might accidentally jab her with his fork. The elder Yvonne, however, willowy in a gray cashmere sheath and matching shawl, chatted amiably with him.

As Sidney had recommended, the musicians played a combination of cool jazz and Baroque pieces for two hours during the meal, allowing their audience to converse easily over a supper of beef Wellington served with carrots and peas, winter squash, mashed potatoes, and fresh-baked bread. Duncan's cook Febe—a name that meant "brightest of women"—had sent generous portions to the performers' rooms prior to the dinner party. The kitchen girl who'd delivered the food explained that the cook wanted to "give the entertainers strength and inspire them."

Throughout the meal, bottles of red wine made their way up and down the table. Lizzie noticed that most of the men and women imbibed. Despite Prohibition, Duncan Fox apparently had no problem procuring the beverage.

As soon as his guests emptied one bottle, another instantly appeared. *I must see about getting my hands on some,* Lizzie promised herself.

After the servants had cleared away the dinner dishes and set a dessert plate of pumpkin pie in front of each guest, The Troubadours launched into the movement Bert had chosen from Bach's *Brandenburg Concerto.* Given his chance to shine, he sparkled. The gawky young man with big ears, unruly brown hair, and gapped front teeth shucked off his shyness and radiated such vitality that he captivated everyone in the ballroom. When he'd finished, Lizzie hugged him and insisted he take a bow, to enthusiastic applause that caused him to blush profusely.

Next, it was her turn to impress. The difficult aria from Mozart's *Magic Flute* challenged her beyond any of the jazz tunes she usually sang. And yet, or perhaps because, she loved performing it. Although she would have appreciated the accompaniment of a full orchestra, their small ensemble had adapted Mozart's score as best they could. With Bert's French horn carrying the bass line and Melody's flute imitating Lizzie's sylvan soprano, her strong, clear voice soared through the octaves like an eagle set free to fly to the heavens.

This is why I perform, she reminded herself. *What could be better than doing what you love most and sharing it with other people?*

When she finished, Duncan Fox stood and clapped loudly. One by one, his guests joined him. Helen shouted, *"Brava!"* The muscular young fellow stuck his fingers in his mouth and whistled, as if he were at the ballpark. Lizzie bowed, thrilled not only by her audience's response, but at knowing she'd pushed her artistic limits to the utmost and excelled.

One by one, the diners began easing away from the table. Duncan, his gray hair radiating like a frizzy halo around his head, approached the stage. He opened his arms wide as if embracing everyone in the room.

"Magnifico!" he cried and held out both his hands to Lizzie.

Grasping them, she stepped down from the stage. "I'm glad you enjoyed the evening's entertainment."

"Enjoyed it? I was enthralled. I'd heard good things about you, but tonight far surpassed my expectations."

Sidney draped an arm around Lizzie's shoulders. "We aim to please."

"My guests are going to repair to the parlor downstairs," Duncan said. "I can understand that you may be tired after such a lively performance, but if you care to join us, you'd be most welcome."

Melody's big blue eyes pled for an excuse to decline. Lizzie knew the flutist probably wanted to retire to write letters to her beau and her parents back home. Bert, she realized, was wary of socializing with these strange people. Sidney always liked to spend an hour or so after playing, mentally going over everything that had transpired. What went well and what could be improved upon. Each begged off politely.

Lizzie, however, still buzzed with her post-performance high. "Although my colleagues want to rest, I'd be delighted to join you and your guests."

"Splendid," Duncan said and shook hands all around. "Thank you again for a most impressive evening."

* * *

"I'm going to see what's what," Lizzie told Sidney after Duncan and the others had gone downstairs. "Sure you don't want to come along?"

He shook his head. "I hired on to entertain these people, not to befriend them. Frankly, this whole scene's made me feel kind of grummy. Nose around in their weirdness if you must, Bearcat, but watch yourself, will you?"

"You sound as though you think they might be dangerous." The idea had crossed her mind too, but it hadn't diminished her curiosity.

"A woman died this morning of unknown causes, remember? I don't know what to think."

Lizzie threw her arms around his neck and gave him a sisterly hug. "You played splendidly tonight, as always. See you in the morning. Have a good rest-ski."

"All the best-ski," he said.

Instead of walking down the sweeping staircase, Lizzie decided to try out the elevator. As the kitchen maid had explained, operating the lift was a simple matter of pushing a button. With a groan and a shutter, it slowly descended to the ground floor.

Electric light fixtures with amber-glass shades hung from the parlor's ceiling. To block autumn's nighttime chill, heavy drapes had been drawn across the sea-facing windows. A fire warmed the spacious room. Duncan's friends lounged in the wine-colored velvet sofas and leather armchairs. Tonight, however, no one sat at the game tables or dabbled in esoteric amusements.

Lizzie didn't see Duncan or the widowed Gregory Talbot or the deceased's alleged lover, Roger Young, among those gathered in the comfortable room. All the women, however, as well as Duncan's son-in-law Jonathon Matthews and Ophelia Wraith's bearded husband Kevin, were present. Yvonne leaned toward the fireplace seeking warmth, and held her palms up toward the flames.

Thank goodness for the fireplaces, Lizzie thought. Even though the castle had modern heating, it was only marginally effective at chasing the ever-present chill. *I wouldn't want to live here in January.*

Cora stroked her mink as if it were a pet. Sabine chewed her fingernails. Helen Simms smoked a cigarette and leisurely blew smoke rings toward the ceiling. Jonathon lit his own cigarette, but puffed on it with a sense of urgency. Lizzie wondered if he had something pressing to attend to or wanted to get away from the others.

Ophelia had claimed an armchair near the fireplace. Toying with her peculiar feathered necklace, she waited patiently while her companions settled themselves. Lizzie slid quietly into the room and took a seat on one of the velvet sofas. In the uncertain ambiance, she sensed the inky-haired woman in her pumpkin-orange gown slowly taking charge.

"What do you say we try to contact Natalie on the Other Side?" Ophelia asked. "Maybe she can tell us what happened to her."

"This is all so upsetting. I'd really like to know the truth," Sabine said, her eyes wide with curiosity. "Do you really think you can channel her, Ophelia?"

"I can certainly try."

Helen stubbed out her cigarette. "Why not give it a whirl? What harm can it do?"

I guess that depends on what the dead woman has to say, Lizzie thought.

"Yes, please do try," Sabine said.

She looked at each guest in turn, as if seeking their approval. Kevin, Cora, and Yvonne nodded in agreement.

"All right." Ophelia closed her eyes and began breathing slowly and deeply. She rested her hands on the arms of the leather chair, palms up. Her reddened lips twitched. A few moments passed, then she slumped in her chair and tilted her head slightly toward her left shoulder.

"Heavy, so heavy," Ophelia muttered. Her voice sounded deeper than usual, and she slurred her words as if she were drunk.

"What do you see?" her husband Kevin prompted her.

Ophelia's blue-shadowed eyelids fluttered. "Murky... dark."

"Natalie, are you here?" Cora asked. "Tell us how you feel. Are you okay?"

"Tired. Very tired." Ophelia's head dropped backward to rest on the chair.

The group waited eagerly for her to say more, but after a few moments, Ophelia began to snore. Cora and Yvonne exchanged confused glances. Sabine bit a fingernail. Kevin Wraith toyed with his beard and stared at his wife. He nudged her arm gently, willing her to either speak or snap out of her trance, as if she'd disappointed her audience by failing to provide more information. She didn't respond.

Jonathon stood. "Well, I guess that's that. I'm going to have an after-dinner glass of port. Anyone care to join me?"

Sabine and Yvonne shook their heads.

"I will," Helen said. She got up and straightened the creases in her trousers. "Lizzie, want to come with us?"

"Ab-so-lute-ly."

"Cora?" Jonathon asked.

"Maybe in a bit."

Slowly, Kevin unwound his aged body, stood, and bent over his sleeping wife. He shook her shoulder gently to rouse her. Ophelia snorted. Her eyes snapped open like window shades.

"Okay, folks. Show's over," Jonathon said. "We'll be across the hall in the billiard room if anyone wants to stop by for a nightcap."

Lizzie and Helen followed him. He flipped a switch on the wall, and electric lights illuminated a curved mahogany bar. Another switch sparked lamps with stained-glass shades that hung above a billiard table. Wall sconces glowed a soft gold that might have been romantic under different circumstances.

Jonathon strolled behind the bar and selected a bottle from the array lined up in front of a huge mirror. "What's your pleasure?"

"I'd like a glass of that port you mentioned," Lizzie said.

Helen positioned herself on a barstool. "Got any scotch back there?"

"I'm sure old Duncan's stashed some brown plaid around here somewhere. He can get his hands on just about anything." Digging into the cabinets, Duncan's son-in-law found a bottle of Lagavulin and poured a few fingers worth into a glass, then handed it to Helen.

Lizzie gathered up the long skirt of her evening gown and climbed onto the stool beside Helen as gracefully as she could. *How much easier it would be if I were wearing trousers too*, she thought. Jonathon set a glass in front of her, his eyes dropping to the cleavage exposed by her dress's plunging neckline. When she placed her hand to her chest, covering as much skin as possible, he raised an eyebrow, then turned away and poured himself a glass of port.

"Cheers," he toasted, and the three clinked glasses.

After taking a sip of the rich, sweet wine, Lizzie nodded in the direction of the parlor and asked, "What was that all about?"

"Just a little show that fizzled," he said.

"You're always so skeptical, Jonathon," Helen said. She pulled a cigarette out of a handsome silver case and offered one to Lizzie.

"Oh, no thanks. I have to take care of my voice."

"Smart girl."

Jonathon whipped out a lighter and lit Helen's cigarette. She inhaled deeply and blew a plume of smoke toward the ceiling.

"Ophelia has a flair for the dramatic, even though she bombed tonight," he said and lit his own cigarette.

"True. Still, she's a pretty good psychic," Helen said. "She's been right about a lot of things."

"Like what?" Lizzie asked. She wasn't sure if she believed in any of this, but she was definitely intrigued.

"She predicted President Harding's sudden death from a heart attack."

"I heard his heart quit because he stopped drinking," Jonathon said. "Too much of a shock after a lifetime of boozing."

Helen continued, "She predicted the big earthquake in Santa Barbara, California, this past summer and the tornado in Illinois in March that killed 700 people. When Sabine was just a girl, Ophelia told her she'd marry a banker, and here you are, Jon. Ta-da."

He held up his hands and laughed. "Okay, I surrender. But I'm not convinced. Nor do I believe you can tell what's going to happen simply by looking at the stars."

"That's because you haven't studied astrology. If you had, you'd understand."

"Are you an astrologer?" Lizzie asked Helen. She'd never met an astrologer before—or a psychic either, for that matter. Despite her wariness, she couldn't help being fascinated.

"I am," Helen said and took a sip of her scotch. "Mmm. I could get ossified on this."

Jonathon leaned his elbows on the bar and stared hard at Helen, challenging her. "If both you and Ophelia are so good at reading the future, how come neither of you knew Natalie was going to die? Or why?"

"I might have seen it in her birth chart if I'd been so inclined. Except it's been years since I looked at Natalie's chart."

"Hmpf." Jonathon emptied his glass of port and poured himself another. "A splash, Lizzie?"

"Yes, please."

Cora's heels clicked on the parquet floor as she entered the billiard room alone.

"And here's our resident tarot card reader, come to join our little party," he called out to her. "You're just in time. We're discussing the art of divination."

"The others have all gone off to bed," she said as she slid onto the stool beside Helen.

Jonathon reached across the bar and patted the glassy-eyed head of Cora's mink stole. "How's the little weasel tonight?"

"It's a mink," Cora said, slapping his hand away. "Pour me some of whatever you're drinking."

He grabbed another glass, filled it, and handed it to her. "Why, do all you prognosticators want to know about the future anyway?"

"People have always wanted to see what lies ahead," Cora said. "Thousands of years ago, people from all over Greece traveled to Delphi to consult the oracle there. And early seers used bones, stones, even animal entrails to give them insight into the future."

"But if you can't do anything about it, why concern yourself?"

"I'd think that, being a banker, you'd want to know what lies around the bend, so you could make wise investments," Helen said.

"I'll rely on my business acumen, not what some soothsayer tells me."

The astrologer shrugged. "Suit yourself, but don't come crying to me if you lose a bundle one of these days because you didn't ask my advice."

"I'd like to hear your advice," Lizzie said. "But don't tell me if you see I'm going to die soon."

They bantered a while longer, lingering over their drinks and smokes, until Helen glanced at her Laco watch with its black face and unfeminine leather wristband.

"Holy moly," she said. "It's already tomorrow."

They finished their drinks and exchanged goodnights. As they climbed the stairs to their individual rooms, Lizzie wondered what Natalie Talbot had been thinking on her last night as she lay down alone in her bed, never to wake again. Before she fell asleep, did she cast her gaze into the future and see death waiting for her just around the corner?

Chapter Five

"There are no secrets that time does not reveal."

— Jean Racine

Lizzie had just dozed off when a pounding on her bedchamber door startled her. She threw off the eiderdown and grabbed her robe. Melody stood at the door, her blue eyes wide with fear. She pushed past Lizzie without waiting to be asked in.

"I heard the men's voices in my bedroom again."

Tired and annoyed at having been awakened, Lizzie snapped, "It's just your imagination, Mel. Stop acting like a baby and go back to bed."

"Really, I did hear them." She'd tied up her hair with rags to make it curl, and when she shook her head, she reminded Lizzie of a blond hydra.

"There's no place for men to hide in your room. We've already checked." But Melody looked so childlike and vulnerable and scared that Lizzie relented. "All right, let's have another look."

Together they entered the flutist's bedchamber, where every available light burned brightly. *If any spirits really were here, Mel's surely chased them away.* Lizzie opened the mahogany wardrobe, but saw only Melody's clothing hanging inside. She knelt and peered under the bed. Nobody hiding there either. She opened the door to the shared bathroom between their two bedrooms, but it, too, was empty.

"You don't believe me," Melody said.

She didn't doubt Melody had heard something, but what? And where could the noises be coming from? Lizzie crouched in front of the fireplace and tilted her head, listening, but heard only the crackling of burning wood.

"Who's in the bedroom beside this one?" she asked.

"Yvonne," Melody said.

That rules out men's voices from next door, Lizzie thought, longing to snuggle back in her warm bed. *I'm sure there's a logical answer to this. I'm just too tired now to dwell on it.* "Plenty of strange goings on around here," she said, trying to humor Melody. "How about we sit quietly for a bit and see if I hear what you heard?"

Melody agreed, and both women sat on the four-poster bed, waiting and listening. Five minutes passed. Then five more. Tired after a long, stressful day and woozy from the wine, Lizzie started to doze. Suddenly, Melody grasped her arm.

A rustling seemed to come from behind the headboard. *Squirrels in the walls?* Lizzie wondered. A moment later, a knock pounded nearby. *Most likely caused by steam pressure in the radiator pipes that heat the castle,* she decided. Then a man's voice mumbled something too low for Lizzie to understand. Another voice replied. She froze, straining her ears to catch more. Although the words were muffled, she thought she heard him say "tomorrow."

For ten minutes more, the two women sat in anticipatory silence on Melody's bed. When no more sounds arose, Lizzie patted her younger friend's hand.

"I heard them too," she said.

"Are they ghosts?"

"Haven't the foggiest."

"What are we going to do?"

Lizzie wished she had an answer. "Well, we've checked your room, so we know there aren't any creepy guys in here waiting to harm you. And there's a heavy iron bolt on the door. That's reassuring, right?"

"I guess so."

"Despite how eerie this castle may seem, you don't really believe vampires or ghosts or evil spirits live here, do you? That's all made-up, fantasy nonsense."

Melody shrugged, but she didn't look convinced.

Grasping at straws, Lizzie said, "I'm sure there's a reasonable explanation. Maybe we're hearing the voices of servants stoking the coal furnace in the basement, coming up through the ductwork along with the heat. If that's the case, we better be careful what we say—they might be able to hear us too."

Her young friend nodded, wanting to believe. "What about that lady who died?"

"What about her?"

Melody fingered the lace on her nightgown. "Do you think there's any connection?"

"Between the voices and her death? Poor little bunny, of course not. The police are doing an autopsy. They'll probably discover she had a heart condition or some other ailment and died peacefully in her sleep, just as it appears." She had no intention of scaring Melody further by telling her about Cora's tarot reading. "Do you want to swap rooms with me? Would that make you feel better?"

"You'd do that for me? I'd be ever so grateful."

"Sure, go sleep in my room. I'll stay in here. In the morning, we'll ask one of the chambermaids to move our belongings."

"Thanks, Lizzie," Melody said and gave her a quick hug. "You're the bee's knees."

* * *

Lizzie and Sidney had arranged to meet with their host after a late breakfast to discuss the evening's entertainment. They were still lingering over coffee when Duncan entered the dining hall.

After wishing them a good morning, he said, "As musicians, I thought you might like to see the pipe organ my grandfather imported from Austria soon after he built this castle. It's truly an amazing instrument. He played it rather well, in fact, and so did my father."

"Yes, I would," Sidney said, his brown eyes shining with interest.

"I'm an amateur musician myself," Duncan said.

Oh no, Lizzie groaned inwardly. A patron who fancied himself a musician. That could get awkward. Would he expect to participate in their performances? Would they be required to humor his childish attempts or encourage his fantasies? Or worse yet, give him lessons?

"Did you know the pipe organ's origins go back to ancient Greece?" Duncan said. "Even today it's considered one of man's most complex creations."

He led them down the central hallway into a grand chamber that resembled the sanctuary of a Gothic church. A round rose window and five tall, peaked, stained-glass windows set in one of the stone walls let in jewel-colored light. From an arched ceiling, three stories high and supported by heavy wooden beams, hung iron lanterns—unlit at this time of day. Rows of oaken pews faced an apse dominated by a magnificent pipe organ.

They approached the instrument with awe and mounted the steps that led up to its mahogany console. Four keyboards, arrayed one above the other, begged to be touched.

"The wooden pedals on the floor provide yet another 'keyboard' that let the organist produce low-pitched sounds," Duncan explained. "And these knobs are called stops. They allow the musician to direct pressurized air to the ranks of pipes positioned on a balcony above us."

Sidney ran his fingertips over the ivory keys. "Holy moly, this is spectacular!"

"Can you play it?" Lizzie asked her friend.

"Probably, but not very well. It's ever so much more complex than a piano. And unless it's electrified or driven by gas or water pressure, I'd need a calcant in order to make this beauty sing."

"What's a calcant?"

"Someone who pumps air into the pipes with a bellows."

"It's electrified," Duncan assured them.

Sidney rubbed his thumbs and fingertips together, as if eager to discover what sounds they might coax from the keyboards. He looked up at a balcony above the organ and the rows of pipes—some as tall and thick as a man's body—standing side by side like stalwart soldiers. Their mouths hung open, ready to emit the tones prescribed to them. His face glowed with reverence and amazement. "There must be a thousand pipes up there."

"Eleven hundred and twenty, to be exact," Duncan said.

"That sounds like a lot," Lizzie said.

"The big organs in Europe's great cathedrals have tens of thousands of pipes. But yes, this is a lot for a privately owned instrument," Duncan answered proudly.

Lizzie's only prior exposure to organs had been in the church she attended as a child and in the local movie theater, where an organist banged out overly dramatic music to accompany a silent picture. But those clumsy instruments bore little resemblance to this treasure. When she got back to New York, she planned to visit the big cathedrals there and listen to their pipe organs.

"Duncan, you must play it while we're here," she insisted.

"And so I shall, dear lady."

"Would you let Sid play it too? This is the first time I've seen a spark in him since before Mrs. Talbot died."

Their host grinned. "Of course. That's why it's here, to be played and enjoyed."

* * *

As Lizzie passed the castle's spacious parlor on her way upstairs, she spotted Duncan's friends Cora and Yvonne, his daughter Sabine, and Melody at a game table playing cards.

Oh good, Mel's making friends, she thought as she stepped inside and greeted the women. *Maybe she'll feel more comfortable here now.*

Near the fireplace, Ophelia sat in one of the leather armchairs, dressed in a cream-colored smock with bright embroidery at the neck, wrists, and hem. It reminded Lizzie of Mexican garments she'd seen in *National Geographic*.

The medium looked up from a magazine she was scribbling in. "What's a six-letter word for displace? Starts with U and ends with T."

Lizzie thought for a moment. Upset only had five letters. "How about unseat?" she suggested.

"That fits." Ophelia penciled the answer into what Lizzie realized must be a crossword puzzle. "How about a five-letter word for opponent, fourth letter A?"

After a bit, Lizzie came up with "rival." As she said the word aloud, a picture of Roger Young emerged in her mind. But before she could give Gregory Talbot's competitor much thought, Ophelia tossed out another question, "Fall, six letters, ends in LE?"

Does the clue refer to the season or the action? Lizzie wondered. Plays on words were one of the appealing challenges of crossword puzzles. Going with the latter, she offered, "Tumble?"

"Hey, you're good at this," Ophelia said.

"Ophelia, we're trying to play bridge," Cora said, a hint of annoyance in her voice. "We need to concentrate. I'm sure you can find a *Roget's* around here someplace."

"Sorry," the overweight medium said, but she didn't sound sorry at all.

Lizzie took the opportunity to leave the women to their amusements and climbed the stairs to her second-floor bedroom. There she found a chambermaid busily shuffling her belongings into the room Melody had previously occupied. While she collected her cosmetics and jewelry, she thought about the brilliant and troubled man who'd compiled the popular thesaurus. Peter Roget had been a nervous youth who'd calmed himself by making lists of words. He'd become a medical doctor and professor and probably never suspected that crossword puzzles would make his uniquely personal form of therapy a household essential. *Who knows what we'll be remembered for, or what legacy we'll leave behind for future generations?* she thought as she handed the chambermaid a coin.

* * *

Even though bright flames crackled in the fireplace, the grand ballroom on the castle's third floor seemed gloomy and colder than Lizzie remembered.

The electric chandeliers were lit, yet they couldn't lift the darkness that hung over everything like a shroud. Approaching the stage, she felt a draft on the back of her neck. *A ghost?* She tried to brush it away, then scolded herself for such foolishness. *This balled-up mess has thrown me into a dither. I need to pull myself together and focus on my music.*

Sidney sat at the Steinway, his fingers trilling Chopin's "Nocturne Opus 9 No. 2 in E-flat Major." Duncan had asked them to perform pieces by one of his favorite composers tonight instead of their usual jazz tunes. Most of the evening's entertainment would fall to Sidney, although The Troubadours also planned to play the composer's "Variations for Flute and Piano" to showcase Melody's talent, plus a few of his Polish songs—translated into English—so Lizzie could sing. Unfortunately, Chopin didn't write music for the saxophone or trumpet, which left Bert out.

Lizzie felt a twinge of guilt at excluding Bert. Ever since she'd come upon him playing for change in Central Park, she'd felt protective toward the gawky youth who was only four years her junior, but seemed much younger. At the time, he was living a hand-to-mouth existence on the city streets after his father died and his mother took up with another man. Five minutes into listening to the skinny young man with the big ears play saxophone, she knew she had to convince him to join The Troubadours.

She took a seat beside Bert. "I hope you don't feel bad about not performing tonight. It's just this one time."

"I don't," he said. "I'll be here anyway, playing in my mind."

After Sidney finished Chopin's beautiful piece, Lizzie stood up and clapped her hands. "Lovely. Say, do you think we could break from tradition and have Bert play sax in 'Trio for Piano, Violin, and Cello' since we don't have a cellist?"

"Not so good. The horn's too bold." He slipped a cigarette into his silver holder, lit it, and waved it in dismissal. "Don't worry, Bert won't get in a lather. He's not an egomaniac like me."

"You just want to hog the whole show," she teased him. "Hey, wait a minute. What about the 'Clarinet Melody'? Scrap the Trio. You can't do it justice with only two musicians anyway. You fellas can play that instead."

Sidney snapped his fingers. "You're right, Bearcat. I forgot that one."

"What do you say, Bert?" she asked.

A lopsided smile brightened his face. "Sure, I'm game. My dad and I used to play that song together when I was a kid."

"Okay, you're on," Lizzie said. "And how about a waltz or two? Maybe we can get some of these flat tires up to dance." She leaned into the grand piano's curve, propping her elbow on its ebony body. "I wish we could put on a few humorous, dramatic sketches to lift the mood. I wonder why Duncan only hired us to play music instead of including our usual skits and dance routines."

"It's too cold for your infamous bathtub scene from *Porcelain and Pink*, Bearcat, and we'd never manage to get a motorcar up here for *While the Auto Waits*." He blew a few smoke rings. "I agree, it's damned depressing around here. But we're professionals. We made a commitment, and we're going to honor it. Besides, we need the money."

You don't. You're a trust-fund baby. But I sure do, Lizzie thought. "Don't I know-ski," she said.

"Then on with the show-ski."

Melody's footsteps echoed on the wooden floor as she entered the ballroom, carrying her flute case in one hand and her violin case in the other. "Sorry I'm late for practice. After our card game, Duncan's daughter Sabine cornered me and asked me a million questions. She wants to learn to play the flute."

"I hope you didn't offer to give her lessons," Sidney said.

The blond flutist blushed. "I did, actually."

He rolled his eyes. "Next, she'll want to perform with us."

"It's okay, Mel," Lizzie said. "You couldn't refuse. Besides, even if Sabine does want to play with us, what can it hurt? This isn't the New York Philharmonic, you know. And as you often say, Sid, we're paid to please."

She felt the draft on her neck again and turned up the collar of her woolen blouse. *Jeepers, creepers, where's that coming from? I hope Melody doesn't sense this eerie cold—I don't want her to panic and swear off performing tonight.*

"Fine, fine," Sidney said. "All right, let's get to it."

For the next hour, as her colleagues worked through Chopin's compositions, Lizzie strolled about the ballroom listening to how the music sounded in different parts of the commodious hall. To her satisfaction, Duncan's grandfather hadn't skimped on the acoustics when he built this castle. She tried to imagine what entertainments that long-ago music lover might have held in this space and promised herself she'd find out more about him.

Promptly at four o'clock, the elevator rumbled up its shaft and stopped at the third-floor ballroom. The door swung open, and the brawny kitchen maid, who'd introduced Lizzie to the elevator yesterday, stepped out bearing a silver tray of refreshments. She tiptoed across the room, trying not to disturb the musicians, and set the tray on the long oak trestle table.

Sidney stopped playing, and Melody followed suit. "Thank you," he called out to the servant. "The cavalry has arrived just in the nick of time."

The girl looked confused, and Lizzie laughed. As the maid returned to the elevator, the chandeliers blinked, not once but three times in succession.

* * *

When the afternoon's practice ended, Lizzie went downstairs to her bedchamber to rest for a while before the evening's performance. But as she turned into the hallway that ran the length of the second floor where Duncan housed his guests, she heard men's voices arguing.

"If it weren't for you, she might still be alive," one man said.

Lizzie flattened herself against the wall, just outside their range of vision, and eavesdropped.

"I have no idea what you're talking about," another said. His English accent tagged the speaker as Gregory Talbot.

The first man shot back angrily, "You got Natalie into this occult bushwa."

"Natalie made her own choices. I never forced her into anything—not that I could have anyway."

"She could've lived a normal life—"

"With you?" Gregory uttered a low, condescending sound that was part laugh, part growl. "Roger, what do you understand about any of it?"

"More than you think," Roger said. "I know she wanted to leave you."

"Really, my man? If she'd wanted to leave me, she would've done it a long time ago."

"You're a con artist. A cheap charlatan."

"And you're a low-life ruffian. At the moment, I'm also the grieving widower, so my position trumps yours—as it always has. Now move aside and let me pass."

"Don't be so sure of yourself. Crimes have a way of coming back to bite you on the ass."

Gregory laughed again. "You ought to know. Perhaps you should watch your own ass, eh?"

Footsteps muffled by carpeting thumped down the hall. Lizzie heard a door open and shut, and then another. When all grew quiet, she peeked around the corner. The hallway was empty. As she passed closed doors, wondering which guests occupied which bedrooms, she glanced at the door to the room where Natalie Talbot died and noticed it was ajar. *Perhaps a chambermaid is cleaning it,* she thought.

Tentatively, she pushed the door open. A bedside lamp illuminated the space, but she saw no one inside. The bed pillows and quilt had been plumped, and the deceased woman's belongings removed. The room appeared ready to receive another occupant.

Lizzie stepped inside. She didn't know what she was looking for as she circled the chamber, casting her gaze on one object after another: a chaise longue covered in flowered chintz, a mirrored vanity with an upholstered bench, a graceful writing desk. She inched open the desk's single drawer, which held stationery and a boxed pen-and-pencil set. Beside them lay a framed photograph.

Lizzie lifted out the black-and-white picture, faded with age. It depicted a scene of a gentleman and a young lady on horseback. The woman sat sidesaddle, her long full skirt billowing down over the horse's belly. Dressed for the hunt, she wore riding boots, a hat with a short veil, gloves, and carried a crop. Lizzie switched on the desk lamp and studied the photograph more closely. The faces, shadowed by the riders' hats, were unclear. As she puzzled over why the old picture had been tucked away in this desk drawer, she heard a sound behind her. She turned to see Gregory Talbot standing in the doorway.

"Why are you in my wife's bedroom, Miss Crane?"

Startled and squarely caught in an act of indiscretion, she couldn't think of a reasonable response.

The pale, thin man stepped toward her. "What have you there?"

"Just an old photograph."

"Let me see it." Gregory held out his hand, and Lizzie gave it to him. "Where did you find this?"

"Here, in the desk drawer."

"I'll keep it, thank you," he said.

"Who are the people in the picture?"

Gregory slid the photograph into his jacket pocket. "I think you should leave my wife's room now."

"Yes, of course."

He stepped aside to let her pass, and Lizzie walked to her own bedchamber next door. As she fit her key into the lock, she heard the door to what had been Natalie's room shut.

Chapter Six

"Narcotic drug addiction is one of the gravest and most important questions confronting the medical profession today. Instead of improving conditions the laws recently passed have made the problem more complex."

— American Medicine, November 1915

The burly policeman with a barely healed scar on his cheek stood at parade rest, his hands clasped behind his back, as Duncan's friends filed into the castle's lecture hall. In recent years, this space had hosted speakers in the arts, science, metaphysics, the Suffragist movement, and many more subjects. Standing beside the big copper, Duncan tugged nervously at the bottom of his Irish fisherman's sweater. His gray hair poked out in all directions like magnetized metal filings. His dark eyes studied his guests.

Lizzie sat on a straight-backed wooden chair between Sidney and Bert, waiting for what could only be bad news. The gray afternoon light filtering through the windows did little to chase the room's bleakness or musty odor. She crossed her arms over her plaid woolen blouse and shivered, not only from the cold.

Cora, dressed in a sporty, two-piece burnt-orange outfit, entered last. When she'd seated herself behind Ophelia and Kevin, Duncan cleared his throat and adjusted his spectacles.

"Friends, I apologize for dragging you away from your activities, but I'm afraid Sergeant O'Quinn here has some disturbing information for us."

The policeman unfolded his meaty hands and stepped closer to the front row of chairs, where Sabine and Jonathon Matthews sat. Beside them, Lizzie spotted a gray-haired woman she hadn't remembered meeting before. Wrapped in a heavy black shawl, her shoulders hunched, she listed awkwardly to one side, almost touching Sabine. *Could this be Duncan's reclusive sister Frances?*

"Ladies and gentlemen," Sergeant O'Quinn began. "You're all aware that a woman, Mrs. Gregory Talbot, died here Sunday night. To determine the cause of her untimely death, her husband agreed to an autopsy. We now have the results of the autopsy, which show that Mrs. Talbot died from an overdose of heroin."

Murmurs and cries of surprise arose from the group. They looked at one another with raised eyebrows. Sabine grasped her husband's hand. Duncan tugged at the cuffs of his sweater. Roger Young cracked his knuckles, his eyes fixed on the doorway as if judging whether he could reach it before the policeman tackled him.

Sergeant O'Quinn nodded at Gregory. "Mr. Talbot has stated that his wife never used drugs of any sort, and he suspects foul play. The police will be conducting an investigation into Natalie Talbot's death from an illegal narcotic. As Mrs. Talbot's friends, I ask you to come forward with any information you may have that might help the police resolve this situation. Even something you consider trivial might be useful. Until we know more about what happened here, I must ask you all to remain at Halcyon Castle."

"I can't believe this," Sidney grumbled.

Like Sid, Lizzie was stunned. She hadn't expected the police to determine the cause of death so quickly or to arrive at this conclusion. Perhaps they'd found needle marks in the woman's arms, and that aided their investigation? *Jeepers creepers. We've only been here two and a half days, and already a lady's been murdered, and we're all suspects.*

Kevin Wraith stood up. His wrinkled tweed suit looked as if he'd slept in it. "Sergeant, surely you don't suspect us of harming Natalie. She was our friend."

"No accusations have been made, sir," the policeman said. "I'm requesting that you, her friends, make yourselves available for questioning."

"What about the castle's staff?" Jonathon asked.

"I've already advised them to stay on site. My fellow officer will question them. I'll try not to keep you longer than necessary."

Duncan held his hands outstretched in a manner that conveyed his helplessness in the situation. "Please, everyone. I beg you to assist Sergeant O'Quinn in any way you can. I'm sure you feel, as I do, that the sooner we get to the bottom of this unhappy matter, the sooner Natalie's soul can rest in peace."

"Duncan's right," the woman with the long gray braid said. "Sergeant, I'm willing to answer your questions."

"And you are?"

"Yvonne Pasqual. I've known Duncan Fox for more than thirty years. His daughter Sabine is my goddaughter."

"Please come with me, ma'am." The policeman held out his hand to her, but she was as limber as someone half her age and needed no assistance getting up.

Duncan approached the hunched woman in the black shawl seated beside his daughter, and crooked his arm for her to grasp. Jonathon placed his hand on her back and helped her rise. Slowly, the bent woman, supported by the two men, shuffled out of the room. Sabine followed close behind them.

A few moments later, Lizzie saw Roger Young get up and slip away without a word to the others. Sidney and Bert agreed to speak to the policeman and asked to be notified when their turns came. Then they excused themselves on the pretense of having to practice for the evening's performance. After they'd left the lecture hall, a flurry of conversation broke out.

Ophelia shifted in her seat so she could see the others and adjusted her Indian-printed caftan to cover her thick ankles. "Am I all wet, or is that Irish cop insinuating that somebody killed Natalie? Maybe one of us?"

"Sounded like that to me," Helen said. "He's definitely treating this as a crime."

"What crime are we talking about? Possession of heroin? Trafficking? Murder?" Cora asked.

"Nat never used drugs," Gregory said. "Something's amiss."

With the strain of his wife's death, his pallid complexion seemed even more blanched than usual. *He looks like a corpse himself,* Lizzie thought.

"Where would a person get heroin anyway?" Melody asked, her blue eyes wide with confusion.

Lizzie knew plenty of musicians in New York used the drug, as well as opium and cocaine. But Melody was as naïve as a child about such things.

"Where does anyone get anything that's banned?" Ophelia asked, then answered her own question. "The black market, of course. Making something illegal doesn't make it unavailable, just a lot more expensive. You see how ineffective Prohibition has been at stopping the flow of booze."

"Thankfully," Helen said.

Several people laughed uneasily.

"Seriously, it wouldn't be hard," Kevin Wraith said. "Until a couple years ago, doctors prescribed heroin for all sorts of ailments. When Bayer first introduced it, parents gave it to their children as cough medicine. Cora, didn't your father use heroin to treat his tuberculosis?"

She nodded. "My mother bought it from the local chemist. It came in a glass vial along with a hypodermic needle, packaged in a pretty engraved tin."

Sergeant O'Quinn poked his head back into the lecture hall after interviewing Yvonne, and the conversation stopped abruptly. He glanced at the men and women and said, "Who's ready to talk with me next?"

"I guess I may as well get this over with," Kevin said, tugging his pointed beard.

After her husband and the policeman had disappeared down the hallway, Ophelia asked, "Greg, are you still planning to go through with Natalie's funeral?"

"Yes, if the police give the okay. Now that the autopsy's finished, it shouldn't be a problem." Despite the lecture hall's chill, beads of sweat dappled the spectral man's high forehead. He pulled a handkerchief from his pocket and dabbed at his face. "This morning I spoke with a minister from the Universalist Church in Gloucester, and he agreed to perform the service. Duncan's been generous, offering to host a memorial gathering here at the castle, but Nat's family have been members of that congregation for more than a hundred years. I've decided to hold the service there."

Lizzie studied Gregory's drawn face, his slumping shoulders that made his thin body appear as if it were imploding, and felt compassion for him. She brushed off the curt meeting she'd had with him yesterday in the bedroom where Natalie died. Even if the Talbots had reached a stumbling block in their marriage, even if Natalie had become romantically involved with Roger Young, this awful situation had taken a toll on her husband. *It's hard enough to lose someone close to you*, she thought, *but to lose her due to a possible crime or treachery must be dreadful beyond belief.*

When it was her turn to talk to the scarred policeman, Lizzie followed him into a small anteroom furnished only with a table and four wooden chairs like the ones in the lecture hall. No windows, no pictures on the wall. She couldn't imagine what purpose it had, unless it served as a storage area. Sergeant O'Quinn had commandeered it for his interrogations. She hadn't had time to change out of her casual attire before the policeman called the household to order. Now she watched him eyeing her tweed knickers, her dark bobbed hair, and rouged cheeks, and tried to imagine what picture he might be forming of her. Gloucester was a provincial town, a long way from Manhattan—culturally as well as geographically—and she questioned if that might work against her.

"You're a musician from New York City," O'Quinn said. "What brought you here?"

She folded her hands in her lap and forced herself to appear calm. "Mr. Fox hired my colleagues and me to provide entertainment for his fiftieth birthday party."

"Is this your first trip to Massachusetts?"

"No, we performed at a party in Ipswich in August."

The sergeant wrote in his notebook and tapped his pen on the table. He narrowed his eyes, as if trying to recall something just outside his range of memory. After a few moments, he gave up and asked, "You were here the night Mrs. Talbot died?"

"Yes."

"Your bedroom was next to Mrs. Talbot's?"

"Yes."

He scribbled in his notebook again. "New York's Chinatown is a center for the heroin trade in this country."

"I wouldn't know about that, sir."

He laid down his pen, folded his hands atop his notebook, and frowned at her. "You're a New York musician and you don't know that illegal drugs flow through Chinatown and the rest of the City, all day, every day? Forgive me, Miss Crane, but I find that hard to believe."

"Whether they do or don't is none of my business."

"You were the first person to enter Mrs. Talbot's bedroom after her death, correct?"

"Except for the housemaid who found her."

Her eyes traced the scar on his face, a ragged red line that ran from the outer corner of his eye down to his jaw, and wondered how he'd gotten it. *He's not much older than me, early thirties maybe,* she thought. O'Quinn was an Irish name, and he certainly looked as if he hailed from the Emerald Isle. However, he spoke without a brogue—barely even a Massachusetts accent.

A glimmer of recognition lit in his eyes, and he leaned toward her, resting his elbows on the table. "The Troubadours. Now I know why that name sounded familiar. A member of your group was killed at Zachary Winslow's Ipswich estate in August."

"Yes, but—"

"Sorry, I can't discuss the case. It hasn't come to trial yet." He tapped his pen rapidly on his notebook. "Still, one wonders about the coincidence of you being present at two suspicious deaths within a period of two months, Miss Crane, and in a state where you don't reside."

Fear burned in Lizzie's chest, but she struggled to keep it from showing on her face. The stigma of her former colleague's murder hung over her like the sword of Damocles, casting suspicion on her for Natalie Talbot's death.

"Is there anything else you'd like to tell me, Miss Crane?"

Lizzie shook her head. "There's nothing more to tell."

"If you remember anything, I'll expect you to contact me."

* * *

Returning to her bedchamber for a warm jacket, Lizzie noticed the door to the room next to hers, the room where Natalie Talbot had died, hung open. Inside she saw a policeman opening drawers and poking into cabinets.

"Hello there," she said.

The officer, a middle-aged man with a ruddy face and bulbous nose, turned and held up his hands, signaling her to stop. "Don't come into the room."

"Why not?"

"I'm examining a crime scene. I don't want you contaminating it."

But Lizzie had already explored the bedchamber, and her fingerprints were on its writing desk. How many of Duncan's guests and servants had already traipsed through this room? She tried to recall which curious friends had entered the morning they'd discovered Natalie's body.

From the doorway, she asked, "What are you looking for?"

"Evidence. Who are you?"

"Elizabeth Crane, one of Mr. Fox's guests. I'm the one who insisted on calling the police when the maid found Mrs. Talbot's body. Sergeant O'Quinn said Mrs. Talbot died of a heroin overdose. Have you found any drugs?"

"I wouldn't tell you if I had. This is a police investigation, Miss Crane. Everything is confidential."

Lizzie leaned against the doorjamb. "I understand, sir. It's just, well, I got the impression from Sergeant O'Quinn that Mrs. Talbot might have been murdered. I'm not familiar with these things as, of course, you are. But it would seem that if the lady accidentally overdosed, she might have left behind some of the drug or perhaps a syringe. On the other hand, if someone killed her, that person would probably have taken the 'evidence' away with him."

The policeman raised an eyebrow, but otherwise kept his face expression-less. "You aren't involved in law enforcement, are you, Miss Crane?"

"No, I'm an entertainer."

"Then please go entertain someone else and leave me to my work."

Chapter Seven

"I am all in a sea of wonders. I doubt; I fear; I think strange things, which I dare not confess to my own soul."

— *Bram Stoker, Dracula*

Her conversations with the two policemen had left Lizzie desperate to escape the darkness within the castle's walls. Her mind spun as she puzzled over Sergeant O'Quinn's revelation: Natalie Talbot had died from an overdose of an illegal drug. How would the discovery affect The Troubadours? Did the big Irish cop suspect her and her colleagues because of a previous scandal?

She hurried outside where she could breathe fresh air and walked briskly toward the tip of the rocky promontory that overlooked the ocean. As she passed the saltwater swimming pool, she spotted Yvonne Pasqual. Seated on a wooden lounge chair, Yvonne was wrapped in a gray shawl and reading a book. The older woman waved, and Lizzie waved back. *How many of the other guests has Sergeant O'Quinn questioned by now?* she wondered.

The wind nearly whipped Lizzie's cloche hat away, and she pulled it down more securely until only the ends of her chocolaty hair peeked out below the felt brim. She glanced back at the castle. Had the policeman interviewed Sidney yet? Halcyon's high stone walls reached down to the ocean, as if the castle grew organically out of the rocky coastline. Its turrets and arches and peaked slate roof reminded her of the fairy tale castles in Maxfield Parrish's paintings.

I hope O'Quinn went easy on Sid. She worried that her friend's current state of frustration and disappointment would arouse suspicion. Sidney's rather effeminate and fussy behavior might also give the tough, burly copper reason to pick on the pianist.

From the promontory, she watched a few small sailboats cutting across the water. Closer to shore, a lobsterman chugged along, checking his traps. A sleek wooden motorboat with a dark green cabin slowed to minimize its wake as it approached the lobsterman. Seagulls scavenged among the sea-blackened rocks far below, searching for a meal. The rhythmic motion of the waves lulled Lizzie into a meditative state. Her mind began to drift.

Suddenly, she realized the motorboat had disappeared. She couldn't hear the roar of its motor anymore either. *That's odd,* she thought. *Where did it go? Did I nod off?* The other boats were still there, however. She stood and walked around the edge of the promontory, looking in every direction, but saw no sign of the missing craft. For a moment, she toyed with the idea of climbing down the cliff to the water's edge, but the risk of tumbling into the sea below made her reconsider.

For half an hour, she sat on a boulder, watching the waves break on the rocks below. The elusive motorboat didn't reappear. The lobsterman finished checking his traps and putted away. She stood up, brushed off the seat of her pants, and walked back toward the castle. *All these peculiar goings on must have addled my brain,* she decided. *I def-in-ate-ly need a drink.*

* * *

Lizzie found the formidable housekeeper, Mrs. Beane, in the medieval-designed dining room, barking orders to the German maid Inge and another girl with dark curls and creamy skin.

"Mrs. Beane, I'd like to speak with Mr. Fox. Would you please see if he's available?" Lizzie asked.

The buxom woman smoothed her starched white apron and frowned. Her face, pinched and ashen, revealed the stress of the past few days. Without answering, she strode out of the room and down the central hallway to where a boxy wood-and-metal intercom sat on a table. She lifted the receiver, turned a dial, and spoke into the Bakelite mouthpiece. After a brief exchange, Mrs. Beane signaled Lizzie to follow her into the elevator. The matron pressed a button, and the lift rumbled up to a section of the castle's third floor where Duncan Fox and his sister Frances had their private quarters.

Trailing behind the stout housekeeper, Lizzie couldn't help wondering how Duncan's servants had reacted to the news that a guest had died here from an overdose of an illegal drug, possibly murdered. She worried about the young chambermaids and serving girls hoping to make their way, and the older women struggling to feed and clothe their families. Having come from a poor family herself, Lizzie knew how tenuous their lot was in the world. Would this controversy put a black mark on their employment records? Get them dismissed, or even worse, implicate them in a crime? If any were illegal immigrants, might they be deported?

Although the door to Duncan's study stood ajar, Mrs. Beane rapped on it and waited until her employer waved the two women in.

"Ah, Lizzie Crane. How good of you to come." He rose and motioned for her to take a seat across from his cluttered desk. His voice seemed strained and tired. "Thank you, Mrs. Beane. That will be all for now."

Lizzie sat in a Chippendale chair that seemed incongruently delicate next to Duncan's huge oak desk. Everywhere she looked, she saw stacks of books and piles of papers. Books cascaded onto the floor, perched on windowsills, and spilled over every other surface. A thick tome even served as a doorstop.

What a joy it would be to own so many books, she mused. Although she'd never finished high school, Lizzie thirsted for knowledge. When she was a girl, she snuck away to the public library whenever she could and scavenged newspapers left behind at the barbershop where her father worked. The only book her parents owned was a worn King James Bible.

"I apologize for disturbing you," she said. "I can't imagine how upsetting this whole affair must be for you. My condolences for the loss of your friend. Have you known Mrs. Talbot for a long time?"

"Since she was a girl. She and my sister Frances were friends in school, although Natalie only came back into our lives a few years ago. She and Greg lived in England for two decades," he answered. "I realize this whole sordid mess must be quite unnerving for you. I hope you haven't come to tell me you're going to leave us and drive back to New York at first light."

If only we could, Lizzie wished. "Actually, I came to ask if you wanted my colleagues and me to continue playing for your guests, or if you've decided to cancel the engagement due to all that's transpired."

Duncan steepled his hands on his round belly and forced a smile. His spritely manner that she'd admired upon first meeting him had faded. "Dear Lizzie, nothing would please me more right now than if you agreed to continue entertaining us with your splendid music. Without that to look forward to, I fear we'd all rattle around in this dank and drafty castle, getting on one another's nerves, until the police give my guests leave to go home."

Sergeant O'Quinn wasn't about to let The Troubadours go home yet either, but she didn't point that out. "I was afraid you might think it inappropriate for us to continue performing under the circumstances."

"Good heavens, no. Quite the opposite. You'll rescue us from our doldrums. Now, as I recall, you and your friends play jazz."

"That's our specialty."

"Splendid. Then given today's dreary events, I think we might benefit from a pleasant diversion. Would you be willing to brighten our collective mood with some cheerful songs?"

"Ab-so-lute-ly." For the first time since Natalie Talbot's death, Lizzie felt a spark of optimism. "I'm sure I speak for my colleagues when I say we'd be delighted. Thank you ever so much for this opportunity. I promise you won't be disappointed."

* * *

Relieved that Duncan had asked The Troubadours to continue performing, Lizzie hurried down the castle's second-story hallway. Unlike the third-floor halls with their bare wooden floors, this one was covered with worn oriental runners that looked as though they might have come to Gloucester on clipper ships in the middle of the last century. She hoped to find Sidney in his bedroom working on the opera he'd been composing for more than a year. Instead, she almost literally ran into Bert, leaving his own room with a fishing pole in his hand.

"Oh, Bert, I'm sorry," she said. "I never meant to drag you into such a mess. This isn't what you expected when you signed on with us."

The shy saxophonist shrugged. "I signed on to play music."

"You don't feel uneasy about getting caught up in a police investigation? Or that a woman died here?"

"Got a roof over my head and three squares a day. That's good enough for me." His mouth turned up in a lopsided smile. "I appreciate your concern, Lizzie, but I've been through a lot worse."

"I know," she said. "It's just, well, you're a valuable addition to the group. You've only been with us a month. I wouldn't want to lose you."

"Not a chance, unless you boot me out. But if you're worried about losing someone, look to Melody."

Taken aback, Lizzie asked, "Why do you say that?"

Bert thumped his fishing pole on the toe of his shoe. "She's got this rich daddy she hopes is gonna marry her. A home and kids and all. A nice, normal life."

"She told you that?"

"Not in so many words, but yeah, that's her plan. And no man's gonna let his wife go off for weeks at a time with a bunch of entertainers, to who knows where and what." He paused as if trying to decide how much to share with the woman who was both his protector and employer. After a moment's deliberation, he said, "Hasn't she talked to you about it? You being friends and all?"

The Troubadours without Melody? *Why didn't I realize this?* Lizzie asked herself. *Bert's right. Especially after all the bad press we've gotten, and now we're mixed up in another murder.*

The talented young musician had joined Sidney and Lizzie two years ago, after they heard her perform at the wedding of one of Sid's friends. Although Melody was only seventeen at the time, her musical ability and poise belied her youth. It had taken months to convince her doting parents to let their only daughter hook up with two New York jazz performers, but finally, their desire to see her happy outweighed their apprehension. Until now, however, Lizzie hadn't considered that Melody might be planning another future.

She shifted the conversation to safer ground, until she had time to think about the possibility he'd raised. "What's with the fishing pole?"

"Mr. Wraith's been showing me how to fish here. I used to go fishing in the Catskills and Rangeley Lake in Maine with my dad when I was a kid, but I've never fished in the ocean before."

"Does this mean I can expect fresh bass for dinner soon?"

Bert shook his head. "We don't keep what we catch. We let 'em go."

"Humanitarians, eh?"

"Yeah, I guess. I don't like to see any creature killed just for sport."

Lizzie smiled at the awkward young man she was still getting to know. At least he didn't seem ready to abandon The Troubadours in the midst of all this hoopla.

"I don't know the fishing equivalent of 'break a leg', but whatever it is, good luck and have fun," she said. "See you later in the ballroom for practice."

* * *

After questioning all the occupants, Sergeant O'Quinn and his fellow officer mounted their motorcycles and roared across the drawbridge, away from Halcyon Castle. From her bedroom window, Lizzie watched them pass through the open dragon-guarded gate as the sun's last rays melted into the sea. She sighed with relief, then went downstairs to meet Sidney in the billiard room.

Dapper in a gray tweed lambswool jacket and maroon tie, he smoked a cigarette while jotting notes on a pad of paper. A bottle and two glasses with ice cubes waited at the center of a game table.

"A spot of gin-ski?" he asked. "I liberated it from behind the bar."

"I'm in-ski," she said, even though it was still early in the afternoon. As he poured, she related her conversation with their host. "Duncan asked for 'cheerful songs' tonight, to try to lighten the grummy atmosphere around here. I'm thinking we could do some show tunes: 'Dinah,' 'Tea for Two,' and 'I Want to Be Happy.' "

He scribbled on his notepad. "Got 'em."

"And 'Who Stole My Heart Away.' Duncan and his guests probably haven't heard it yet."

Sidney added the song from the new Broadway musical *Sunny* that had opened last month. "Good idea. Bring a little New York class to the hinterlands."

Although he managed The Troubadours' bookings and finances, Sidney usually deferred to Lizzie when it came to orchestrating their performances. She chose the music they played, choreographed their dance numbers, directed their skits, and selected the outfits they wore. Even at the age of nineteen, when they'd first met while working at a nightspot in Greenwich Village, she'd demonstrated an intuitive ability to tune into an audience's mood and give them what they wanted. That ability, coupled with her arresting beauty and talent, had enabled the group to move up from speakeasies to lucrative private venues in the homes of wealthy people, such as Duncan Fox.

For nearly an hour, they tossed around possibilities, vetoed some, agreed on others, until they'd compiled a repertoire they hoped would surpass Duncan Fox's expectations. Music offered Lizzie and her friends a refuge from this nightmarish scenario. For a few hours a day, they could immerse themselves in it, forgetting the rest. Perhaps they could help Duncan's guests do the same.

Voices echoed down the central hallway. Lizzie easily recognized Ophelia's braying, but the others melded together in a collective muddle. The group turned into the parlor across the hall from the billiard room.

"Are we copacetic here, Sid?" she asked, straining her ears to hear their conversation.

"You're itching to snoop around in their business, aren't you, Bearcat?"

"Ab-so-lute-ly. I want to find out what that policeman asked them and what they think about this whole balled-up mess. The more I know, the better prepared we'll be to fend off the coppers."

"But we're clean as a whistle," he protested.

She shrugged. "I know, but innocence doesn't guarantee safety."

"All right," he gave in, waving her off with his cigarette holder. "See you in the ballroom later." He tossed back the last of his drink, stood, and patted her on the head. "Let me know what you find out, Agatha Christie."

* * *

By the time Lizzie entered, Ophelia Wraith, dressed in a boldly patterned woolen frock that resembled a Navaho blanket and made her look a bit like a teepee, had settled herself on one of the ruby-colored velvet sofas near the grand parlor's fireplace. Her fetish-like necklace hung between her pendulous breasts. Her husband Kevin stood nearby, puffing on his pipe. Duncan's daughter Sabine and Cora, the card reader, had taken up positions in two comfortable leather armchairs. Helen Simms, wearing woolen trousers and a thick cabled sweater that made her appear even boxier than usual, sat on the stone hearth, leisurely smoking a cigarette. Behind her, a fire crackled and shot sparks up the chimney. She waved to the singer, motioning Lizzie to join the group.

Still holding her drink, Lizzie took a seat on one of the sofas. Before she could broach the topic of Sergeant O'Quinn, however, Helen said, "Ophelia's going to try to contact Natalie again."

"In light of today's news, we simply *must* know what happened," Ophelia said.

Kevin nodded. "My wife has agreed to go into a trance and allow our departed friend Natalie to speak through her. If you're all comfortable and ready to begin, I'll serve as Ophelia's guide. I remind you that during her communication with Natalie, none of you shall speak or leave the room."

He stared at each member of the group in turn, as if to make sure they understood before he sat down beside Ophelia. The medium closed her eyes and rested her hands on her lap. She began breathing slowly, deeply. After a few minutes, her head tilted to the left. Her eyelids fluttered. Her mouth hung slack. Her shoulders drooped. Gradually, her breathing took on a rasping sound, much like a snore.

Kevin raised his arms and called out to the dead woman in a commanding voice. He reminded Lizzie of an evangelical preacher, except for the meerschaum pipe he still held in one hand. "Natalie, your friends are gathered here in love and respect. We hope you're at peace now on the Other Side. But we're stunned and confused about your passing. The police suspect murder." He lowered his arms and took a few puffs on his pipe before continuing. "Tell us what happened, Nat. Speak to us through the vocal cords of your friend, Ophelia. We seek to know the truth."

All eyes focused on the entranced woman, whose plump hands twitched in her lap. She turned her head slowly from side to side, like an antenna trying to pick up a signal. Her loose, blue-black hair hung down over her shoulders. When she finally spoke, her voice was soft and sad, nothing like her usual brassy bravado. "I paid for my sin."

Lizzie recalled the argument she'd overheard yesterday between Gregory Talbot and Natalie's alleged lover, Roger Young. Was infidelity the sin the woman meant? Or the crime of using an illegal drug?

"Had to leave," the medium mumbled. "Couldn't stay here anymore."

Kevin lowered his voice and spoke in a more solicitous tone. "Why, Natalie?"

"Too much pain and suffering."

"I understand. Earth is full of suffering."

Suddenly, an idea popped into Lizzie's head, one she hadn't thought of before. Could the lady have killed herself intentionally? Since Sergeant O'Quinn's revelation, she'd considered only two possible causes of death: murder or an accidental overdose. Had Natalie Talbot committed suicide? Used heroin to end whatever misery she referred to now? Lizzie remembered Cora's tarot reading and the sad card that pictured a heart with three swords piercing it.

Kevin leaned closer to his wife until his forehead nearly touched hers. "Natalie, was your death an accident, or did someone do this to you?"

Sabine fidgeted in her chair, waiting for the medium's reply. She glanced around nervously at the others as if trying to read their expressions. Cora fingered her rope of pearls. Helen ground out her cigarette, flipped the butt into the fireplace, and lit another.

"No accident."

The overhead lights flickered twice. Lizzie looked up at the half-dozen fixtures that hung on chains from the parlor's ceiling. *Must be a short in the electrical wiring,* she thought as the lights blinked again. And again.

"Natalie, did someone kill you?" Kevin asked. "Who?"

A loud, whining sound, like an anguished cry, rang out. Then one of the light fixtures at the far end of the parlor crashed to the floor. Amber glass shattered. Sabine shrieked. Cora clapped her hands over her face. Ophelia snapped out of her trance.

"Everyone, stay calm," Kevin ordered, waving his pipe like a conductor's baton.

Sabine jumped up and dashed out of the room.

Lizzie moved from beneath another overhead fixture, just in case it decided to come undone too. Was faulty installation or a rusted-out fastener to blame? Had someone tampered with the hardware to loosen it from the ceiling? But if so, why?

In the confusion, she studied each member of the party in turn, trying to assess their reactions to the unsettling event. Ophelia blinked repeatedly like someone who'd been jarred from a deep sleep. Helen, seated at the hearth, leaned forward, rested her elbows on her knees, and frowned at Kevin as if to say, "What ruse are you up to now?" Cora, after slowly dropping her jeweled hands from her face, stared at the broken glass on the parlor floor with curiosity as if the pattern formed by the pieces might, like tea leaves, offer an explanation.

What was all that about? Lizzie wondered, then answered her own question. If what the Spiritualists believed, that the dead could talk, Natalie Talbot had been about to reveal her murderer's name. Someone or something didn't want that name spoken.

Chapter Eight

"The average man is not hard to mystify."

— *Howard Thurston, stage magician*

Still feeling uneasy after this afternoon's disconcerting experiment in mediumship, Lizzie was glad to escape into music. Duncan's request for cheerful tunes let her sing some of her favorite songs, including George and Ira Gershwin's "Oh, Lady Be Good" and "Somebody Loves Me." "Rhapsody in Blue" gave Bert an opportunity to show his skill at clarinet with Sid at the piano. From the ballroom stage, she studied Duncan and his guests seated around the long oak banquet table. No one had gotten up to dance. However they appeared a bit more animated than last night, and she hoped the music had lifted their spirits.

Unfortunately, there was no one in the audience she wanted to charm with her sultry voice and sensuous figure. *I brought along all these gorgeous gowns, and for what?* she lamented. Her mind flashed back to The Troubadours' ill-fated engagement two months ago at the nearby estate of industrialist Zachary Winslow. Despite the awful events that had occurred there, Lizzie fondly recalled a handsome, wealthy gentleman from one of Boston's elite families who'd seemed taken with her. He'd promised to meet her for dinner the next time he visited New York, but so far, only a few letters had passed between them. Had he forgotten about her or, more likely, found another focus for his attention? Handsome, wealthy, single gentlemen had seemingly infinite possibilities available to them.

After finishing glasses of port and pineapple upside-down cake, Duncan's guests began drifting away from the banquet table to find other amusements. *To consult their tarot cards and talking boards?* Lizzie wondered.

A shiver ran up her spine as she mentally replayed what Ophelia had said only a few hours ago, while supposedly channeling Natalie Talbot's spirit. Thankfully, none of the other Troubadours had been in the parlor to witness that peculiar scene. Lizzie had observed so many strange goings-on at Halcyon Castle already, she had no idea what might happen next. Still, she refused to believe ghosts or other spirits were responsible. *There has to be a logical explanation,* she told herself.

When only Duncan remained seated at the antique trestle table, Melody and Bert packed up their instruments. Sidney's fingers still toyed with the Steinway's keyboard. She suspected Bert longed for some activity, other than fishing, to break the tedium of their confinement in this dark, gloomy castle. On several occasions, she'd spotted him at the billiard table or playing cards with Duncan's son-in-law Jonathon and Natalie Talbot's alleged lover Roger Young. She hoped these were just friendly games, and that no serious money was changing hands. She didn't want The Troubadours to be held responsible if their horn player got himself into debt gambling with people beyond his league. *I should talk to Sid about it. And Bert.*

Then she reminded herself, *you're not his mother. He's twenty-two years old.* Bert had lived on the streets of New York for a couple years before she'd invited him to join The Troubadours. He probably knew more than she did about the dark side of life. Still, she felt responsible for bringing him—and Melody too—here to a situation for which they were ill prepared. Fortunately, the young flutist had calmed down a bit since Lizzie switched bedrooms with her.

Lifting the skirt of her plum-colored gown, she stepped down from the stage and crossed the ballroom to the long trestle table. She took a seat beside their host in the chair vacated by his daughter Sabine.

"What a marvelous performance," Duncan said. "Thank you, Lizzie. You and your friends helped take our minds off our problems for a while."

"I'm glad you enjoyed it. I'm sure I speak for my colleagues when I say we're happy to have given you and your friends a bit of a lift."

The elevator clanked up to the ballroom, bringing two kitchen maids, the hearty girl who'd shown Lizzie how to use the lift and a middle-aged woman with graying hair, to clear away the remaining dishes.

"Duncan, I wonder if I might ask you something? It's about Mrs. Talbot. I don't want to trouble you if it's too painful a subject."

Cora's tarot reading and Yvonne's suggestion that a heart problem might have led to Natalie's death sparked an idea in Lizzie's mind. Then Natalie, speaking through Ophelia about her "pain and suffering," had opened another possibility. Lizzie didn't mention the chandelier that crashed, but felt certain Sabine, Ophelia, or one of the others would tell Duncan about it soon if they hadn't already.

"I think I can handle it, my dear. Ask away."

"Did Mrs. Talbot suffer from an illness that she might have treated with heroin?"

Duncan shook his shaggy gray head slowly. "No, not that I'm aware of."

"It's just that, well, her husband said she didn't use drugs even though the policeman said she died from an overdose of heroin. Doctors prescribed it for all sorts of ailments—until recently, that is."

"Surely Greg would know if his wife were taking heroin for a medical condition." He turned a ring with a big red stone around his finger several times.

"Forgive me if I'm being too bold, but the Talbots didn't seem very close. They had separate bedchambers." *Did Duncan know about the rumored affair between Natalie and Roger Young?* "I just wondered if she might have been trying to relieve the discomfort of an ailment and accidentally taken too much of the drug."

"I'll try to find out. I'd rather believe that than think she was murdered."

* * *

Emulating Jonathon Matthews's ease behind the billiard room bar, Lizzie pulled a bottle of scotch from the lineup and poured golden liquid into two glasses: one for Sidney and one for herself. At this late hour, the rest of Duncan's guests had retired to their bedchambers. But Lizzie felt too keyed up from the events of the day to sleep yet.

Still dressed in her seductive purple gown, she took a seat beside her longtime friend. She raised her glass and toasted. "Here's to jazz. It feels good to get back to it, don't you think-ski?"

"Yes, and thanks for the drink-ski." Sidney clinked his glass to hers, but without enthusiasm.

They'd played well tonight, and their audience seemed pleased. Usually, a good performance boosted Sidney's spirits, but not this time.

"That mulligan cop has it in for us, Bearcat. I'm afraid one of us might go to jail either for murder or drug trafficking, even though we're not involved in either." He took a sip of his scotch, and then another. A worried look darkened his face. Bluish half-moons under his eyes indicated he hadn't been sleeping well. "It's all guilt by implication. Our past taints us. I think we should pack up tonight and beat it back to the city while we still have a chance."

"We'd never get past the dragon gate, and the only other way in and out is by sea," Lizzie said. The tall, iron gate at the property's entrance not only prevented unwanted visitors from coming in, it also kept those inside from leaving.

Sidney fingered his formal bat-wing tie. "There's got to be a way to open it—we just have to figure out how."

He's right, Lizzie realized. The night The Troubadours arrived at Halcyon the gate swung aside to admit them. It opened on its own again to allow Sergeant O'Quinn and his colleague to leave the property. A switch must exist somewhere in the castle, but where?

"What did O'Quinn ask you?"

"It wasn't what he asked as much as what he insinuated," Sidney answered.

"About Henry's murder, you mean?"

"Right. I fear *that* calamity will dog us for the rest of our lives," he said glumly. "Oh, and Melody told me you two swapped bedrooms. What's this about hearing men's voices in the walls?"

"Applesauce, it's all her imagination. You know how impressionable she is. This creepy castle and the lady dying and all, well, Mel's pretty spooked. I didn't want her to get in a panic and not be able to play." Lizzie didn't tell him she'd heard the voices too.

He shook his head. "Still, it's not good. It could raise suspicion. People might think you're trying to hide something."

"If that copper searches our rooms, he won't find a thing out of the ordinary. Well, nothing out of the ordinary for two New York performers." She told him about encountering the second policeman rummaging about in Natalie Talbot's bedroom.

"Bearcat, stay out of it. Don't draw attention to yourself."

She struck a jesting, seductive pose. "That's not easy for a tomato like me. Anyway, I thought we played swell tonight, and everyone seemed to enjoy the show. A break from the doom and gloom of these past couple days."

"We did, didn't we?"

Sidney's face brightened slightly, and she thought, as she had so many times before, *how handsome he is. If only he preferred women instead of men...*

"At least Duncan wants us to stay on for the whole contract. I was afraid he'd cancel and refuse to pay us."

"Yes, that's a relief." He lit a cigarette and exhaled a lungful of smoke. "Lizzie, do you think we're jinxed? I mean, what are the odds of us getting tangled up in two murder cases in two months?"

"I'm not a gambling girl, but I'd guess maybe a million to one. May I point out, however, that Natalie Talbot's death hasn't been declared a murder yet. Despite what her husband claims, the lady may have been on the needle and simply got more than she bargained for."

"True. What do you make of this weird lot?"

"Duncan and his friends?" She considered the talking board incident, Ophelia's attempt to channel the dead woman's spirit, Cora's tarot reading, and Helen's admission of being an astrologer. *You don't know the half of it, Sid.* "They're peculiar, but hey, we're from New York City, home to all the planet's peculiar sorts."

Sidney smiled and clinked his glass to hers. "Touché."

* * *

Still too animated to sleep, Lizzie wandered the castle's eerie spaces. Some, such as the comfortable parlor and the billiard room with its well-stocked bar, had obvious purposes. Others, including the room guarded by the medieval suit of armor and the one filled with stuffed wild animals, seemed to exist only to showcase the owner's collection of oddities. Now that cold weather had set in, whole wings were closed off. What strange things might those contain? Unicorn horns? Egyptian mummies? A torture chamber in the basement?

Duncan had generously offered to let her use his personal library on the third floor. Now seemed like a good time to take advantage of that opportunity. Lifting the long skirt of her evening gown, she climbed the staircase that flowed like a stone waterfall from the ballroom to the castle's central hall. To her delight, the library's door was open. She pressed a switch, sparking the room's electric lights to life.

For a moment, she paused in the doorway, awed by the immensity of what stretched before her. Never, except in the New York Public Library, had she seen so many books gathered together in one place. Shelves that stretched floor-to-ceiling lined the walls of a room that could have held several apartments the size of her Greenwich Village flat. Ladders mounted on wheels provided access to the topmost rows. A refectory table with benches on either side sat in the midst of all this literary wealth. At one end of the vast chamber, in an alcove where windows overlooked the ocean, four upholstered armchairs nestled around an octagonal coffee table strewn with magazines.

As if entering a museum, Lizzie stepped into Duncan's private library. She made her way along the stacks, running her fingertips over the books' leather spines and reading their gold-embossed titles. Works of history, science, and philosophy regaled her. Novels by all the great writers were arranged in alphabetical order according to author. But after a bit, she found herself drawn to a section at one end of the room near a desk with legs carved to resemble griffins. The books here bore titles such as *Knowledge of the Higher World and Its Attainment* by Rudolf Steiner, *The Secret Doctrine* by Helena Blavatsky, and *The Book of the Law* by Aleister Crowley. On others, she saw the names Gurdjieff, Ouspensky, Mary Baker Eddy, and William Butler Yeats.

Reverently, she pulled book after book from the shelves and thumbed through them. Each expressed ideas so unusual she couldn't begin to comprehend their meanings, yet she longed to know more. Hugging three to her chest, she moved on to a rack of magazines and journals. A headline on the cover of one magazine caught her eye: "Psychics Trick Grieving Families." Curious, Lizzie opened the two-year-old publication and flipped through the pages until a picture of Gregory and Natalie Talbot stopped her. An accompanying article claimed:

"This is not the first time the duplicitous duo, Mr. and Mrs. Gregory Talbot, have been called into question for preying upon vulnerable citizens. Mr. Talbot, an English photographer, now residing in Boston, Massachusetts, and his wife Natalie Talbot, a self-proclaimed psychic and medium, faced trial three years ago for attempting to gain control of a widow's assets after convincing her that her deceased husband intended his sizable fortune go to support the Talbots' esoteric research."

Charges were dismissed, Lizzie read at the end of the article. But its author had raised suspicions that set her mind whirring. Supposedly the Talbots had duped numerous people into believing the pair had photographed the ghostly spirits of departed loved ones. The couple also claimed they conveyed those spirits' "messages" to relatives left behind on earth, messages that often encouraged the living to hand over large sums of money or other assets to the Talbots.

Lizzie added the magazine to her armload of books, trying to make sense of what she'd read about Duncan's friends. Had grief-stricken people pressed charges because the Talbots' claims didn't meet up to their expectations? Had greed reared its ugly head when family members discovered their deceased relatives had bequeathed money elsewhere? Or had the Talbots actually tricked unsuspecting folks into signing away their property to a pair of frauds?

While she descended the stairway to the second floor, the last of those musings tumbled around in Lizzie's brain. She recalled Roger Young's hallway confrontation with Gregory Talbot yesterday and his accusation: "You're a con artist. A cheap charlatan." If it was true, might someone who believed Natalie Talbot swindled him have taken revenge on her? But the people gathered here at Halcyon Castle were longtime colleagues of the Talbots, occultists themselves, not unsuspecting clients. They wouldn't have fallen for supernatural tricks. And no one except Duncan's friends and family had access to Natalie Talbot on the night she died. Still, the idea stuck in her mind like a burr.

She opened the heavy oak door to what was now her bedroom, glad to find that one of the chambermaids had lit a fire in the grate and the room was pleasantly warm. She took off her evening dress and hung it in the wardrobe. Then she slipped quietly into the bathroom between her room and Melody's. After washing off her face paint, she curled up in bed with the magazine she'd brought from Duncan's library. Before she managed to get very far into an article about spirit photography, however, sleep overtook her.

Chapter Nine

"The Tarot is a pictorial representation of the Forces of Nature as conceived by the Ancients according to a conventional symbolism."

— Aleister Crowley, The Thoth Tarot

When Lizzie awoke, she noticed two dry, brownish leaves, each about the size of her hand, clinging to the shade of the electric lamp she'd left burning on her bedside table. *How odd,* she thought as she reached to pluck them off. The "leaves" flapped away. She shrieked as the bat circled the ceiling of her bedchamber and then landed on the drapery rod.

The door of the bathroom between their two bedchambers burst open, and Melody rushed in. "What's wrong?"

"Only a nightmare," Lizzie lied. She didn't want Melody to start worrying about vampires again. "Sorry I woke you."

"This place would give anyone the night frights."

"I'm okay now, truly. Go back to bed."

After her friend had retreated, Lizzie stared at the creepy creature perched atop the heavy drapes. It must have flown down the chimney, she reasoned. *Except a fire was burning in the fireplace.* Hot coals still glowed in the grate. *How did it get in? And why was it hanging on the lamp? Bats don't like light.*

She threw off the eiderdown and climbed out of bed. Even though the clock on the vanity showed it was only a few minutes past six, she knew she couldn't go back to sleep now. She slipped into a pair of woolen trousers and a thick sweater, then pulled on warm socks and low-heeled shoes. After running a brush through her bobbed hair, she went downstairs and located a housemaid.

She couldn't remember having ever seen this maid before, a tall, thin woman about her own age with high cheekbones, ruddy skin, and long dark hair tied back from her face. Lizzie explained the problem and asked, "Would you please have someone remove it straight away?"

"Yes, ma'am. Which room is it?"

Lizzie told her and pressed a coin in the maid's palm. "And without a lot of fuss. I don't want to frighten my friend in the adjoining room. She has a delicate constitution."

"Certainly, ma'am. And thank you." The young woman dipped her head deferentially, avoiding eye contact with Lizzie, and said in a low voice, "Pardon me, ma'am, but the bat may be a messenger."

"What?"

"Bats can 'see' in the dark, you know. Perhaps this one has come in a time of darkness to tell you to use your inner sight."

Before Lizzie could make sense of what the maid had said or ask for further illumination, the woman hurried off. *Even the servants here are strange,* she thought as she made her way down the central hallway toward the dining room. Oil portraits of men and women dressed in Victorian clothing, whom she guessed were Duncan's ancestors, stared down from the walls at her. Her heels clicked on the stone floor. Not for the first time, she questioned why Duncan hadn't installed rugs in the long, shadowy corridor to make it seem less bleak.

No one but the servants appeared to be up and about at this hour. A boy who looked to be about twelve years old squatted before the dining room's massive fireplace, coaxing tentative flames to ignite the logs he'd laid in the iron grate. Lizzie had barely seated herself when the freckled kitchen maid greeted her with a pot of coffee.

"Would you like breakfast, ma'am?"

"Yes, thank you. Would you please bring me an egg over easy, some bacon, and toast with gobs of butter and jam?"

"Certainly, ma'am."

Lizzie sipped the strong black coffee, feeling the caffeine nudge away the lingering dullness due to lack of sleep. "Horrid bat," she grumbled. *At least Melody didn't see it. She would've had kittens.*

As the sun made its slow ascent, a soft ochre glow shone through the three lancet windows, whose pointed tops symbolically reached toward the heavens. Even so, the cavernous room with its low beamed ceiling, heavy Jacobean furniture, and stone floor remained oppressive. While she waited for the girl to return, she studied the tapestries hanging on three of the walls. Each was about the size of a bed sheet and featured a hunting scene. To Lizzie's mind, they seemed rather gruesome reminders of how the food one was eating had been obtained.

After what seemed like an impossibly short time, the freckled maid set breakfast on the table and topped off her coffee cup. Lizzie ate her solitary meal in silence, except for the sounds of the servants going about their morning chores. She'd nearly finished her third cup of coffee when Sidney strolled into the dining room, a newspaper folded under his arm.

"Top o' the morning, Bearcat," he said, touching two fingers to his receding hairline in a mock salute.

"You're up awfully early," she said.

"An idea for my opera woke me. I had to write it down so I wouldn't forget it."

He sat across from her in one of the heavily carved chairs, laid the latest edition of the *Gloucester Daily Times* on the table, and fitted a cigarette into his silver holder. After the serving girl finished pouring coffee for him and asked what he'd like for breakfast, Lizzie told him about the bat.

"Jeepers creepers. First, you've got talking walls, now a bat. It didn't bite you on the neck, by chance?"

"Don't be ridiculous. It's just an ordinary bat, not a vampire. Still, it spooked me, I admit." She hadn't told him about the fallen light fixture yesterday, although he'd probably hear of it before long.

Sidney opened the newspaper and passed it to her. "It appears our dead lady's the talk of the town."

At the bottom of the front page, Lizzie read an article that described Natalie Talbot's demise, including the fact that she'd died from a heroin overdose. The writer mentioned that Natalie came from a well-known local family, but omitted anything about her occult activities.

"I wonder what this means for Duncan and his menagerie—and for us?" she asked.

Sidney shrugged. "Hard to tell. At least we're not named in the article. I don't want The Troubadours connected with another suspicious death."

The serving girl set a plate of pancakes with blueberry jam and maple syrup in front of Sidney. While he devoted himself to his meal, Lizzie scanned the newspaper. A local speakeasy had been raided, and more than twenty cases of alcohol seized. A motorcar had hit and injured a boy who darted into the street. A foxhunt would take place on Saturday at the nearby Myopia Hunt Club.

She showed the foxhunt article to Sidney. "Look at this. It says here a ritzy sporting club in a nearby town allows people who can't see very well to ride horses and discharge rifles."

"Baloney. That doesn't make sense." Sidney mumbled through a mouthful of pancakes.

"I hope the hunters' vision is too blurry to see the poor, terrified fox."

* * *

As Lizzie passed the parlor with its red velvet sofas, richly carved mantelpiece, and sea-facing windows, she spotted Cora Delaney seated at one of the tables. Dressed in a well-cut blue woolen blouse and straight calf-length skirt, the woman sat alone shuffling her tarot cards. She glanced up when she heard Lizzie approach.

"I didn't mean to disturb you," Lizzie said.

Cora motioned for the singer to join her at the table. "You didn't. I've finished the reading I was doing."

Lizzie stepped cautiously into the room where yesterday a hanging lamp had mysteriously come unhinged and plummeted to the floor. "About your friend's death?"

"Natalie Talbot was no friend of mine," Cora said. "I know it sounds awful, but to tell the truth, I'm glad she's gone. If there's such a thing as divine justice, she got what she deserved. Don't tell that policeman I said so, though. He might suspect I did her in."

The woman's words surprised Lizzie. However, Duncan's other guests had expressed similar sentiments. How much did they know about the Talbots' duplicity, as reported in the magazine article she'd read? Did any of them actually like or respect, or trust Natalie Talbot? Did the deceased woman have any real friends among this group, except Duncan and his sister?

"We were interested in some of the same things," Cora said as Lizzie took a seat at the card reader's table. "Because we're, well, *different*, people like us tend to cling together. Safety in numbers, you might say. In the bad old days, we got hanged or burned at the stake for doing what we do. That makes us compatriots, but not necessarily friends."

Lizzie's gaze drifted toward the ceiling, to the gap where the shattered lamp had hung. Although a hearty fire blazed in the parlor's fireplace and no windows were open, she felt a cool breeze ruffle her dark hair and brush her bare neck.

"What do you make of that light falling yesterday?" she asked Cora.

"That was rather unnerving, wasn't it?"

"And how! Do you think something out of the ordinary caused it?"

"Why do you say that?"

"Well, don't you think it's peculiar that it came crashing down just when Kevin asked who killed Natalie?"

"It does seem an odd coincidence." Cora shuffled her cards a few times and changed the subject. "Want me to do a reading for you?"

"Only if it's a good one," Lizzie said. She remembered the reading Cora had done the day before yesterday that suggested Natalie Talbot might have been murdered. If bad news lay in her future, she'd rather not know about it just yet.

"I don't have any control over that."

"Okay, but don't tell me if I'm going to get murdered."

Cora shuffled the deck one more time and then slid it across the table. "Cut."

Taking a deep breath, Lizzie cut the deck and nudged it back toward the other woman. Cora turned over four cards and laid them face up on the table. As she set down the last one, Lizzie realized she was still holding her breath.

The tarot reader studied the spread for a couple minutes. With a long, manicured finger, she tapped a card that pictured a man with a crown seated on a golden throne. In his hand, he held a wooden stave that sprouted leaves. "The King of Wands," she said. "There's an illustrious man in your future."

"How far in the future?"

The card reader laughed. "Not far at all. I can only see a few months ahead at most, but in this case, I'd say you could meet your 'king' within a week or so."

Lizzie felt a flutter of excitement in her stomach. Did that mean the police would release The Troubadours from the castle soon, letting her return to New York where a wealthy suitor awaited? No one here at Halcyon fit that description. Then she recalled the empty chairs at Duncan's banquet table. Maybe the man the card reader had referred to hadn't arrived yet.

"Well, that's swell news. Who is he?"

Cora smiled and shook her head. "I don't know. I guess you'll just have to wait and see."

"Hmm. What else do the cards say?"

"You've had a past of deprivation, struggle, and poverty. But you've overcome that through sheer determination." She pointed to a card that showed a cobbler at his bench. Eight yellow circles with stars on them bordered the right side of the card. "You're still working hard to get ahead."

"And how. Will I succeed?"

"Things seem favorable." Cora frowned and narrowed her heavy-lidded eyes. She rubbed the bridge of her nose.

"What is it?" Lizzie pressed, sensing her companion was holding something back.

The card Cora indicated depicted a man carrying five swords in his arms. Two more were stuck in the ground behind him. He appeared to be running away from something or someone.

"This one warns you to be cautious. You'll have to use discretion and discrimination during a period when things aren't clear."

"The card is upside down." Lizzie started to turn it around, but Cora stopped her.

"It's not a mistake. The reversed card suggests deception."

"By whom?"

Cora shrugged. "Do you have a business manager or someone who handles your finances?"

"Sidney, our piano player. But he's like a brother—he'd never deceive me. He's my best friend. Besides, my success and his are all wrapped up together."

Lizzie pondered the idea, trying to think of someone she knew who might not be trustworthy. The music world was fraught with greedy record producers who exploited starry-eyed hopefuls. Tricksters waited at every bend of the long and arduous road to the top. Scandals and swindles were as commonplace as April rain. Add to that the constant threat of being raided by police during a performance at a speakeasy. Of being tossed in the hoosegow *en masse* because a nightclub owner didn't make his payoff. Even her presence at a bust could link her to alcohol or drug trafficking. She contemplated Sergeant O'Quinn's suspicions and her close proximity to a controversial woman who'd died from an illegal substance under dubious circumstances. How much murkier could things get?

"I didn't mean to alarm you," Cora said. "The cards are intended to offer guidance and direction. They show areas you need to pay attention to, including problems you may be able to avoid if you know about them in advance."

Lizzie shook her head, trying to cast out the images that perplexed her. So far, Cora's assessment was disturbingly accurate. "Where does the tarot come from?" she asked. "I mean, who decided this card means success, and that one means watch your step?"

"No one knows for sure. They were popular in Europe during the Renaissance, not only for telling fortunes but for gaming. You can see a connection between the numbered cards in the tarot and our modern poker decks. This particular deck was created by an artist named Pamela Colman Smith in 1909, with direction from the English occultist Arthur Edward Waite. Both were members of the Order of the Golden Dawn."

"You mean there are other decks?"

"Oh yes, a lot of them. The old ones didn't have these storytelling pictures on them, though." Cora scooped up the cards she'd laid out for Lizzie's reading and slipped them into a black velvet pouch.

Lizzie longed to snatch the cards from Cora's hands and study them further. The idea that the tarot harkened back hundreds of years intrigued her. How could it still speak to people today? And how could a pack of cards predict the future? Maybe she could find a book about it in Duncan's library.

"What's the Order of the Golden Dawn?" she asked.

Cora patted her crimped brown hair, toying with a pretty silver comb decorated with mother-of-pearl. "A secret brotherhood. Connected with the Masons and such. It's too complicated to explain in a few words." The card reader pushed away from the table, and Lizzie sensed she wanted to end the discussion.

"Thanks for the advice," Lizzie said. "I hope that rich man shows up soon."

Cora stood and tucked her tarot pack into the pocket of her woolen blouse. "Be careful," she warned.

Chapter Ten

"Since it always happens that one gives form and substance to the dangers upon which one broods to excess, the dread of the possibility became an accurate forecast of the future."

— *George Sand*

On this beautiful fall day, when the sun shone clear and bright and pleasantly warm above the oppressive stone walls of Halcyon Castle, four of Duncan's guests engaged in a game of croquet on a grassy court not far from the saltwater swimming pool. Ophelia Wraith, dressed in a billowy frock striped with bands of red and blue that reminded Lizzie of a circus tent, smacked a ball through a wire hoop. Sabine clapped her hands jubilantly. Ophelia's elderly husband, Kevin, stepped up next, mallet in hand. He stood for a moment, stroking his pointed gray beard, while he contemplated his shot. From the sidelines, Sabine's husband Jonathon urged him on. Apparently, they'd waged a contest pitting the men against the women.

Lizzie watched them play for a few minutes before continuing on to the rocky promontory overlooking the ocean. Nothing more had come down from Sergeant O'Quinn since his initial interrogations. She didn't know whether that was good news or bad.

Gregory Talbot had arranged for his wife's funeral to be held on Friday in the Universalist Church at the corner of Gloucester's Middle and Church Streets. Although the policeman had instructed everyone who'd been in residence at Halcyon at the time of Natalie's death to remain on the estate's grounds until further notice, he rescinded his order temporarily so they could attend her funeral.

Lizzie couldn't help thinking about the deceased's kin and childhood friends who might still live in the town of Gloucester. Did they know she might have been murdered? Once upon a time, Lizzie'd learned from reading publications found in Duncan's library, Natalie's family had occupied a prominent place in this historic seaport. Her grandfather had owned clipper ships that brought precious goods from the Orient to trade here. The fortune he'd amassed had all but disappeared, however, due to Natalie's father's excessive indulgences and bad investments. When her parents died, her older brother inherited what remained and took off for California, leaving his sister nearly destitute. With her life in shambles, Natalie sailed to England. There she married Gregory Talbot and began dabbling in the occult.

When Lizzie reached the granite point at the easternmost end of Duncan's estate, she sat on the boulder she'd become familiar with and gazed out at the horizon. She opened the book she'd brought with her and read George Sand's words ""…since it always happens that one gives form and substance to the dangers upon which one broods to excess, the dread of the possibility became an accurate forecast of the future."

Putting a finger between the pages to hold her place, she closed the book and contemplated what she'd read. Was Sand suggesting that people actually attracted the very things they feared most by worrying about those things? And if so, did their brooding influence the events that followed? The strange idea made her mind spin. Deep in thought, Lizzie didn't hear the woman approach until she spoke.

"May I join you?"

Startled, Lizzie turned around and saw Cora Delaney standing only a few feet behind her. "Oh, yes, of course."

Noticing Lizzie's book, Cora said, "If I'm disturbing you, please say so. I won't be offended."

"Actually, I was just mulling over something that maybe you can clarify."

As Cora sat on a granite block nearby, Lizzie read Sand's words aloud. "Now, here's what baffles me," she said. "When you do a tarot reading, do you see someone's future because it's fated? Or does the person influence the future by dwelling on certain things, as Miss Sand suggests?"

"Ah, you've hit on a much-debated matter. Probably too complicated to go into now, and many minds greater than mine have argued the idea for ages." Cora smoothed her skirt and stared out to sea as a skiff passed by on the blue-green water below. "But if you want my personal opinion, I'm inclined to favor the latter."

The lobster boat Lizzie had grown accustomed to seeing each day motored by, and they watched its captain haul up one trap after another. Beyond him, a small pleasure craft with two white sails skimmed the waves. Lizzie waited to see if Cora would say more. After a while, she did.

"I want to explain why I disliked Natalie Talbot. You'll learn about this eventually. It's no secret, so you may as well hear it from me now. Two years ago, my father died of tuberculosis. After his death, my mother was distraught. She asked Natalie to contact my father on the Other Side. The Talbots had recently returned from England and set themselves up in Boston. Greg supposedly took photographs of spirits while Nat talked to the dead. For a few months, my mother conferred regularly with the Talbots. Natalie painted such a glowing picture of my father's happiness in the place where his spirit now resides that my mother…" Her voice caught, and she paused to get herself under control. "My mother hanged herself so she could be with him."

"I'm so sorry." Lizzie wanted to hug the sad woman, but Cora's stiff posture exuded a stoicism that caused her to hold back. "How awful that must have been for you."

Cora took a deep breath, then exhaled loudly. "In some ways, I blame Natalie for my mother's suicide. Yes, I know, we're all responsible for our actions. My mother made her own choice. But I can't help wondering whether she would've done what she did if Natalie hadn't given her such a glorified vision of the afterlife and insisted my father was waiting there for her."

Maybe Natalie hoped to cheer Cora's mother with her glowing accounts, Lizzie thought, but she decided not to pose that possibility to the obviously bitter Cora. Instead, she said, "It must be hard, being an orphan."

"Yes, it is. I'm a spinster and an only child. I don't have anyone with whom to share this sorrow. In a way, Duncan's group of misfit occultists are my family now."

Just as she was going to ask Cora if she knew about the Talbots supposedly profiting from tricking grieving families, Lizzie heard angry men's voices shouting. She jumped up and hurried toward the castle's croquet court, with Cora following behind.

"You didn't love her," one man shouted.

"What do you know of it?" the other shot back.

As she drew closer, Lizzie saw Roger Young punch Gregory Talbot in the jaw. The frail widower crumpled to the ground and lay there like a marionette whose strings had been cut. Kevin Wraith and Duncan's son-in-law Jonathon quickly intervened, pinning Roger's arms behind his back. Still, the irate man continued squirming and yelling at his adversary.

"I know what you are!"

Gregory wiped blood from his mouth and yelled back, "I know what *you* are too. And what I know could put you behind bars for the rest of your life."

* * *

Roger didn't appear at supper, but Gregory showed up sporting his bruised jaw and split lip like war medals. Lizzie thought he seemed to be enjoying the additional attention the other guests lavished on him. In a perverse way, he shone in the macabre spotlight. Not only was he the grieving widower, now he was also the victim of an unexpected assault, one inflicted at the height of his bereavement.

If Lizzie could believe Ophelia, Gregory knew about his wife's affair with Roger Young. It was also possible that the entire group knew the Talbots had been accused of swindling gullible people. *Is Sergeant O'Quinn aware of the love triangle between Natalie, Greg, and Roger?* Lizzie asked herself. Jealousy had sent many a man to his grave—and many a woman too. Had it been a factor in Natalie Talbot's death? Perhaps Gregory killed his wife because she'd betrayed him. In her mind's eye, Lizzie envisioned Greg on one side of a scale and Roger on the other, weighing their possible guilt. But the scale bobbed up and down without delivering a decision.

As Lizzie stepped down from the stage after The Troubadours finished their performance that evening, the two men's angry words echoed in her memory. *What information does Gregory have that could send Roger to the hoosegow?* she wondered.

* * *

"Nothing like a little fisticuffs to liven things up," Sidney said as he pulled a bottle of scotch from a cabinet behind the bar in Halcyon's billiard room. He served Lizzie first, then himself.

"Boys will be boys," she said, wondering where those "boys" were. On other nights the men had repaired to the billiard room to play a few games of pool or cards. Tonight no one but Sid and Lizzie sat in the comfortable room lit by stained-glass lamps. "By the way, did I tell you Roger was having an affair with Natalie? At least, that's what Ophelia claims. It seems to be common knowledge."

"Ah, the plot thickens. So that's what the beef was about." He sipped his scotch and rubbed his thumbs along the sides of the glass tumbler. "Do you think ol' Greg bumped off his wife because she was cheating on him?"

"I've been thinking the same thing. The husband's usually the prime suspect."

"But why here? I mean, he could've done her in at home and saved the rest of us a lot of bother."

"Maybe he likes an audience. He certainly seemed to enjoy the attention he got this evening after Roger thumped him." Lizzie sipped her scotch, then continued. "Here's another thought. Maybe Greg planned to pin the crime on Roger. That way, he could take revenge on both of them."

"You're playing the sleuth again," Sidney said. "That can only lead to trouble."

She waved her hand dismissively. "Of course, we don't know for sure that someone killed her. I'm still betting the lady accidentally overdosed, and her husband doesn't want people to know she was a doper."

"That's my theory too." He tossed back his scotch and stood up. "Time for me to turn in. 'Night, Bearcat. Sorry to cut this short. Sweet dreams and all that. See you at breakfast. I'm off to my rest-ski."

"All the best-ski."

After he left, Lizzie poured herself another splash of scotch and carried her glass across the hall into the parlor. Only one of Duncan's guests sat there at this late hour: Yvonne Pasqual. The gray-garbed woman bent over a table, writing something on a piece of paper. As Lizzie drew closer, she noticed Yvonne's eyes were closed. Not wanting to startle her, Lizzie waited quietly while the older woman scribbled, paused, and finally laid down her pen.

After a few moments, Yvonne slowly opened her eyes. She rolled her shoulders a couple times and turned her head from side to side. "Oh, goodness me, I didn't realize I had company," she said when she saw Lizzie.

"Sorry, I didn't mean to disturb you."

"No, it's all right." She smiled and motioned for the singer to sit at the table in front of the fireplace, where the coals still glowed a bright vermillion.

"How can you write with your eyes closed?"

Yvonne looked down at her paper and ran a fingertip along the lines she'd written. "What I'm doing is called automatic writing. Have you heard of it?"

Lizzie shook her head.

"It's a method for gaining insight from a source outside myself. A form of channeling."

"How does it work?" Lizzie asked, perplexed.

"I contemplate a question or situation I want to know more about. Then I ask a spirit I've contacted to guide my hand as I write down the answer. I never know what's going to come out of it. Sometimes the result is a complete surprise. Sometimes it's baffling at the time, but later turns out to be accurate."

Lizzie frowned at the peculiar idea. How could a spirit make you write something? How could you even contact a spirit? What, exactly, was a spirit anyway?

Seeing her confusion, Yvonne laughed. "I know, it sounds pretty bizarre. Remember the night Ophelia and Sabine were consulting the talking board?"

"How could I forget?"

"They'd asked a spirit to speak to them by spelling out a message on the board."

"Well, that experiment de-fin-ite-ly went haywire."

"You could see it that way, but in retrospect, I think it clearly predicted the situation. The planchette picked out the letter M before flying off into the fireplace."

Still confused, Lizzie asked, "What do you make of that?"

"I've never seen anything like it before. My guess is we were being warned of Natalie's death. The M stood for murder."

Lizzie sipped her scotch and contemplated what the older woman had said. Warned? By whom? Who or *what* could have known Natalie Talbot would die that night? Who knew she'd be murdered, if, in fact, that were the case? An idea popped into her head. If Ophelia had planned to kill the woman, she could've manipulated the talking board's planchette. But why?

"What did you learn from your automatic writing?" Lizzie asked.

Yvonne pushed the sheet of paper toward her so the singer could read the rambling scrawl on the page. "Forgive my dreadful penmanship," she said. "I write better with my eyes open."

"'I'm sorry, I didn't mean to hurt you,'" Lizzie read aloud, remembering the apology Ophelia supposedly channeled from some unseen source: I paid for my sin. "What do you make of it?"

"I don't know. I'd hoped to understand more about what happened to Natalie. This is what came through."

"Do you think Natalie's trying to communicate with you?" Lizzie asked, sliding the paper back toward her companion.

"That was my first thought. But I didn't get the impression she was apologizing to me."

"Who then?"

Yvonne tapped the table with her pen. "Gregory, maybe. Or Roger. She'd grown tired of him and was going to end the affair. He's quite hurt. But then, Natalie and Greg hurt a lot of people with their phony séances and photographs of ghosts. She could have been apologizing to any of them."

So the Talbots' peers do *believe the couple engaged in chicanery,* Lizzie thought. She recalled what Cora had revealed earlier about Natalie's role in her mother's suicide. She wanted to ask Yvonne more questions, but the older woman folded the piece of paper, capped her pen, and stood up.

"It's late. I think it's time I turned in," she said, pulling her shawl tight around her thin shoulders. "A good night to you."

"Thanks for showing me this. If you figure it out, I'd like to hear more."

For a while, Lizzie sat alone in the spacious parlor, contemplating the new piece of the puzzle Yvonne had revealed. Natalie planned to dump Roger. Had the volatile young man lashed out in anger and murdered his lover? Although Lizzie didn't know much about Roger Young, he seemed the type who'd choose a more aggressive method to kill someone, stabbing or bludgeoning, perhaps, not secretly injecting her with heroin. She tossed back the last of her scotch and pushed herself up from the table.

As she climbed the wide stone staircase to the castle's second floor, Lizzie heard a grandfather clock in the hallway below strike one o'clock. Despite the late hour, she didn't feel sleepy. A book she'd borrowed from Duncan's library promised to entertain her until the buzz of the evening's performance diminished enough that she could finally doze off.

She slid the lock on her bedchamber door into place and stripped off her silk evening gown. Once again, she regretted the fact that she had no chance of finding a suitor here. The only single fellows present, if one didn't count the widower Gregory Talbot, were Duncan—who was older than her father and too odd to even consider—and Roger Young—who was both coarse and angry, not to mention a suspect in the possible murder of Natalie Talbot. *I'm twenty-six years old. How much more time do I have?* She contemplated the tarot reading Cora had done for her and the cartomancer's words: "There's an illustrious man in your future. You could meet your 'king' within a week or so." Was there any truth to any of that? Or was it all just wishful thinking?

After washing up, Lizzie plumped the feather pillows on her bed and settled herself against them. She opened a book about local architecture, which included a chapter on Duncan's grandfather who'd built Halcyon Castle seventy-some years ago. *It may look ancient, but it's an imitation,* she realized. *No people of European descent lived on the Massachusetts coast during the Gothic era.*

According to the text, Quentin Fox descended from a long line of English aristocrats. He immigrated to the States, where he became involved in the abolitionist movement and the Underground Railroad. He optimistically named his Gothic Revival residence south of Gloucester "Halcyon" because he hoped it would be a place of happiness where people of all races, nationalities, and creeds could find peace.

How idealistic, Lizzie thought as she closed the book. She wished she could have met Quentin Fox and heard him speak about his views, which according to the book, he did publicly and often. Apparently, he also invited many other progressive thinkers to share their ideas, including Susan B. Anthony, William Lloyd Garrison, and Elizabeth Cady Stanton. Lizzie tried to imagine these eminent men and women speaking in the drafty lecture hall where Sergeant O'Quinn had questioned her and the other guests at the castle after Mrs. Talbot's death.

Maybe Duncan's forward-thinking grandfather had inspired him to explore the unconventional path he'd followed. How would Grandpa Fox feel about the situation that now troubled his idyllic retreat? She considered Yvonne Pasqual and Ophelia Wraith, and the rest of Duncan's friends, all trying to commune with the spirits of dead people. Could they connect with Quentin Fox? And if so, what might he have to say about this whole sordid business?

Chapter Eleven

"It is time, therefore, that you should apply for aid to such helpful Spirits. But will you have the strength of mind, the courage to endure the approach of Beings so different from mankind?"

— *William Beckford, Episodes of Vathek*

In the morning, Lizzie returned the architecture book to Duncan's third-floor library and began searching the shelves for information about communicating with spirits. Among the array of texts, she found one about a photographer named William H. Mumler, who became famous for taking pictures of spirits during the 1860s and '70s. He even claimed to have captured an image of Abraham Lincoln's ghost shortly after the president was assassinated. Mumler was accused of fraud, but never found guilty. After reading Mumler's personal account and the testimonies of photographers, Spiritualists, and scientists familiar with his work, Lizzie concluded that his pictures were most likely legitimate, despite his many critics. He seemed an honest man who believed in what he was doing.

Another book, however, explained how charlatans duped people into believing they saw images of departed loved ones. Sometimes, while a subject sat for his photograph, another person stepped quickly into the scene and then away again. The camera's slow shutter speed couldn't capture the moving person clearly; only a blurry, ghost-like shape appeared in the finished print. Double exposures and lighting tricks also produced "spirits" in photographs.

Did Natalie and Gregory intentionally fool grieving and gullible people, like Cora's mother, capitalizing on their vulnerability? Or was the couple persecuted unjustly? Like Mumler, the Talbots were never convicted. Yet many people—including their own colleagues—believed them guilty. Lizzie slid the books back into place on Duncan's shelves, more confused than ever.

* * *

When Lizzie arrived for breakfast, Sidney was waiting for her at the heavy oak table in the dining room, silver cigarette holder in one hand, coffee cup in the other. Over her tweed trousers, she wore a suede jacket of a russet color that complimented her smoky eyes and provided some visual warmth in the dark, chilly space.

"How did you sleep-ski?" she asked, seating herself across from Sidney.

"In the deep-ski," he said, his eyes sparkling.

"You look chipper this morning. What's up?"

"I'm going to play Duncan's pipe organ. And since it's electrified, you're off the hook as calcant."

"Whew," she said, running a finger across her forehead, pretending to be relieved. "Thank goodness, considering I haven't the foggiest what that job entails."

An Irish serving girl brought coffee. The thin, freckled maid set out chafing dishes of scrambled eggs and rashers of bacon on the Jacobean sideboard. A third girl, whom Lizzie didn't recognize, placed a platter of hotcakes dripping with melted butter and golden maple syrup on the dining table.

Lizzie helped herself to three hotcakes, a scoop of eggs, and two thick slices of bacon.

"Watch your figure, Bearcat," Sidney teased her.

She sat up straight and arched her back, causing her unfashionably full breasts to press against the fabric of her jacket. "Something wrong with my figure?"

"Not a thing," he laughed, and for the umpteenth time, she wished he could see her as more than a business partner.

After the serving girls left, Lizzie asked, "When do you plan to acquaint yourself with the illustrious pipe organ?"

"Right after we finish breakfast."

Hearing footsteps behind her, she turned to see Ophelia and Kevin Wraith enter the dining room. Ophelia wore a black, floor-length dress with long pointed sleeves and a high neck that made her hair seem blue by contrast. The dress billowed around her like a sail as she walked. Her husband was attired in a black suit, decades out of date and in need of a good pressing, with a black shirt buttoned at the neck, but no tie.

I probably should have dressed in something more somber on the day of Natalie Talbot's funeral, Lizzie realized in retrospect.

"Hallooo," Ophelia said as she took a seat in the high-backed chair at the head of the table.

"Morning," Lizzie and Sidney replied in unison.

The Wraiths had barely settled themselves before Cora, followed by Yvonne, appeared in the doorway. Cora, too, wore black, a fashionable pleated skirt that stopped mid-calf and a hip-length woolen blouse with a velvet collar and mother-of-pearl buttons. Yvonne had shunned her usual gray garb for a long black cardigan and straight skirt that brushed her ankles. As everyone exchanged greetings, the freckled serving girl returned with a pot of coffee and filled their cups, then set a basket of fresh-baked pastries on the table.

"Finally, we can get away from this depressing castle for a while," Ophelia said.

"But you've come here before, lots of times," Cora said. "Surely you didn't always find it depressing?"

"It's not the same now. I've never been here under such morbid circumstances." The medium speared a stack of pancakes with her fork and slid them onto her plate. "In the past, visiting Halcyon was always an exotic adventure. Especially when I was young, I loved coming here. But ever since that bossy policeman ordered us confined to quarters, I've felt like a prisoner."

"Halcyon always seemed elegant and magical to me," Yvonne agreed. "Not this time, though."

"Natalie ruined Halcyon for me, just like she ruined so many things," Ophelia said bitterly. "Duncan and I had such fun here when we were children. We loved exploring all its rooms, playing among the odd treasures his grandfather collected from the four corners of the earth. You never knew what you might find when you opened a door. It was a fantasy world, a place where anything could happen."

Kevin Wraith frowned at his wife, but remained silent. Cora reached for a cranberry muffin and buttered it. Yvonne sipped her tea.

"Nat and Greg tainted us all," Ophelia said. "It's hard enough to get people to view us and our work as legitimate. Most of them think we're evil, cracked, or carnival show hucksters out to steal their hard-earned cash. Then the Talbots came along with their tricks and discredited the rest of us."

The rotund medium stopped talking momentarily to add four strips of bacon to her plate. After eating several bites, she continued, "I've spent my life teaching people that death isn't the end, that we live on in the spirit world after our bodies die. I sincerely want to help others and, well, yes, earn a living in the process. What's wrong with that?"

Kevin laid his hand on his wife's arm to quiet her as Melody entered the dining room. The flutist glanced nervously at the black-garbed group seated around the table, as if trying to decide whether to stay or run away. Lizzie waved her colleague in. Tentatively, Melody eased into the room and sat in a chair beside Lizzie.

Yvonne took the opportunity to shift the conversation to a more immediate and practical subject. "How shall we travel to Natalie's funeral? I'm willing to drive. Anyone who wants to ride with me is welcome."

"That's sporting of you, Yvonne. Ophelia and I accept your offer," Kevin Wraith said.

"Me too," Cora said. "No sense in all of us driving our cars."

"Funeral's at noon, and it'll take about twenty minutes to drive into town," Ophelia said. "Let's meet out in the parking area at eleven. I want to be there in time to get a good seat."

"Do you think a lot of people will be there?" Yvonne asked.

Ophelia shrugged. "Who knows? Natalie came from a noted Gloucester family, although they fell on hard times. She still may have people here, maybe even a few friends. Of course, a scandal always draws a crowd."

Lizzie noticed Melody's wide-eyed appraisal of Duncan's guests. She nudged her friend in an attempt to get the girl to reveal her thoughts. "What is it, Mel?"

"I don't know if I should attend the funeral," Melody said. "I mean, I didn't know the lady, but I don't want to be disrespectful." She glanced from one guest to another, seeking advice.

Ophelia waved her hand, a hand that held a half-eaten muffin, in dismissal. "You needn't bother. I can't imagine Natalie would care one way or the other."

"I want to go, though, out of respect for Duncan," Lizzie said and turned to Sidney.

"I'll go too," he said.

Melody studied Ophelia's broad, unartfully painted face and frowned. "How did all of you know to bring black clothing to wear to Mrs. Talbot's funeral? Did you guess she was going to die?"

The women exchanged glances. After a few moments, Cora realized why Melody was perplexed. "It's traditional to wear black on Samhain, or what you call Halloween," she explained. "We'd already planned to celebrate the holiday, which also happens to be Duncan's birthday, tomorrow evening. That's why we all came here in the first place, before this business of Natalie's death."

In the confusion that surrounded Natalie Talbot's demise, Lizzie had nearly forgotten the original purpose for coming here to Halcyon Castle. To mark Duncan's half-century of life on earth. It was supposed to be a joyful celebration, not a dirge.

"Now our gathering has taken on a more poignant meaning," Yvonne told the blond flutist. "Samhain, you see, is a time for honoring those who've left the physical world and gone to the Other Side. Tomorrow, we'll recognize

Natalie in addition to our departed family members and other loved ones."

Melody's face clouded over in bewilderment.

Lizzie patted her friend's arm and whispered, "Don't worry, Mel, it's got nothing to do with you."

She glanced at Sidney, but couldn't penetrate his thoughts. His handsome face was as blank as a clean sheet of paper. After breakfast, she'd ask Bert if he wanted to attend the funeral. So far, he hadn't seemed upset by the death of Natalie Talbot, and Lizzie hoped it would stay that way. Nor had he shown any qualms about joining a group of musicians whose previous saxophonist had been murdered. Maybe, as he'd said, he was just glad to have a roof over his head, three meals a day, and a little extra cash to spend as he wished. Still, he must wonder why death seemed to dog the entertainers.

All Lizzie cared about right now was keeping The Troubadours together through this crisis, so they could complete their engagement, collect their pay, and go home with positive reviews. And stay out of prison.

* * *

Lizzie and Sidney entered the sanctuary where the pipe organ presided. As they approached it, Sid's fingers twitched involuntarily. She watched him throw various switches and stops to engage the instrument. He stroked each of the organ's four keyboards, making friends with them. He tapped his feet on the wooden pedals. He raised his eyes to the vaulted ceiling, as if petitioning the muses for assistance. Then, reverently, he placed his long, elegant fingers on the ivory keys.

The first unexpectedly loud notes startled them both. Lizzie actually felt, as well as heard, the overwhelming sound resonating from the pipes perched on the balcony that ran the width of the sanctuary above the organ. Sound rippled through her body, a deep resonance that reminded her both of thunder's rumble and the ocean's roar. She stepped down from the platform that held the organ and sat in a front-row pew while Sidney explored the keyboards, trying to get his bearings. After stumbling for a bit, he managed to grasp the basics of the complex instrument.

As he eased into one of Handel's familiar pieces, Lizzie closed her eyes and let herself be swept along with the music. When he finally stopped playing, she had no idea how much time had passed. Ten minutes? Half an hour? More?

Sidney practically danced down from the organ's platform and slid into the pew beside her. His face glowed with excitement. He grasped her hands.

"I did it! What do you think, Bearcat?"

"Outstanding," she answered. "An amazing experience."

"And how!"

"You were magnificent."

He grinned. "You really think so?"

"I do. Say, did you notice there's a ladder leading up to the pipes?" She pointed to a series of rungs attached to the wall. "I'm going to see what they look like up close. Want to come with me?"

Sidney shook his head. "I just want to sit here for a bit and luxuriate in this 'amazing experience' as you called it."

Grasping the ladder, Lizzie placed her foot on the first rung. Cautiously, she pulled herself up step by step until she reached the balcony, which hung more than a dozen feet above the sanctuary's apse. Pipes of all sizes, some taller and bigger around than she was, were mounted in ornate mahogany frames decorated with gilt.

Even though the pipes were made of metal, they seemed oddly sentient, as if imbued with mystical properties, even life itself. She stroked the gleaming pipes with her palms. Her fingers traced the intricate carvings of vines and gargoyles that decorated the balcony. She could easily imagine angels in heaven playing this awe-inspiring instrument instead of harps.

When she finished her exploration, she climbed back down the ladder. Sidney still sat on the pew with his eyes closed, just as she'd left him.

"Sid?" she said softly.

His eyes blinked open. "Hmm?"

"You really should go acquaint yourself with the pipes. They're even more majestic up close."

"Another time."

"I'm glad you got to play the organ."

Sidney smiled, obviously pleased with himself. "So am I."

* * *

While Sidney drove, Lizzie read from a tourist guidebook of Gloucester. "Did you know we're going to the oldest Universalist church in America? Its congregation was founded in 1779."

"Nope, I don't even know what a Universalist is."

"It says here, 'Universalism is founded on the belief that God wills the salvation of all, emphasizing the inherent goodness of human beings.'"

"Even those who murder their friends?"

Ignoring him, she continued reading, "'Construction of the church was completed in 1806.' That makes it older than a lot of the churches in New York."

Sidney turned onto Gloucester's Church Street, where motorcars lined both sides of the street. Black-garbed mourners made their way toward the church, a pale yellow, clapboard building with clean, simple lines and an impressive steeple.

"Looks like Natalie Talbot was pretty popular," he said as he parked the Buick.

Or much hated, she thought, glad Melody and Bert decided not to come along. "People love a scandal. Maybe they're just curious how a woman from a prominent family ended up dying from a drug overdose."

Lizzie took his arm as they followed the others down a long sidewalk and into the church. Because the only black dress she'd brought with her from New York was a low-cut evening gown totally inappropriate for a funeral, she wore a smart midnight blue suit, a pretty felt hat, and plain pumps. Around her neck hung a single strand of expensive pearls, a gift from a long-ago admirer. Sidney, as usual, looked smashing in a Savile Row three-piece black suit with a diamond stickpin on his lapel. She noticed appraising looks from several people and thought *we'd make a handsome couple. If only there was even the remotest possibility of us being a couple.*

Unlike Ophelia Wraith, who wanted to "get a good seat"" as if she were attending the theater, Lizzie preferred to sit near the back of the sanctuary. From there, she could watch everyone who came and went. She quickly spotted Duncan with his daughter and son-in-law seated three rows back from the front of the church. To her surprise, the bent and wizened woman, whom Lizzie supposed was his reclusive sister, sat with them. Despite her physical difficulties, Frances Fox had come to pay her respects to her old friend. Duncan's guests occupied the pew behind them. Gregory Talbot and a few people, most likely Natalie's extended family, sat in the front pew. A casket, draped in black and festooned with flowers, rested before the pulpit and chancel.

At the rear of the church stood Sergeant O'Quinn and another policeman in uniform, overseeing the crowd who'd gathered to mark Natalie Talbot's passing. *How many of these people realize Natalie may have been murdered?* Lizzie wondered. *Maybe they think the coppers are just here for crowd control.*

Promptly at noon, the minister entered and began the service. Lizzie tuned out most of what he said. Except for standing to sing several hymns, she spent the hour observing the people in the sanctuary. Didn't mystery novels say the murderer always showed up at the victim's funeral? Of course, *if* Natalie had been murdered, which the police had yet to prove, the most likely suspects were those in residence at Halcyon Castle at the time of her death. Duncan's friends.

Unless someone else had managed to sneak into the castle that night. Someone who figured out how to get past the dragon gate or who accessed the estate from seaside. Maybe someone who wasn't human? The idea made her cringe. Plenty of strange things had already happened since The Troubadours arrived at the castle, and Duncan's peculiar group of friends claimed to consort with spirits. Could a demon have slipped into the castle and killed Natalie Talbot?

You're going loony, she scolded herself. *A demon wouldn't inject a woman with heroin. A demon would bite her on the neck and suck her blood or stop her heart cold or eat her brain.* Lizzie's thoughts circled back to her early suspicions. *Natalie Talbot was on the needle, and her husband's trying to cover that up with this charade.*

Chapter Twelve

"Many men go fishing all of their lives without knowing that it is not fish they are after."

— Henry David Thoreau

Even before she saw them, Lizzie heard the malcontents outside the church.

"Natalie Talbot bilked me out of three hundred dollars," a woman claimed.

"She cheated me too!" another shouted at Gregory. "You and your wife are con artists!"

A man yelled, "You deserve to die like her."

By the time Lizzie and Sidney emerged from the sanctuary, Sergeant O'Quinn and his uniformed colleague had cordoned off a small group of angry men and women who continued to hurl insults at Gregory Talbot. Greg, looking pale, scared, and vulnerable, held his head high as he walked past the throngs of tormenters, refusing to be drawn into an argument with them. His face still bore the bruises Roger Young had inflicted on him yesterday, and it appeared that other people might enjoy getting a few licks in, too, if they could. Although Lizzie hadn't found much to like about the widower before, she admired his stoicism now.

She'd expected to follow the mourners to the cemetery, but Sidney grasped her elbow and steered her toward his automobile.

"I've had enough of this circus. Let's get out of here," he said. "You don't feel like standing around a gravesite in this cold weather, do you?"

"Not especially. I need to find a post office while we're in town, though. Melody asked me to mail a letter to her parents and one to that fella she's been seeing."

"Okay. Let's get some lunch too."

They motored several blocks to Gloucester's waterfront and parked near the inner harbor. Sidney helped her out of the breezer, and they walked uphill to an eatery whose tantalizing aromas drew them in.

Two dozen patrons stared at the duo when they entered. Lizzie felt their animosity like fire ants stinging her skin. Her fashionable outfit, bobbed hair, and face paint marked her as someone from away, someone whose wanton ways didn't belong in this town. Sidney's expensive suit and effeminate grace raised the hackles of the hard-bitten fishermen seated at the bar, who claimed this as their territory.

Before they could turn around and leave, however, a heavy-set woman who was missing a front tooth showed them to a table in the back of the restaurant. She gave them handwritten menus and asked, "What's yours?"

Sidney scanned the menu. "Fish and chips."

"The same," Lizzie said. "And coffee, please."

After the waitress had poured their coffee and the locals had stopped gawking, Sidney asked, "What do you make of that fuss back at the church?"

"Seems like the Talbots had more than a few enemies. Maybe Natalie Talbot crossed the wrong person, and it cost her her life."

"You really think someone murdered her?"

"I don't know what to think," Lizzie said.

She remembered the chandelier that crashed on the parlor floor when Ophelia tried to channel the dead woman's answer to Kevin's question: "Natalie, was your death an accident, or did someone do this to you?"

Sidney fitted a cigarette into his silver holder and lit it. Cringing, Lizzie wished just this once he'd dispense with his foppery and hold the smoke between his fingers the way other men did. In towns like this, three-letter fellows like Sid got pommeled simply for being there. But the burly seamen seated at the bar had turned their attention back to other matters.

"I read a couple articles about the Talbots in a magazine," she said. "They were charged with fraud once, but the case was dismissed."

Their waitress brought plates of delicately fried fish with crispy sliced potatoes and set them on the table. She refilled their coffee cups and asked, "Something more?"

"Not at the moment, thanks," Sidney said.

"I keep wondering," Lizzie said after the waitress retreated to tend to other customers. "Assuming Natalie Talbot really *was* murdered, was it because she hoodwinked the wrong person? Because she dabbled in the occult? Or for the most commonplace of crimes: adultery?"

Sidney forked a flaky piece of fried cod and held it aloft for a moment. "Are you fingering Gregory Talbot? Or Roger Young?"

* * *

On their way back to the castle, Sidney and Lizzie drove south along Cape Ann's coast, enjoying stunning views of the ocean and ogling the spectacular estates that overlooked it.

"Wouldn't it be the bee's knees to live there?" she asked, pointing to a mansion made of native stone complete with turrets and a widow's walk, guest cottages, stables, and a carriage house.

"And how. Better snag yourself a rich man, Bearcat. You've got champagne taste."

"I'm trying, but I haven't spotted any eligible candidates at Halcyon Castle."

Sidney switched subjects. "We need to nail down what we're playing this evening. Everyone seemed to enjoy the jazz last night, but I don't suppose that's appropriate après-funeral fare."

"How about Liszt? Duncan included him on his list of favorites. You'll dazzle them with your skill at the ivories, Sid. Maybe some Mendelssohn to showcase Melody's violin? We can sing a couple of his duets too." She pulled a small notebook from her purse and began scribbling in it.

"Might work," Sidney said. "A respectful blend of elegance and drama."

"Unless Duncan wants to lighten the mood, which I'm all for."

He nodded in agreement. "I'll sure be glad to get back to New York. Shuck off all this darkness and return to our normal lives. How about we drive straight home now, instead of going back to the castle? Are you game?"

"We can't abandon Melody and Bert," she said. "And if we bolt, Duncan won't pay us."

"You're right, Bearcat. As usual."

When they reached the turn-off that would take them to Halcyon Castle, Lizzie laid her hand on the breezer's steering wheel. "While we've got the chance, though, let's motor on."

"Where to, oh Mistress of Unplanned Adventures?"

"Remember that newspaper article I showed you about Myopia Hunt Club's foxhunt?"

"Yeah, so?"

"It's not far from here. I thought we might check it out. It's just too bizarre to be believed. Imagine, blind people hunting."

Sidney frowned at her. "You want to go to a place where blind people are riding around on horseback, shooting guns at each other? I don't know, Bearcat."

"I doubt they're actually blind. Myopic means nearsighted. They probably wear glasses. Besides, the hunt doesn't start until tomorrow."

"Meaning we're not likely to get picked off today?"

"Probably not." She pulled out her visitors' guidebook and studied the enclosed map. "Stay on this road for another five miles."

After crossing into the town of Hamilton, they turned onto a road bounded by a split-rail fence and lovely old trees. Even this late in the season, some of them still displayed leaves as bright as flames. Endless green pastures stretched in either direction.

"Are we trespassing?"

She waved her hand dismissively. "Ish kabibble."

"You may not care, but I don't want to trade one lock-up for another."

"If anyone questions us, we'll say we're lost. They'll see the breezer's New York license plate and give us the bum's rush." She read aloud from her guidebook. "It says here, the club was started by four wealthy, short-sighted brothers in the town of Winchester fifty years ago as a gentlemen's sporting club. They relocated here in 1882 because they needed more room for foxhunts. They began holding polo matches in 1888. Six years later, they put in a golf course. Four U.S. Opens have been played here."

"Okay, I'm impressed," Sidney said as they pulled up in front of a rambling three-story mansion with a pillared front porch that seemed a mile long. A perfectly groomed putting green stretched in front. He parked the Buick and shut off the motor. "Now what?"

"Now we go inside and see what's what."

Before he could change his mind, Lizzie opened the passenger side door and jumped out of the car. Sidney hurried after her.

"Are we sightseeing, Bearcat, or do you have another agenda?"

She stopped to let him catch up and smiled sweetly. "Whatever do you mean?"

"Damn it, I should've known."

They entered the Colonial manse, now Myopia's clubhouse, and began exploring its interior. Everywhere they looked they saw examples of the understated elegance for which New England was known. None of the show-stopping sparkle of Manhattan, but rather a confident, timeless, we-don't-need-to-prove-ourselves proclamation of class.

Lizzie veered into a room hung with scores of photographs, some dating back to the club's early days in the 1880s. Glass cases held an array of trophies. As she gazed at the sepia-toned images of men and women dressed in tennis outfits, riding horses, holding golf trophies aloft, and hamming it up for the camera, she spotted one that reminded her of the picture she'd discovered in Natalie Talbot's bedchamber the morning after the lady died. The faded photograph Gregory Talbot had demanded she hand over to him. This one showed a young woman seated sidesaddle on a dark horse and a handsome young man beside her riding his own mount. Like many of the people in the photographs on the clubhouse walls, the woman wore spectacles.

"Spill," Sidney said.

"All right." She told him about her encounter with Gregory and the photograph he'd taken from her.

"Do you think what you found was an early picture of the Talbots?" He tapped his index finger on the framed photo hanging on the clubhouse wall.

"I have no idea. I guess I'd hoped to find out more by coming here. Duncan told me Natalie and his sister Frances were school chums. One of Halcyon's housemaids said Frances had been injured in a horseback riding accident in her youth. Both ladies came from money, although Natalie's family squandered theirs. Maybe they belonged to this club, rode here together." She stretched out her arms to take in the trophy room. "Ob-vi-ous-ly this is a playground for the rich."

He grabbed her arm and pulled her toward the clubhouse's entrance. "No more sleuthing, Lizzie. Poking your nose deeper into this affair can only cause trouble. If need be, I'll tie you up and stuff you in a closet and only let you out to sing for your supper."

Before she could respond, a balding man wearing gold-rimmed eyeglasses stopped them in the hallway. "May I be of assistance?"

"No, thank you," Sidney said. "We were just leaving."

* * *

The dragon gate at the entrance to Halcyon Castle remained open to allow the guests who'd attended Natalie Talbot's funeral to reenter the premises. In the west, the sun hung low in the sky. Purple shadows were already spreading over the estate. Sidney drove across the drawbridge and into the parking area, where Lizzie spotted Yvonne's gray Studebaker. That meant some of Duncan's guests had returned. Beside it sat a motorcar she hadn't seen before: a black Oakland sedan.

Lizzie opened the Buick's passenger-side door and stepped down onto the parking area's granite paving stones. "I'm going to get a breath of fresh air. Okay-ski?"

Sidney shrugged. "What can I say-ski?"

"You can stop being a grumpy old bear, for starters. At least we had a brief excursion into the real world this afternoon. Bit of a diversion."

"But where did it get us?"

"Does everything have to get us someplace?"

"Right now, I just want to get away from here and back home to Manhattan. We should've bolted when we had the chance."

Lizzie thumped on the auto's passenger side door. "Meet me in the ballroom in half an hour."

Crisp, tangy air blew in off the ocean. She strolled along the dirt path that led past the croquet court and the saltwater pool. Nearing the promontory at the end of the estate, she spotted Bert standing on a rocky ledge overlooking the sea, holding a fishing rod. She called to him, and he waved.

"Have you caught our supper yet?" she said.

"Naw. Caught a couple stripers, but I let 'em go." The chilly wind had nipped his nose and his prominent ears bright red. "How was the funeral?"

She decided not to tell him about the ruckus after the church service or the accusations people had hurled at the Talbots. "Okay, all in all."

"I hope you don't mind that I didn't go. Funerals, well, they remind me of my dad."

"I understand." A sudden gust of wind caught Lizzie's hat and almost whipped it into the sea. Clutching it to her head, she said, "I'm glad you've got fishing to occupy your time."

Other than music and the odd game of billiards or cards, there was precious little at Halcyon to amuse a young man. Except, perhaps, pretty serving girls, and she didn't want to have to worry about that on top of everything else. Kevin Wraith with his pretentious Van Dyke beard and meerschaum pipe didn't fit her image of a fisherman, especially when compared to the rough-hewn men she'd seen this afternoon in the Gloucester restaurant where she and Sid ate lunch. However, she was grateful to him for taking Bert under his wing.

Lizzie heard the unmistakable motor of a lobster boat and shifted her sights to watch the one she'd become familiar with chugging through the shallow water off the end of the estate. She pointed at the craft. "Maybe you could try your hand at lobstering while you're at it. I'm quite fond of lobster."

"That's grueling work." Bert shook his head and wriggled his fingers. "Don't want to hurt my hands hauling up traps."

"Or risk having a lobster snap off a digit or two?"

"Or that," he agreed.

Fishing these waters wasn't something to take lightly. On her previous visit to Gloucester two months ago, she'd seen the recently erected Fisherman's Memorial overlooking the town's harbor, a monument to the thousands of men from this country's oldest fishing community who'd died at sea during the past two hundred years. Its bronze plaques didn't list the names of the thousands more who'd been injured, sometimes crippled for life, while performing their dangerous jobs.

"Be careful, Bert."

Chapter Thirteen

"If the doors of perception were cleansed every thing would appear to man as it is, infinite."

— *William Blake, The Marriage of Heaven and Hell*

Mrs. Beane, the stalwart housekeeper, met Lizzie when she entered the foyer with its gas-lit streetlamps and antique wooden choir stalls. "Mr. Fox asked me to intercept you when you arrived," she said. "Would you kindly come with me, Miss Crane?"

"Of course."

She followed the buxom, broad-hipped woman to the elevator and rode it to the third-floor ballroom. When they emerged, Mrs. Beane led Lizzie down the hall with its unadorned wooden floors to Duncan's office. The housekeeper rapped lightly on the door and waited for her employer to admit them. After a few moments, the castle's owner opened the door. He'd changed out of his black funeral suit into rumpled trousers and a tatty gray sweater that was missing a button. His wiry hair stood out as if he'd just received an electric shock. He removed his glasses, wiped them with a handkerchief, and invited Lizzie in. Mrs. Beane, having delivered her charge, retreated to tend to other matters of the household, a formidable task under the best of circumstances, Lizzie realized, and these were hardly the best.

"Ah, Lizzie. So good of you to come," Duncan said. *"Entrez, s'ils vous plait."*

As she entered the spacious room with its overladen bookshelves, cluttered desk, and graceful Gothic Chippendale guest chairs, she saw that Sidney had preceded her to Duncan's office and now sat waiting for her to arrive. Lizzie raised an eyebrow at her friend, as if to ask *what's this about?*

"I wish, once again, to extend my condolences for your loss," she said to her host.

"Yes, thank you." Duncan nodded and gestured for her to sit. "That's not why I asked you here, however. It's my hope that you might once again help my friends and me to shuck off today's sadness by performing uplifting music this evening."

"Certainly," Sidney said. "We are at your disposal."

Duncan clapped his hands in a childlike manner, though without the enthusiasm he'd shown prior to Natalie's death. "Good. Could you play some tunes made popular by that young sensation, Louis Armstrong?"

Sidney beamed. "And how! Our trumpet player, Bert, does Satchmo like nobody else. He'll wow you and your guests."

"Duncan," Lizzie said, "are you sure your friends wouldn't prefer something more subdued, considering the circumstances?"

"Dear Lizzie, I know most people perceive death as a frightful thing and dread it. But my friends and I have a different perspective. Tomorrow, at our Samhain celebration, you may come to understand more. Nonetheless, it's been an unpleasant day and I'd like to end it on a cheerful note." He chuckled at his bad pun.

Lizzie wanted to ask about Samhain, but sensed Sidney hoped to finish this meeting as quickly as possible. Duncan, too, seemed tired from the demands of the day.

"Your wish is our command," Sidney said in the voice he used to cajole clients. "We're here to please. I'm sure I speak for my colleagues when I say we'd be delighted to do all we can to honor your friend's passing and soothe the sadness of those who loved her."

Duncan steepled his hands in front of his chest. "Thank you, dear ones. Until this evening, then."

* * *

Lizzie heard voices coming from what Duncan's friends called the "little parlor," a garish room with red-flocked wallpaper and tufted Victorian velvet settees that made her think of a bordello's reception room. She approached the chamber and peered inside. Duncan's daughter and most of his friends had gathered here, all except Roger Young and Sabine's husband, Jonathon. At the center of the hubbub stood a very tall, very thin elderly man dressed in a long, brown robe that reminded Lizzie of a monk's garb. His long white hair hung down between his shoulder blades, and his equally white beard reached to the middle of his chest. A multicolored rope circled his waist, tied in numerous knots. On his shoulder perched a black cat.

Another odd duck joins the flock, she thought and started to back away. She'd hoped to get in a quick nap before it was time to prepare for the evening's entertainment. Then she noticed the thick, gnarled stave on which the old man leaned. It resembled a stout tree limb. It even sprouted leaves, just like the one held by the King of Wands in the card reading Cora had done for her. The card that predicted a man in Lizzie's future.

Oh no, that can't *be him! He's ancient! And he looks as poor as a church mouse.*

"Yoo-hoo, Lizzie," Ophelia invited her in. "You simply *must* come here right this minute and meet our dear friend Thaddeus Blake. He's from New York too."

Duncan's childhood friend, still dressed in her voluminous black funeral dress and floor-length woolen cape that protected her from the evening's chill, stepped toward Lizzie. Her painted face was flushed with excitement. She grasped the singer's wrist firmly and pulled her toward the group.

"Thaddeus owns a bookstore in Manhattan—perhaps you know of it? The Chalice and the Sword?" Ophelia said.

Lizzie shook her head. She didn't want to appear rude, but she didn't feel like socializing with these peculiar people at the moment. All she wanted was a nap, a bath, and some supper. When her eyes met those of the old man, however, she felt pinned in place like a butterfly in a collector's case, unable to move.

"Lizzie hails from Greenwich Village," Ophelia told the elderly man. "She's a singer."

"Please to meet you, sir. I'm Elizabeth Crane," she said politely. "Mr. Fox hired my colleagues and me to provide musical entertainment for his guests this week."

The man gripped his stave with a gnarled hand and appraised her. Beneath shaggy white eyebrows that rose and fell as if performing calisthenics, his blue eyes glinted like sapphires. "My friend Duncan has good taste," he said with a smile that got lost in his beard.

"Have you come to mark Duncan's birthday? Or because of Mrs. Talbot's death?"

"I regret the conditions of Natalie's passing, but I'm here for other reasons."

Before he could elaborate on those reasons, Cora and Yvonne approached Thaddeus Blake, one on either side, and linked their arms through his. The black cat on his shoulder batted at the card reader and hissed, then rearranged itself around the old man's neck like a fur boa.

"Come with us. Duncan's going to play the pipe organ," Cora said.

Lizzie wasn't sure if the invitation included her, but she couldn't resist the opportunity to hear Duncan's performance. Sidney had managed reasonably well to coax simple melodies from the magnificent instrument, but perhaps the organ's owner, being more familiar with it, could do better. She followed the gaggle of guests down the castle's central hallway and into the neo-Gothic sanctuary.

As she slid into a pew, Lizzie wished she'd had time to let Sid know about this impromptu concert. Surely, he would have wanted to hear Duncan play. Their host sat caressing the keyboards as if charming them to do his bidding. He looked up only once and nodded as his friends took their seats. When they'd all settled themselves and grown quiet, he reverently laid his hands on one of the organ's four keyboards and began to play.

From the first chords of Handel's concerti to Bach's preludes to Mendelssohn's sonatas, Lizzie sat entranced. She closed her eyes and let the music wash over her. Duncan may not have been the most talented of performers, but his enthusiasm and the pipe organ's beautiful timbre stirred in her a respect for both the instrument and the man.

For a time, she drifted on the waves evoked by the music. When she opened her eyes, she looked up at the balcony where the organ's pipes stood in erect symmetry, their open throats singing to the heavens. In front of the central bank hovered a hazy form, its arms outstretched as if to embrace the people in attendance. For a minute or so, she watched it flutter there—white-gold, so brilliant she couldn't make out any distinguishing features, just a glowing light that shone like a star and then, gradually, faded.

Had Lizzie been a religious person, she might have interpreted the radiant image as an angel. *Could it be a ghost?* she wondered. *Natalie Talbot's ghost, reaching out to her old friends on the evening of her funeral?* Lizzie longed to ask the others if they, too, had seen the apparition. She certainly wouldn't mention it to her fellow Troubadours, however. No need to upset them further.

When Duncan stopped playing, stood, and took a modest bow, she pushed herself up from the pew and quietly left the sanctuary.

* * *

Although she'd meant to take the elevator to the second floor, Lizzie accidentally pressed the down button. The elevator groaned and began to descend. *Holy moly,* she thought, *I'm still discombobulated from seeing that ghost, angel, or whatever it was.* For some reason, the unexplained vision hadn't scared her—and not only because she doubted that it was, in fact, a ghost. Rather, its appearance had comforted her. For a brief moment, she'd felt calm in the midst of the storm swirling about Halcyon Castle. *None of this makes sense, nothing that's happened since I got here makes sense,* she argued with herself. *There has to be a rational explanation for everything. I just haven't found it yet.*

When the lift thumped to a stop, she opened the door, curious to see where she'd inadvertently ended up, and stepped out onto a platform. She found herself in a tunnel of sorts. Below, a channel of seawater lapped at the pilings that supported the platform. Briny air tickled her nostrils. One end of the tunnel opened to the ocean. Partway down the platform, a heavy wooden door hung ajar. Curious, Lizzie walked toward it and, seeing no one else in the vicinity, stepped into a dimly lit storeroom.

Shelves reached from floor to ceiling along the walls, laden with all manner of provisions: wooden crates of root vegetables, jars of canned fruit, wheels of cheese, row upon row of tins, boxes, and crocks. Smoked hams hung from hooks. Barrels clustered at the far end of the room. The underground chamber, kept cool by the ocean, made a perfect larder.

The roar of a motorboat's engine caught her attention, and she remembered the boat that had inexplicably disappeared while she watched from the promontory at the end of Duncan's property two days ago. When she exited the storeroom, the noise grew louder. She hurried back to the elevator and stepped inside, just as a handsome wooden craft with a green cabin eased into the slip beneath the castle. The same boat that had "vanished" before her very eyes.

Its captain cut the engine, and Lizzie smiled at her foolishness. Boats don't just disappear into thin air. The mysterious motorboat must have been bringing provisions to Halcyon Castle and pulled in here to make its delivery. Mystery solved.

Through the window in the lift's door, she saw a husky man with skin darkened by long days at sea emerge from the cabin and move to the boat's stern. To her surprise, Roger Young followed him and then climbed onto the platform where she'd stood only moments ago. For several minutes she watched as the man in the boat handed up crates of bottles to Roger, who stacked them carefully on the platform.

Looks like they're ferrying something other than cheese and smoked hams, Lizzie surmised. *I bet anything those bottles are full of hooch.*

Although possessing alcohol wasn't a crime, transporting it was. Gregory Talbot's words, after Roger punched him yesterday, echoed in her head: "I know what *you* are too. And what I know could put you behind bars for the rest of your life."

She couldn't let the two men catch her witnessing their illicit activity. She pressed the lift's button for the second floor. They'd hear the contraption rumble away, but they wouldn't be able to stop it. And they hadn't seen her, she was sure of that. As the elevator lumbered upward, she realized Duncan must know what was going on. That would explain the incongruous association between the castle's owner and Roger Young. Maybe Duncan was doing more than merely acquiring libations to entertain his guests. Maybe a business venture between him and Roger was helping to support Duncan's lifestyle.

The lift bumped to a stop at the castle's second floor. Lizzie stepped out into the hallway and hurried to her bedchamber. As she closed the door and slid the lock into place, she realized that if Roger knew where to procure alcohol, he might know where to acquire heroin too.

Chapter Fourteen

"Do you not think that there are things which you cannot understand, and yet which are; that some people see things that others cannot?"

— Bram Stoker, Dracula

Without much success, Lizzie struggled to sort out the tangle of thoughts and feelings brought on by the day's events. The hubbub at Natalie Talbot's funeral. Duncan's organ performance and the appearance of what might have been a ghost. The arrival of the elderly monk-like man, Thaddeus Blake, and his black cat. And on top of it all, Roger Young's suspicious delivery to the castle's underground storeroom. It was enough to make her pine for the peculiarities of New York City.

She ran a hot bath and slid into the soothing water. She needed to relax, calm her mind, and focus on tonight's entertainment. At least Duncan had requested jazz numbers; that was a relief. The Troubadours could play jazz in their sleep. Louis Armstrong's lively music promised to lift the strange mood that hung over this place, plus it would give Bert a chance to shine. Although the young horn player seemed chipper enough during performances, he'd kept to himself for the most part since their arrival at Halcyon Castle except for his recent foray into fishing. She was glad he'd found a diversion to occupy himself during the long, empty days, even though she couldn't understand his new friendship with Kevin Wraith, whom Lizzie found both stuffy and pretentious. Bert, she knew, still missed his deceased father. Maybe Kevin served as a grandfather substitute for the lonely young man.

When the bathwater began to cool, Lizzie stepped out of the tub, toweled off, and pulled on her Chinese silk robe. No sooner had she taken a seat at her vanity than she heard a knock at her bedroom door.

"Your supper, ma'am," a serving girl called.

Lizzie opened the door, and the Irish housemaid set a tray of aromatic dishes on a side table between the bedroom's two armchairs. The singer fished in her purse for a coin and pressed it into the girl's hand. Duncan might be swimming in money, but that didn't mean he paid his staff adequately. Wealthy people often seemed oblivious to the struggles poor folks faced. Having grown up in a Bronx tenement with her hard-working parents and six younger siblings, Lizzie felt a kinship with the girls in service here who were trying to make their way in the world. Befriending the servants could produce unforeseen benefits too. The staff knew everything that went on in a household, and she might need to tap their knowledge at some point.

"Thank you, ma'am," the girl said and curtsied.

Peeling back the linen cloth that covered her dinner tray, Lizzie saw a plate of smoked ham cut, perhaps, from one of the very same shanks she'd seen hanging in the underground storeroom only a couple hours ago. Another dish contained sliced potatoes in a cream-and-parsley sauce. A third held a medley of summer squash, onions, and mushrooms. She hesitated and poked at the mushrooms. *What if they're poison?*

Not willing to take a chance, she shoved the vegetables aside and opened the other dishes on the tray. One offered Parker House rolls, named for the famous Boston hotel; another an apple cobbler. *A gift of the grape to go with this would be sublime,* she thought wistfully. *Would Duncan give me a bottle if I asked? Maybe I could sneak downstairs to the underground larder and appropriate one.*

* * *

Half an hour before show time, Lizzie heard a knock on her bedchamber door. "It's open," she said.

Melody entered and took a seat near the fireplace. She held her hands outstretched before the flames to warm them.

"What's up?" Lizzie asked as she leaned toward her vanity mirror and fluffed her face with powder.

"Would it be okay if I wore another gown tonight?"

"What do you have in mind?"

Lizzie usually organized the troupe's performances, from the order of the songs they played to the garments they wore. In some of their venues, she designed stage sets, directed skits, and choreographed dance routines. Each detail played a part in creating ambiance and enhancing the audience's enjoyment.

"I thought, well, instead of the yellow one, maybe the dark blue silk with the sequins."

"Okay. Any particular reason?"

"My monthly visit from Aunt Flo. It's just, well, I don't want to take a chance…you know. Besides, it seems more proper after the lady's funeral."

"Poor little bunny, of course. Are you well enough to perform? You can sit this one out if you don't feel up to it. I have a bottle of Lydia Pinkham's Vegetable Compound if you want some."

"I want to play."

As Lizzie applied scarlet lipstick to her lips, drawing a fashionable cupid's bow, a man's voice seeped through the wall behind her canopy bed.

"Did you hear that?" Melody asked.

Lizzie paused, lipstick in hand. "Hear what?"

"A man talking."

No use denying it, Lizzie decided. *Better to deal with it head on.*

"It sounded like that to me too." She tossed her lipstick tube into the vanity drawer and dabbed at her lips with a tissue. "Strange people, ghostly voices. Things that go bump in the night. Honestly, there's so much weird stuff going on in this castle I can't explain, well, I'm inclined to just ignore it all and go about my business. Concentrate on the music, Mel. That's our job.

That's why we're here."

"Aren't you afraid?" Melody asked, twisting a lock of blond hair around her finger.

Drawing upon her acting skills, Lizzie squashed her own concerns in an attempt to calm her younger friend. "Ab-so-lute-ly not. I'm sure there's a logical explanation, even if I don't know what it is. And I'm sure it has nothing to do with us."

"But a lady died."

Lizzie turned away from her mirror to face Melody. "People die all the time. Hardly any of them are the victims of foul play—and probably *none* are done in by evil spirits, vampires, or ghosts."

Although foul play still figured into the matter of Natalie Talbot's death, Lizzie wasn't going to admit that to Melody. And although she still questioned the validity of evil spirits, vampires, and ghosts, her skepticism had certainly diminished since her arrival at Halcyon Castle.

The blond flutist looked dubious, but she stood up and forced a half-hearted smile. "If you say so."

"I do," Lizzie said. "You haven't heard any voices in your bedroom since we swapped, have you?"

"No."

"Okay then. And Mel, you'll look smashing in that blue sequined silk." She reached into her jewelry box, withdrew a sapphire choker, and handed it to her friend. "Here, this will look stunning with your gown. Now get a wiggle on. I have to finish dressing."

* * *

When all his guests had seated themselves at the oak banquet table in the castle's ballroom, Duncan stood and raised his glass in a toast to Natalie Talbot. Gazing at that glass, Lizzie couldn't help but recall the scene she'd witnessed only hours ago: Roger Young stacking crates of what she suspected might be contraband on the dock outside the castle's subterranean storeroom. She'd assumed Duncan must know what was going on, but now she wondered if perhaps Roger had arranged for the deliveries without telling his host. Maybe he was taking advantage of Duncan's good nature. Although Duncan certainly had his oddities, she liked him well enough and didn't want to think he might go to prison if his secret were discovered. And she certainly didn't agree with the Temperance movement or the Volstead Act.

Duncan and his guests seemed more ebullient tonight than they had since Natalie Talbot's death, which they referred to as her "transition." They bantered among themselves with an easiness that had been missing these past few days. Perhaps the funeral and burial had brought closure to the group. Roger Young had rejoined them, though he and Gregory avoided eye contact. The newest arrival, the elderly Thaddeus Blake, had brought his black cat with him to dinner. It perched gracefully on his shoulder, where he and Helen took turns slipping it bits of meat.

Yet Lizzie wondered how these people could rest, how Natalie's spirit could rest, if spirits actually existed, while her suspicious death remained unsolved. Once again, she recalled Cora's tarot card reading and the picture of the man with the swords sticking in his back. *How many of these people believe someone killed Natalie?* Struggling to push the disturbing thoughts out of her head, Lizzie brought her attention back to her music.

Louis Armstrong's songs turned out to be just the ticket. Bert was in his glory, belting out tunes on his trumpet and sax. A few times during their performance, Lizzie and Sidney broke into an impromptu Charleston on stage. Although Duncan hadn't asked them to do any dance numbers, it felt good to move her body again. Despite the ballroom's chill, she was glad she'd worn a beaded, knee-length flapper dress tonight that allowed her to literally kick up her heels. Their audience showed approval by clapping enthusiastically. Even Gregory Talbot smiled.

When the evening ended, and the guests began to disperse, Duncan approached the stage. "That was brilliant, simply brilliant," he beamed and clapped his hands. "Thank you, dear people, for providing such a delightful diversion for my guests and me."

Sidney bowed. "It was our pleasure."

"I'm glad you enjoyed the show," Lizzie said.

"Yes, indeed," Duncan said. "And now, I must bid you *adieu*. Tomorrow we'll discuss your role in the Samhain ritual. *Bon soir.*"

"Sweet dreams," Lizzie called after him.

But their "role in the Samhain ritual" worried her. Not because she had any qualms about it, but how would her colleagues react if they knew they were participating in what she suspected was a pagan ceremony? A ceremony devoted to the dead—including the woman who'd died here only a few days ago? Who might have been murdered by someone right here in this castle?

The last guests to leave were the two elders in the group, Yvonne Pasqual and Thaddeus Blake. Despite their advanced ages, both moved with ease and grace. The old man, who'd exchanged his brown monk's robe this evening for a black one, seemed to carry his walking stick for effect rather than as an aid. At one point, Lizzie could have sworn he wasn't holding it at all. The wooden stave seemed to follow along beside him like an obedient dog.

Jeepers creepers, she thought and blinked several times. *I haven't even had a drink tonight, and my vision's already muddled.*

Turning to Bert and Melody, she said, "Superb job, both of you. You sure played a hot horn tonight, Bert."

"And how!" Sidney agreed.

The young man blushed and grinned broadly at their praise, revealing the gap between his two front teeth. "Satchmo's my favorite musician."

"You were darb too, Melody," Lizzie said. "I'm going to ask Duncan about putting in some dance numbers if we end up hanging around here beyond tomorrow. To liven things up a bit. We might even get these old fuddy-duddies up to dance. What do you say?"

Melody smiled, her cheeks dimpling. "That would be swell. It was fun, wasn't it?"

"This place could sure do with some livening up," Sidney said.

"Good, we'll talk about it more tomorrow. Get some shut-eye, kiddos."

When they were alone, Sidney asked, "What are you up to now, Bearcat?"

"I'm going downstairs to scare up a drink-ski. Care to join me?"

"Let me think-ski. It's tempting, but I want to go over tonight's performance while everything's still fresh in my mind. See you at breakfast?"

"You're on. Sleep tight, then, and don't let the bedbugs bite." She gave him a quick hug and laughed. "Or the vampires either."

* * *

Still soaring high on the music and the evening's success, Lizzie rode the elevator down to the first floor. She longed to talk to Sidney about the voices that continued to speak behind the walls, the ghostly figure she'd seen on the balcony above the pipe organ, and the possibility that Roger Young was smuggling booze, perhaps in cahoots with Duncan. However, she couldn't guess how her friend might react. Would he pooh-pooh it or get in a lather? Neither would help her figure things out and spring them from Sergeant O'Quinn's imposed house arrest.

The lift clunked to a stop, and she made her way down the central hallway to the billiard room, where she'd first raised a glass with Duncan's guests only a few nights ago. To Lizzie, it seemed like years. The electric lights above the bar and the golden sconces on the walls invited her in. Helen, Cora, and to Lizzie's surprise, Ophelia's husband, Kevin Wraith, had preceded her. They sat at one of the game tables, drinks in hand, a bottle between them.

"Get a glass and join us," Cora said.

Lizzie grabbed a glass from the bar and sat down with the others. "What have you got there?"

"Top shelf bourbon from my old Kentucky home," Helen said and poured Lizzie a generous amount.

"I happen to know your home's in Beverly, Massachusetts, barely fifteen miles from here," Cora said. "I bet you've never even set foot south of Connecticut."

Helen ignored her and toasted Lizzie. "Swell show tonight. I would've gotten up to dance, but with whom? Man or woman?"

Lizzie laughed as she eyed Helen's close-cropped hair and pin-striped suit with its double-breasted jacket and trousers. "I'll dance with you. Melody and I dance together all the time. Or, if you prefer, you could dance with

Sid."

"We'd make an interesting couple, wouldn't we? He's a sheik, all right. I'll give him that." Helen chuckled and winked at the singer. "And you're a doll. Okay, next time you're on."

"I believe I speak for the others, Lizzie, when I say I'm glad for tonight's brief reprieve from this ghoulish nightmare," Kevin Wraith said. His spectacles enlarged his watery eyes, and his fingers, clamped around the tumbler of bourbon, were gnarled with arthritis. His evening suit, though of good quality once upon a time, hung in need of a good pressing from his rounded shoulders. "If Ophelia wasn't so devoted to Duncan, I would have insisted we return to Boston straight away, after Natalie's body was discovered."

"Except that police dick won't allow it," Helen said. "None of us will get out of here until the whole balled-up mess is settled and we're cleared of guilt."

"Where is Ophelia anyway?" Cora asked.

"If you must know, she's indulging a bit of a sulk," Kevin said. "She'd expected to preside at tomorrow night's Samhain ritual. As it turns out, Duncan asked Yvonne and Thaddeus to do the honors."

Lizzie sipped her drink, hoping they'd provide more information about the Samhain ritual and Thaddeus Blake. She longed to ask Cora if the octogenarian was the "king" in her tarot reading. She'd located a book about the tarot in Duncan's library that described the King of Wands as a strong and charismatic leader, a person of wealth and position, a mature, upstanding, and loyal man, not necessarily a lover. Relieved, Lizzie was determined to find out more about the elderly man and how he might figure into her life.

"No surprise, really," Helen said. "Natalie will be a major focus, and it's obvious Ophelia wasn't fond of Nat."

"That's putting it mildly," Cora said, fingering her string of pearls. "She thinks Natalie discredited the whole field of mediumship."

"It's hard enough to make people trust and believe us," Kevin said. "To add insult to injury, Nat and Greg took away many of Ophelia's clients with their trickery."

"You mean the spirit photography?" Lizzie asked.

He appeared surprised. "You know about that?"

"I read about it in some magazines. They suggested the Talbots swindled gullible people out of their money. It doesn't seem that many people liked Natalie."

"You're on the trolley there," Helen said. "I'm not even sure her husband did. Duncan did, I suppose. They go way back. And Yvonne, but Yvonne likes everyone."

"Don't forget Roger Young," Cora said.

Helen snorted. She seemed about to say something, but lit a cigarette instead and sucked back her words with the smoke.

"And now we're all confined here because of Natalie," Kevin grumbled.

Helen reached for the bottle and topped off their glasses. "I just wish she'd show up and spill the beans, so we could get this farce over with."

"You mean, show up like a ghost?" Lizzie asked. "Because I think I may have seen a ghost today while Duncan was playing the pipe organ. A whitish blur, human-shaped with arms outstretched or maybe wings. It hovered in front of the overhead balcony, you know, where the pipes stand."

Cora stroked her mink. "It was probably Rebecca."

"Who?" Lizzie asked.

"Duncan's wife, Sabine's mother. She died not long after Sabine was born. Rebecca loved music and shows up sometimes when he plays the organ."

"You've seen her before?"

All three of Duncan's friends nodded.

So I'm not crazy, Lizzie thought. But the idea that a ghost really did inhabit the castle was less than comforting. She decided to press for more. "What about the men's voices in the walls?"

Helen and Cora exchanged confused glances. Kevin puffed on his pipe and frowned.

"I hear them at night sometimes," Lizzie said. "My friend Melody does too. They seem to come from behind the walls of my bedchamber. Who are they? Have any of you heard them?"

Kevin shook his balding head and tapped his left ear. "No, but I don't hear very well anymore."

"I haven't, but I'm intrigued. If you hear them again, come bang on my bedroom door, even if it's the middle of the night." Helen ground out her cigarette butt in an ashtray and chuckled. "Of course, you can bang on my bedroom door in the middle of the night anytime you want, Lizzie."

Deflecting the Sapphist astrologer's teasing invitation, Lizzie said, "Do you think they're ghosts too?"

"You never know around here," Cora said. "Have you tried talking back to them?"

The idea surprised her. "No, what would I say?"

"Ask them what they want. Who they're trying to communicate with. Whatever you care to know."

"You mean, talk to them like they're ordinary people?"

"Yes. Just because they've left their physical bodies doesn't mean they're not sentient," Cora said.

As Lizzie contemplated that idea, another came to her. "What if they're not ghosts? What if they're human voices?"

Again, Helen and Cora exchanged glances. Again, Kevin puffed pensively on his pipe.

Finally, Helen spoke. "Well, then, I'd say you've got yourself a whole different kettle of fish to fry and you might prefer ghosts."

* * *

After saying goodnight to Duncan's friends, Lizzie made her way down the castle's central hallway, where stern portraits of old men stared down at her from the walls. Could the voices behind the wall belong to Duncan's father and grandfather? And what did Helen mean by preferring ghosts to humans?

Her first thought was of Roger Young and his clandestine delivery. Instinctively, she'd scurried to the elevator to escape from him, making sure he didn't see her near the underground storeroom. She recalled how Roger had attacked Gregory Talbot. The dark, muscular, square-jawed young man exuded a menacing energy. His tense countenance—his clenched fists, scowling manner, the way he restlessly and continually scanned whatever area he found himself in, as if he expected enemies to appear and attack him at any moment—reminded her of the gangsters she'd seen in New York.

What had attracted Natalie Talbot to a man like Roger Young? she asked herself. His vitality? Passion? Danger? Did she think he might be someone who'd protect her? Her wan husband Gregory exhibited none of those traits.

By the time Lizzie retired to her bedchamber the clock on her night table said quarter past one. Not late by a New York musician's standards, but she'd had a long and trying day. She stripped off her flapper's dress and hung it in the wardrobe with her other frocks and evening gowns. Then she rummaged around in the mahogany chest of drawers for her nightgown.

In the shared bathroom between her bedroom and Melody's, she slathered Pond's cold cream on her face and wiped away her theatrical makeup with a tissue. She brushed her teeth and used the commode. Just as she climbed into the canopy bed and drew up the eiderdown, she heard a man's voice behind the wall say, "Tomorrow."

Chapter Fifteen

"Nothing… would in the least change my opinion, nor would it that of any one else who had become profoundly convinced that there is an occult influence connecting us with an invisible world."

— Sir Arthur Conan Doyle

Lizzie had learned a little about Samhain's history from Duncan's guests and from reading books borrowed from her host's extensive library. One book described it as a harvest festival, dating back to the days of the ancient Celts in Ireland. The word meant "summer's end" and it marked the beginning of the winter season. Yvonne had called it an occasion to honor the dead. Duncan and his friends considered it the best time to communicate with entities in the spirit world.

This morning she'd come to the library on the castle's third floor to return two books she'd borrowed and to see what other information she could find. From the alcove windows that overlooked the ocean, she spotted Yvonne Pasqual near the saltwater swimming pool, dressed in a gray coat and scarf, gathering dried vegetation from Halcyon's grounds. The older woman held a basket in one hand and a pair of gardening shears in the other.

As Lizzie plucked a book about Irish mythology from a shelf, she heard creaking and rumbling sounds behind her. She turned to see Duncan's sister in the doorway, seated in a rattan wheelchair. Frances Fox wore her gray-streaked hair pulled back from her face in a tight bun. An afghan covered the woman's lap, and her gnarled fingers pulled a blue knitted shawl tight around her bent shoulders. As she studied Lizzie, her dark eyes narrowed under heavy eyebrows.

"What are you doing in here?" the crippled woman demanded.

"Hello, Miss Fox. I'm Lizzie Crane."

"I know who you are. I asked what you're doing in my brother's private library."

"Borrowing a book. Duncan has kindly allowed me to use his library during my stay here."

Frances Fox scowled, not attempting to hide her disdain. "What does a showgirl want with books?"

Lizzie felt herself bristling, but tried to feel compassion for the woman who'd been badly hurt in her youth and still suffered from those injuries. Who'd been deprived of a husband, children, the life most women hoped for. *How hard it must be for her. How lucky I am to be healthy,* she reminded herself.

"I beg your pardon, Miss Fox, but not all 'showgirls' are foolish floozies. I, for one, seek to educate myself, and your brother has been generous in helping me further my goal."

"Ridiculous man." Her angry eyes appraised Lizzie's pretty face and hourglass figure. "They all have only one thing on their minds. Surely you should know that, Miss Crane." She spun her wheelchair around and rolled out of the room, still muttering to herself.

A good morning to you, too, Lizzie thought as she tucked the book of mythology under her arm and hurried downstairs to catch up with Yvonne in the backyard.

* * *

"Good morning, Yvonne," Lizzie said to the gray-garbed woman who bent down to cut a clump of what looked like grass blanched white with frost. She hugged her coat tight against the near-freezing morning wind. "Whatever are you harvesting there? I can't imagine you'll find any pretty flowers this time of year."

Yvonne straightened up. Wisps of gray hair had escaped their single braid and blew loose around her face. "Oh, hello, Lizzie. I'm collecting material to make an effigy of the King of Winter."

"Who?"

"The deity who governs the dark half of the year. He'll preside at our Samhain ritual tonight."

"Ah, yes. I understand you're to direct the ceremony," Lizzie said. "Ophelia's got her knickers in a twist over that, you know."

Yvonne smiled. "So I've heard. Between you and me, Ophelia's had her 'knickers in a twist' as you say, for quite a while now. Ever since Natalie and Gregory came back from England and started 'stealing' her clients. Her accusation, not mine. She's envious, too, that Nat and Greg got to hobnob with MacGregor Mathers, William Wescott, and some of the other well-known English occultists while they were over there. Even Sir Arthur Conan Doyle and Aleister Crowley, if one can believe the Talbots."

The names sounded familiar, and Lizzie searched her memory for information about them. *Aleister Crowley. The Golden Dawn. A secret brotherhood of Victorian-era magicians.*

"Mathers, didn't he die recently? And Crowley, he's rather scandalous, isn't he?" *And a heroin user to boot,* Lizzie recalled.

Again, Yvonne smiled. When she did, her lined face showed hints of the strikingly pretty woman she must have been in her youth. "You've been studying, I see."

"Duncan has graciously opened his library to me. But I ran into his sister there just a little while ago, and she wasn't at all pleased about it."

"Got her 'knickers in a twist'?" Yvonne said, apparently enjoying the phrase.

"And how!"

"Frances has had a hard time of it. First, the riding accident that crippled her, then rejection by her fiancé. And now she's sequestered here as her brother's ward, unable to enjoy a normal life. She's very bitter. Don't let her upset you. I certainly don't envy her, but she makes it harder on herself, wallowing in her misery and self-pity. At least, that's my opinion. If only she could take a more philosophical viewpoint."

The older woman turned away and went back to cutting clumps of long, dry grass, as if she feared she'd said too much. For a few minutes, Lizzie watched her, trying to ascertain why Yvonne chose to snip certain plants and passed over others. Finally, she gave up. Although the morning sun shone brightly, the wind off the ocean blew cold, and it cut through her light jacket. Another cup of coffee by the fire would be more than welcome.

"I'll leave you to your King of Winter. I didn't mean to interrupt," Lizzie said.

"You didn't," Yvonne said. "Oh, by the way. When you get back to New York, you may want to visit Thaddeus's shop. He has an even larger collection of esoteric books than Duncan. If you're interested, he can teach you some things too."

"Thanks, I'll keep that in mind."

Inside the castle, Lizzie made a beeline for the dining room, where the servants were clearing up after breakfast. She caught sight of the German maid Inge and asked for a cup of coffee.

"Yes, ma'am. Anything else?"

"If you spy an odd bit of pastry in the kitchen, perhaps you might snatch it?"

Inge smiled, her rosy cheeks dimpling. "Oh, I'm certain our cook, Febe, has baked numerous 'odd bits of pastry' for your enjoyment."

Lizzie sat in one of the high-backed chairs near the fireplace and held out her hands toward the flames. This evening promised to be unusual, to say the least, and she worried about her colleagues. Despite their exposure to New York's eclectic music world, they'd never encountered people like Duncan's guests or an environment such as this before, replete with ghosts, illegal drugs, and perhaps a murderer. The fact that they'd held up thus far made her feel proud of them.

Duncan had asked The Troubadours to play traditional Irish folk tunes tonight, but none of them knew any. Instead, they'd decided to fall back on Baroque pieces by Bach, Mozart, and Vivaldi that would encourage a peaceful mood as a backdrop to the evening's events. He'd also asked them to gather in the ballroom earlier than usual. Supper would be served at sunset, and he wanted The Troubadours to begin their performance at five o'clock.

"You're welcome to join us for the ceremony after supper," he'd said.

Only Lizzie had accepted his invitation. She could tell her colleagues found the whole affair more than a little eerie and wanted no part of it. *If they see me taking it all in stride, maybe they won't consider any of this worrisome,* she thought. *We can't afford to have anyone panic at this stage of the game.*

* * *

Lizzie rode the elevator to the third-floor ballroom. She could've climbed the wide, sweeping staircase easily, but she liked using the lift that, for her, was still a novelty.

In the area that would have been designated for dancing in many other stately homes, she saw Thaddeus Blake assembling what looked very much like an altar. The elderly man was once again garbed in his brown monk's robe, its hood pushed back, leaving his long white hair free. He'd draped a refectory table with a black cloth and, when she entered, was in the process of setting out a number of items on it. Some she recognized, some not.

The black cat on his shoulder turned to face her before he did.

"Hello, Mr. Blake," Lizzie said.

"Oh, hello, Miss Crane."

"I hope I'm not disturbing you. If I may ask, what are you doing?"

"Exactly what you think."

How can he know what I'm thinking?

"I'm setting up an altar," he said. "Do you want to know more?"

"Yes indeed." She stepped closer. "Why are you setting up an altar here?"

"It will serve as a focal point for tonight's ceremony, as well as a workbench to hold the tools we'll use to enact the Samhain ritual."

The black cat he'd named Bast after an Egyptian goddess arched its back and hissed at her. Thaddeus scratched the cat under her neck, and she settled down, but didn't take her wary golden eyes off Lizzie.

"I've draped this altar in black because black pigment contains all the colors of the visible spectrum," he continued. "Black is also symbolic of mystery and, of course, death and the realm beyond."

A black candle the size of a Thermos, positioned on an ornate candle stand, sat on the altar at Thaddeus's left. A white one in a matching holder stood at his right. Between them, he'd set a silver chalice, a brass dagger with a hilt shaped like a snake, and a round earthenware plate with a star on it. He held out a wooden rod about a foot long and, as he released it, the rod appeared to float gracefully down to settle on the altar among the other objects.

Jeepers creepers. How'd he do that? Lizzie wondered. *The old fellow must have studied stage illusion,* she decided. Even though she suspected a trick, Thaddeus Blake's demonstration intrigued her.

He continued speaking, as if nothing odd had occurred. "The candles symbolize the masculine and feminine forces in the universe. And these," he said as he pointed to each of the other objects in turn, "represent the four elements: fire, earth, air, and water."

"I've seen them before," Lizzie realized. "They're pictured on Cora's tarot cards."

Thaddeus's blue eyes sparkled. "Correct."

"What will you do with them?"

"You'll see tonight. Now, off with you, Miss Crane. I have work to do."

He turned away and faced the altar. The cat, however, kept watching Lizzie as she retreated, leaving Thaddeus Blake to his esoteric ministrations. At the ballroom's entrance, she stopped and stared back at the strange old man. A whitish halo glowed around his head. It reminded her of Early Christian paintings she'd seen in the Metropolitan Museum. Slowly, the white light expanded until it surrounded his entire body.

I must be getting daft. Maybe some fresh air will help clear my mind, she told herself as she descended the stairway to the second floor. She grabbed a coat from her bedchamber and hurried outside.

* * *

Lizzie decided a brisk walk might sharpen her senses and cut through the confusion that swirled in her brain. She didn't see Yvonne as she strode along the dirt path to the end of the estate. Apparently, the gray-haired woman had finished gathering the weeds she needed to fashion her effigy and sought warmth again inside the castle. Warmth, Lizzie reminded herself, was a relative term, for at no time since her arrival at Halcyon Castle had she felt truly warm except in bed snuggled under her eiderdown.

At least the sun shone brightly. As she passed the saltwater swimming pool, she noticed it was nearly empty. *Do they close it off somehow in the winter months,* she wondered, *or does it continue throughout the year to fill and empty with the tides?* Near the end of the rocky promontory, she spotted a man wearing an overcoat and a plaid cap. Drawing closer, she saw he was smoking a pipe. Kevin Wraith. She waved to him, and he waved back.

"Out for a bracing stroll?" he asked when she drew close enough to hear him.

"Just a little fresh air," she said. "By the way, I wanted to thank you for fishing with my colleague, Bert. It's meant a lot to him."

She appreciated the fact that Bert had found a companion in Kevin and that the older man had shown an interest in the young saxophonist. At this time in his life, Bert could benefit from the presence of a father figure, even though Kevin Wraith might not be the man she would have chosen for the job.

Kevin pulled his pipe from his mouth and knocked the ashes onto the ground at his feet. "Good chap, Bert."

"Why aren't the two of you out here fishing this morning? Because it's Samhain?"

"No, because it's too bloody cold. These old fingers of mine would tie themselves in knots if I tried to hold a fishing pole."

Lizzie had intended to inquire about Ophelia's mood today, but before she could ask, Kevin shoved his arthritic hands into his pockets and turned to gaze out at the sea. She hoped his wife had gotten over her fit of pique and that tonight's ceremony would go off without a hitch. On one hand, she was eager to witness the event and learn more about the practices Duncan's friends engaged in. On the other, she couldn't completely squelch her apprehension.

She worried about Melody and Bert—and even Sidney—if things got really weird. What if they noticed Thaddeus Blake's staff moving about by itself or saw a halo of light glowing around the elderly man's head? What if a flock of bats fluttered into the ballroom? She could easily imagine Melody shrieking and running to hide under the banquet table. Although her young friend showed unflappable panache when it came to performing, never a twinge of stage fright, the goings on at Halcyon had clearly rattled the girl.

At the end of the promontory, Lizzie sat on her favorite boulder. No recreational sailors had braved the chilly waters today. The lobsterman she often watched checking his traps had either made his circuit earlier in the morning or would wait until afternoon to haul in his catch. After a few minutes, however, a motorboat roared across the sparkling sea toward the tip of Halcyon's land. When it drew closer, Lizzie recognized its dark-green cabin. *Another delivery?*

She glanced back at Kevin Wraith, who still stood about fifty feet away, smoking his pipe and looking out over the water. During the time he and Bert had spent fishing from the rocks here at the end of the estate, surely he'd seen the craft making deliveries. Had he come to the same conclusion Lizzie had? *Why didn't I think to discuss this with Bert before now?* For a moment, she considered asking Kevin what he knew, but changed her mind. Nothing about him, other than his recent interest in Bert's fishing, had made her want to pursue an acquaintance with the older man, and she felt no desire to approach him now.

Lizzie waited until the sleek wooden craft slipped into the tunnel beneath the castle and cut its motor before she crept out to the edge of the promontory. She leaned over as far as she dared, but couldn't see a thing. *Is the motorboat ferrying ordinary provisions or contraband?* she wondered. She debated going inside and taking the elevator to the subterranean larder to find out, but the noise of the lift would alert whoever was down there and ruin her chance of discovering what was going on. The faster and more direct route was to climb down to the water's edge.

Remembering what she'd read about Duncan's abolitionist grandfather, she realized that runaway slaves might have been brought to the castle in this way, by boat, on their road to freedom. Now Halcyon's nether regions welcomed another type of illegal cargo.

She inched her way down the rocky bluff, gripping stone outcroppings and feeling out tenuous footing on the steep incline. Her toe found a support, and she slid her hand over to grasp a protruding chunk of granite. Waves lapped at the rocks below.

Just as Lizzie realized it would be harder to climb back up that bluff again and began questioning her sanity, the rock on which she'd been standing came loose. In an avalanche of sand and stones, she slipped down the bank into the icy sea.

Chapter Sixteen

"You are always nearer to the divine and the true sources of your power than you think."

— John Burroughs, Studies in Nature and Literature

The bitter cold took her breath away. Her water-soaked clothing felt like heavy weights dragging her down. Her arms and legs flailed about wildly. Not for the first time, Lizzie wished she'd learned how to swim. A wave washed over her, then she bobbed to the surface again, gasping and spitting out seawater.

"Help!" she shouted.

Damn it, why wasn't Bert fishing here now when she needed him? Was Kevin Wraith still near enough to respond to her cries of distress, or was the old man too deaf to hear? Would the motorboat's captain come to her aid, even if he did hear her? She lashed out against the frigid waves, struggling to grasp something solid. As the sea threatened to sweep her away, she kicked as hard as she could until she touched a boulder slimy with seaweed. But she couldn't get a purchase on the slippery surface. Each time she tried to pull herself out of the roiling surf, she slid back, and the shockingly cold water slapped her in the face.

"Help!" she screamed again.

If only she could find something to hold on to. Already her fingers were growing numb. A wave broke over her head. She sputtered and choked. The tide sucked her out to sea and then washed her back again, slamming her body against the rocky wall.

"Hold on!" a voice above her called.

Lizzie looked up in the direction of the voice, her vision blurred by the surf. Was that Bert, ready to haul her in like a huge fish? Or Kevin? Salt stung her eyes. She coughed and spat out seawater. She tried again to grasp the slippery rock wall but failed. All she could make out was a figure inching down the bank toward her. The wind whipped away the man's hat, and she saw a flash of copper-colored hair.

Another wave broke over her head. She felt the sickening undertow pull her down, away from shore, away from life. Her lungs screamed for air. Then something splashed in the water above her.

A man's voice shouted, "Grab it!"

Lizzie did.

With frozen fingers, she clung to the wet coat. She felt herself being tugged upward. Her shoulders, then her chest, emerged from the icy sea. Her feet found a narrow ledge to stand on, but she was too weak to climb. Just as she feared she'd slide back into the water, strong hands grasped her arms and dragged her up the cliff.

"Hang on, you're almost there," the man said.

At last, he pulled her over the edge and wiped her face with a handkerchief. Lizzie stared in disbelief as he removed her wet coat, then took off his suit jacket and wrapped her in it. She tried to say his name, but her chattering teeth made it impossible. Gathering her up in his arms, he rushed toward the castle.

Inside, he shouted for the housekeeper, Mrs. Beane. "Get her into a warm bath right away," he ordered. "Bring a cup of hot tea with brandy and telephone for a doctor."

"Yes, Mr. Peabody."

Mrs. Beane called out for Inge, and the housemaid hurried to assist. As they guided Lizzie into the elevator, she turned to look back at the red-haired man who'd saved her life.

***

A doctor with soft white hands took Lizzie's temperature and then pressed a stethoscope to her chest. "You're a lucky lady."

"Don't I know it," Lizzie said.

After a long bath, two cups of strong tea liberally laced with good brandy, and a mustard plaster on her chest, she felt much better. She'd stopped shivering and hadn't even lost her voice, although the doctor warned that might still happen. The danger of pneumonia lurked too. *If Alan Peabody hadn't come to my rescue...* She didn't want to think about what would have happened. *What's he doing here anyway? How did he even know where to find me? Maybe he's just a figment of my delirium, another apparition.*

The doctor packed his instruments into his black leather satchel. "I want you to stay in bed for a few days."

"But it's Duncan's birthday.... The Samhain celebration."

"No buts, young lady. Doctor's orders."

He opened the door just as Melody and a housemaid carrying a bed tray arrived. Along with a steaming crock of chicken soup, the tray held an engraved calling card on which were written the words "Please let me know you're all right. Alan."

"Alan...is that the man you met at the Winslows' estate?" Melody asked, her face scrunched in a frown. "Did you know he'd be here? How did he know you'd fallen in the ocean?"

"Yes, no, and I don't know."

"I don't understand."

"Neither do I, but I'm sure glad he was here when I needed him." Still staring at the card, Lizzie said, "After I eat, I want to take a nap before tonight's performance."

"You can't perform tonight."

"Applesauce. I wouldn't miss it for the world. I don't have to sing. The three of you can handle things perfectly well without me. I'll just sit quietly in a corner with a lap rug and shawl like an old lady and watch."

"Lizzie..."

"Get a wiggle on now. And tell Sid everything's copacetic. You know how he worries and I don't fancy him coming here in a lather to check on me."

She'd barely finished the soup when another knock sounded on Lizzie's door. "It's open," she called.

Duncan's daughter Sabine entered, carrying a tapestry bag with a drawstring. "My father wanted me to come check on you. How are you feeling?"

"I've felt better, but at least I'm still alive. Thanks to Mr. Peabody."

"How fortunate that he could be there just in the nick of time."

Lizzie recalled the few letters he and she had exchanged during the past two months. Had she told him of The Troubadours' engagement at Halcyon? She must have. Had she hoped they might meet while she was in Massachusetts again? Yes, surely, but she'd held no expectations. Not of a man like Alan Peabody, whose wealth, social position, and good looks gave him access to every available woman in the region.

Sabine pulled the dressing table stool up beside Lizzie's bed and sat down, cradling the bag on her lap. "Alan says he met you this past summer at Zachary Winslow's home in Ipswich. What an odd coincidence."

"Yes, isn't it?" *He rescued me then and now again here. What a coincidence indeed.*

"Father asked me to give you this. He hopes it might bring some comfort." Sabine placed the tapestry bag on the bed, and Lizzie noticed the pretty young woman's fingernails were badly chewed.

Lizzie opened the bag and withdrew a bottle of wine. An exceptionally good bottle of Burgundy, older than her own twenty-six years. "Please thank your father for me."

She slid the bottle back into the bag and tightened the drawstring. It would take a lot more than wine to wash away the day's trauma. Even though she'd come through with only scrapes and bruises, the terror and the realization that her life could be snuffed out in one careless moment would remain with her for a very long time. Maybe Sidney was right to worry about her. She really should stop sticking her nose into dangerous places.

Lizzie sensed Sabine wanted to ask something more, but the nervous young woman held back. Instead, she said, "I should leave you now, so you can rest. Please let us know if you need anything. My father feels awful about your accident."

He's probably worried I'll sue him, Lizzie thought. "Thanks, I will."

* * *

Lizzie didn't know how long she'd been asleep when a knock on the door awakened her. *I hope I haven't missed the ceremony,* she thought as she called out, "It's open."

The maid Inge entered carrying a tray. "Your supper, ma'am. Where shall I set it?

Lizzie patted the bed. "Here, please."

Every muscle in her body cried out as she pushed herself up into a sitting position. Even though her coat had provided some protection during her ordeal, she'd endured quite a lot of battering from the waves and from the sharp rocks as Alan Peabody hauled her up the cliff. Her hands were crisscrossed with cuts. Bruises blossomed like dark roses all over her body.

"Thank you, Inge. And thank you for taking care of me this morning after my accident."

The girl nodded. "You're welcome, ma'am. I'm glad I could be of help."

Lizzie remembered how gently the patient housemaid had bathed her and applied camphor oil to her chest to chase away the cold. How she'd held Lizzie's injured hand and encouraged her with soothing words, beseeching her not to give up and assuring her that all would be well. More than the doctor, this girl—who couldn't be more than eighteen years old—had provided healing aid that perhaps had prevented more serious complications.

"Inge, would you please fetch my purse from the wardrobe?"

The girl obeyed. Lizzie withdrew a bill and pressed it into the girl's calloused palm. As Inge registered what she'd been given, her blue eyes grew wide with surprise.

"Ma'am, you needn't pay me for my services. Mr. Fox pays my wages. I only did what anyone would under the circumstances."

Lizzie closed her hand over Inge's. "I come from a humble background too. I know what it's like for a girl to earn her way in the world."

"Thank you, ma'am," Inge said and pocketed the money.

* * *

Dressing turned out to be more difficult than she'd imagined. Tonight, Lizzie eschewed her elegant gowns and flapper dresses in favor of comfort. She wouldn't sing, and she didn't want to display her patchwork of bruises, scrapes, and lacerations. With effort, she pulled on a charcoal-gray wool skirt and black silk blouse, then topped it with a black cashmere cardigan. Even fastening the blouse's rhinestone buttons hurt. She stepped into low-heeled pumps and hooked a string of pearls around her neck.

By the time she'd finished painting her face and arranging her hair, she wondered if it was all worth the bother. She grabbed a lambswool shawl in case the drafty banquet hall became too uncomfortably cold and thought *I look like a dowager. What will Alan Peabody think when he sees me like this instead of the glamorous showgirl he remembers?* She puffed a bit more powder on her bruised left cheek, then turned away from her mirror. *It will have to do.*

After locking her bedchamber door, Lizzie minced down the hall to the elevator. Each step required supreme determination. Her body ached in places she'd never given thought to before. When the lift ground to a halt on the third floor of the castle, she pushed the door open. The Troubadours were finishing up a piece from Mozart's *Requiem,* and she regretted the mechanical disturbance in the midst of such beauty. As quietly as possible, she closed the elevator's door and inched along a wall until she found a chair in a dark corner where she could remain unobserved.

Duncan and his guests sat around the banquet table, apparently engrossed in the music and the solemnity of the evening. Even the crippled Frances Fox was there to celebrate her brother's birthday. The servants had cleared away the dishes and the meal's leftovers. Except for the flames in the fireplace and a row of thirteen tapers on the mantel, the only illumination in the dark chamber came from the candelabra on the dinner table and on the piano, positioned so The Troubadours could see to perform. Not that they needed light; they felt the music in their bodies, minds, and souls.

Lizzie wrapped her shawl around her shoulders and closed her eyes. Her colleagues' music swelled around her, each note a joy that lifted her above the day's turmoil. As the *Requiem* came to an end, she heard footsteps approaching and opened her eyes. A tall, handsome, copper-haired man dressed in an elegantly tailored tuxedo stood before her.

"Lizzie?"

She reached out a battered hand to him. "Alan! How can I ever thank you? Once again, you're my knight in shining armor."

Gently, he lifted her hand to his lips and kissed it. "I thank my lucky stars that I was nearby and heard your cries of distress."

"But how did you know I'd fallen in the water? How did you even know I was here?"

"Let's just say I was headed your way when you slid down the embankment."

"What brings you to Halcyon Castle? This is ever so far from Boston's Beacon Hill." His appearance here, now, in this unreal situation, still seemed like a dream from which she hoped she'd never awaken. "How do you know these odd ducks anyway?"

"Ah, well, that's a complicated story. Better left for another time." He shrugged and released her hand. "Have you eaten?"

She nodded.

"Are you going to take part in the Samhain ritual?"

She nodded again. "I hope to."

The elevator creaked into action. After it came to a stop, two serving girls wheeled a cart with a multi-layered cake on it into the ballroom. They pushed the cart to the head of the oak banquet table and stopped. Together, they lifted the cake and placed it in front of Duncan.

Sabine rose and stood behind her father. She laid her hand on his shoulder as she addressed the others. "Thank you for coming here to celebrate my father's fiftieth birthday. Thank you for remaining here during this time of crisis, confusion, and sorrow. Your friendship means more than you can imagine.

"Although many questions remain, we gather here tonight not only to honor my father but to reach out to our colleague, Natalie Talbot, whose recent transition has left us all in a quandary. Perhaps tonight, we'll gain insight into her passing and into the world that lies in our future too. After we finish marking my father's birthday by eating this celebratory cake, we'll enact a ritual in keeping with the most sacred of holidays, Samhain, led by our dear friends Thaddeus Blake and Yvonne Pascal. I hope you'll choose to participate."

Sabine kissed the top of her father's frizzy gray head. Although Lizzie had considered her a nervous, frivolous, rather spoiled young woman before, she was impressed with Sabine's composure now. Dressed in a floor-length black velvet gown devoid of ornament, Duncan's daughter seemed older than her twenty-some years and more poised than Lizzie had ever seen her before.

The Troubadours struck up a lively rendition of "Happy Birthday" as Sabine lit the candles on her father's cake. While they burned, his friends joined in the singing.

Duncan took a deep breath and blew. Several candles went out, but it took three more breaths to extinguish them all. Everyone clapped, and Sabine signaled to the serving girls. One approached holding a stack of glass plates, the other carried a large kitchen knife. As they cut the cake and arranged slices on the plates, Sabine passed them around the table, first to her father, then her aunt Frances, until each guest had received one.

Alan asked Lizzie, "May I bring you a piece of cake?"

Before he could do so, however, Duncan left the table and approached them, carrying two dessert plates. He handed one to Lizzie and the other to Alan.

"Dear Lizzie, words can't express how happy I am to see you here with us tonight. When I heard you'd nearly drowned, well, I was devastated! Simply devastated! How fortunate we all are that our illustrious friend Alan was there to pull you from the drink."

"Ab-so-lute-ly," she agreed. "I'm ever so grateful for his bravery and kindness."

"Alan, you're a prince among men," Duncan said, slapping him on the shoulder in a comradely fashion.

"Hardly. I'm just glad I was in the right place at the right time and could come to Lizzie's aid."

Duncan placed a hand over his heart. "After Natalie's death, well, to think Lizzie, too, might have perished while visiting my home. It's more than I could bear."

Chapter Seventeen

"Magick is the science and art of causing change to occur in conformity with will."

— *Aleister Crowley, Magick in Theory and Practice*

After the servants had cleared away the dishes, Roger Young excused himself from the group. Frances Fox rolled away in her rattan wheelchair, followed by one of the housemaids. Except for Lizzie, The Troubadours departed. She thought she noticed worried looks on the faces of Sidney and Melody. Both had visited her in her bedroom after the accident and again before supper to check on her condition. Both had insisted she stay in bed. She'd dismissed their anxious concerns with more confidence than she felt. Now she hoped she could make it through the rest of the evening without falling flat on her face.

The rest of the guests moved to the section of the banquet hall where Thaddeus Blake had set up the altar earlier in the day. Lizzie leaned on Alan Peabody's arm—not only for support, but for the pleasure of his closeness—and they joined the others.

"I don't know what I'm supposed to do," she whispered.

"Mostly just watch. It's Thaddeus and Yvonne's show," he said. "I'll let you know when it's your turn to participate. If you see or sense anything strange, don't let it worry you. Wait until we're finished here to speak of it."

Lizzie recalled the many peculiar things she'd already witnessed at Halcyon

Castle. "Strange? In what way?"

"Nothing harmful, just not, well, ordinary. Don't be afraid." Alan patted her hand gently. "I'm going to release you now. Can you stand on your own?"

"Yes," she answered, wishing she didn't feel so sore, anxious, and vulnerable. *Maybe taking part in this ceremony wasn't such a good idea after all.*

"I'm right beside you. Try to relax."

Duncan and his guests formed a circle around the black-draped altar. All were dressed in black. Yvonne had unbraided her long hair, so it hung down her back in rippling silver waves. Ophelia sported the tent-like outfit she'd donned for Natalie Talbot's funeral. Sabine's beautifully cut velvet gown was certainly elegant, but Cora's silk sheath with matching cape, trimmed at the hem with dyed ostrich feathers, far surpassed it. Helen, to Lizzie's surprise, had eschewed her usual trousers for an ankle-length dress with long sleeves and a high neck. Between her breasts hung a silver star with a circle around it.

Thaddeus Blake had exchanged his brown monk's robe for a black one. Like him, Duncan, Gregory, and Kevin wore simple black robes. Sabine's husband Jonathon had dressed in a stylish black evening suit, and he looked quite handsome in it. Not as handsome as Alan, though. *How brilliant his red hair glows amid all this black,* Lizzie mused as she admired the man beside her.

Yvonne stood in front of the altar, where Lizzie noticed a crude figure made of dried grasses, about half the size of a human man. Around its neck hung a necklace of pinecones. An evergreen crown rested on its head. The King of Winter. *Yvonne must have fashioned the effigy and positioned it on the altar, so he could enjoy the show,* Lizzie decided. How long ago their morning conversation seemed!

Thaddeus began walking a slow circuit around the participants, holding a sword on its side with its tip pointing outward. To Lizzie, it looked as if the sword spewed forth a faint white wisp, like a tendril of smoke that hung in the air and formed a foggy circle around the group. When he'd come 360 degrees around, Yvonne lit the candles on the altar.

"Spirits, departed loved ones, angels of life and death, you who are with us always, I bid you join us tonight in this sacred circle," she called out. "Lend your energies to this Samhain ritual. Share with us the secrets of the worlds beyond."

Yvonne picked up a wooden rod from the altar and pointed it toward the east. "Guardian of the east, come, we seek your presence here. Guide and protect, bless and empower us on this sacred eve."

She turned clockwise, pointed the outstretched wand toward the south, and called, "Guardian of the south, come, we seek your presence here. Guide and protect, bless and empower us on this sacred eve."

Turning again, she repeated the call to the guardians of the west and north.

At each compass point, Lizzie thought she saw a spark of light at the wand's tip. *How can a wooden rod produce light?* she wondered. *It must have a battery, like a flashlight.* Although the castle was always drafty, she sensed a stronger breeze than usual wafting through the room—except now the wind brought a welcome warmth, rather than the dank chill she'd come to expect.

"Tonight, we honor those who have gone ahead," Yvonne continued. "We wish you safe passage into the next world. May you be embraced by peace, joy, and friendship. May you abide in a world of perfect love. We ask that tonight you share the secrets of the world beyond with us who seek your counsel and guidance."

She picked up a pomegranate that lay on the altar. In her other hand, she grasped the dagger Lizzie had seen earlier. "Pomegranate, mythology likens your seeds with death. Just as Persephone entered the Underworld to live beneath the earth during its season of death, so we turn inward now, at summer's end." She sliced the fruit with the dagger, laying its seeds open. She speared one with her blade and touched it to her tongue. "I taste the seeds of death, and now so shall ye. In so doing, we plant within ourselves the seeds of hope. We reach into the darkest regions of our beings and transform our fears into light."

The gray-haired woman handed the pomegranate to Thaddeus, who, like her, ate a seed before passing the sliced fruit to Duncan. In turn, each member of the group consumed one or more seeds. When the pomegranate reached Lizzie, she looked to Alan for direction. He nodded. She plucked one seed with her fingernail and dropped it on her tongue.

"Now I eat of the fruit of wisdom, the fruit that Eve partook of in the Garden of Eden. The fruit of the Goddess." Yvonne sliced an apple in half. She held it up for the others to view, although, in the dim candlelight, they couldn't see much. "See how the apple's seeds form a star, its five points symbolize the human body's—arms, legs, and head. They represent our passage from the realm of perfection into human form on earth. As we partake of this fruit, we accept that our lives on this planet have meaning, even though we may not fully comprehend that meaning. Eat, and embrace this stage in your journey, knowing that physical death is not the end. Indeed, there is no end."

When each member of the group had taken a small bite from the apple, Yvonne continued, "We exist in the cycle of life, death, and rebirth. Each turn of the wheel is part of the Cosmic Plan. As the dying fruit goes to seed, its seeds foment new beginnings."

Now Thaddeus stepped in front of the altar, raised his arms toward the ceiling, and called out, "Spirits of the Summerland. We honor you on this sacred night. Guide and protect the souls of those who have left this world and come to you. We ask that you grant our recently departed sister Natalie Talbot safe passage into the world beyond. May she find peace among you. Beloved spirits, on this sacred night when the veil that hangs between the worlds is pulled aside, we seek to communicate with you. We beseech you to speak to those of us who are gathered here tonight to respectfully remember you."

Yvonne moved to stand beside the bearded old man, clasping wax tapers in both of her hands. He took one, turned to position it on the altar, and lit it. "Natalie Talbot, may you be surrounded by love, joy, and peace. May you abide blissfully in the world of the spirit, where all is known, and all is one. Tonight, we honor your life on earth and in the hereafter."

Lizzie heard bells tinkling, but she couldn't see anyone ringing bells or playing any other instrument that might produce a similar sound. *My head must be ringing after today's ordeal,* she thought.

"Come forward now, dear friends," Yvonne said when he'd finished. "Take a candle and light it in memory of a loved one who now abides on the Other Side."

Gregory Talbot was the first to approach her and receive a candle. He fitted his taper into a waiting holder and lit it. For several long, poignant moments, he stood before the altar with his head bowed before returning to his place in the circle.

Is he truly grieving or going for effect? Lizzie wondered.

One by one, Duncan's guests stepped forward and accepted a candle from Yvonne. When Lizzie's turn came, Alan nudged her gently. Nervously, she approached Yvonne. Each step sent pain shooting through her body. Like the other members of the circle, she placed her taper in a candleholder on the altar. She thought about The Troubadour's former saxophonist Henry Ives, who'd been murdered two months ago. Had he gone to the Summerland, as Yvonne and Thaddeus called it? She'd never heard of such a place before. *This is for you, Henry,* she thought as she lit the candle. *Rest in peace.*

She limped back to her place in the circle, and Alan grasped her elbow. His dark eyes searched her face. She nodded, answering his unspoken question: *I'm okay.*

When everyone had lit a candle, Thaddeus said, "Before we leave this sacred space, this world between the worlds, let us also honor one another and the immutable bond that exists between us."

From a wooden platter that sat on the altar, Yvonne selected a small square that, to Lizzie, looked like a chunk of dark bread. The gray-haired woman fed it to Thaddeus as she said, "May you never hunger." He then echoed her gesture and uttered the same words to her.

Yvonne picked up the platter with many squares of bread on it and carried it to Duncan. She held one out to him and repeated the phrase, "May you never hunger." Continuing around the circle, she stopped at each of the guests in turn to offer a morsel and the same blessing. When she reached Lizzie, the singer hesitated a moment, wondering if Yvonne's offering might contain eye of newt or toe of frog. Again, she glanced at Alan for direction. When he nodded, she accepted what turned out to be fruitcake, lavishly laced with brandy.

After all had eaten, Thaddeus lifted the ornate silver chalice from the altar and held it out to Yvonne. "May you never thirst," he said as she accepted it and drank. She passed the chalice back to him and repeated the blessing while he sipped. Thaddeus turned to Duncan next. He offered the chalice to his host and said, "May you never thirst." After Duncan had taken a sip, Thaddeus continued around the circle until each member had tasted the delicious red wine.

Despite her earlier apprehension and the frightful events of the day, Lizzie felt an inexplicable peace descend around her. Even though she hardly knew these people and didn't like some of them, at the moment she experienced a sense of camaraderie with everyone in the room. It was as if she'd found a clan she hadn't realized she belonged to, and she felt awash in love.

The rest of the ceremony passed in a blur for Lizzie. She was vaguely aware of Yvonne calling out to the spirits she'd evoked at the beginning of the ritual and thanking them for their assistance. She saw Thaddeus holding his sword outstretched as he traced his circular path in reverse around the group, vacuuming up the faint white glow that had surrounded them throughout the ritual. She heard Yvonne directing anyone who wished to communicate with beings on the Other Side or to consult oracles to gather in the castle's parlor on the first floor.

Suddenly, Lizzie felt as lifeless as the straw effigy of the King of Winter still propped up on the altar. Every muscle in her body ached. She longed to crawl into bed and snuggle beneath her eiderdown.

Alan grasped her elbow. "Are you all right?"

"I'm very tired. I think I should go to bed."

"Of course. I'm surprised you held up this long. May I escort you to your chamber?"

She flashed him the best smile she could muster under the circumstances and twined her arm through his crooked elbow. "Yes, thank you."

They rode the elevator down to the second floor of the castle, Lizzie still clinging to him and hoping she didn't appear too melodramatic. Men usually fell for the damsel-in-distress act, she knew, but tonight it wasn't an act.

"Do you have someone to look after you tonight?" he asked as he guided her down the carpeted hallway.

"Yes, my friend Melody, our flutist. Her bedchamber is next to mine," she said, wishing he could lie in bed beside her throughout the night.

"My room is the fourth one on the right," he said, pointing down the hallway. "Will you ask her to alert me if you need anything? Anything at all?"

Her imagination toyed with possibilities that might fall into the category of *anything at all*. "Thank you, Alan. I will indeed."

They reached the door to her bedroom, and she turned the key in its heavy iron lock. For a fleeting moment, she considered inviting him in, but she hadn't the energy to entertain him tonight.

"Sleep well, Lizzie. Until the morning."

After locking the door, she undressed, removed her face paint, brushed her teeth, and eased her aching body into bed. Just as she started to drift off, she heard a noise from behind the wall. It sounded like someone rolling a heavy cart. But before she could give it much thought, sleep overtook her.

Chapter Eighteen

"The whole world is an omen and a sign."

— *Ralph Waldo Emerson, "Demonology"*

The radio playing in the corner of her bedroom woke Lizzie. She didn't remember turning it on last night, but she'd been so tired she must have forgotten. The tune wasn't one she recognized. Trying to make out the song's words, she thought she heard "false friends" and "things aren't what they seem" before the music degenerated into static.

When she tried to push herself up from the bed, her whole body cried out in pain. If possible, she ached even more than she had yesterday. Purple bruises splotched her arms, crisscrossed by red scratches and scrapes. At least her throat didn't hurt, and her chest was free of congestion. *That's a blessing,* she thought, thankful the frigid water hadn't done more harm. Slowly and with great effort, she eased herself into a sitting position, propping herself up against a pile of bed pillows. Maybe a hot bath would soothe some of the soreness. Gritting her teeth, she reached to pull the velvet cord that hung beside her bed to summon a housemaid.

After a few minutes, she heard a knock on the heavy oak door. Lizzie opened it to let the blond German maid who'd bathed her yesterday step inside.

"Good morning, ma'am," Inge greeted her. "How do you feel today?"

"Awful. I hurt in places I didn't even know I had."

"You're lucky to be alive, if you don't mind me saying so, ma'am."

Lizzie nodded. "And how! Inge, would you kindly bring me some breakfast, and then run a hot bath?"

"It's good you're feeling well enough to eat. What would you like?"

"Anything, so long as it's hot. And plenty of strong black coffee, please."

"Yes, ma'am." The girl smiled, and her plump pink cheeks dimpled.

After the housemaid left, Lizzie let her mind drift back in time, before she toppled into the sea. Three days ago, Cora had done a tarot reading for her that pointed to danger. Although she still had plenty of doubts about the paranormal in general and the supernatural skills Duncan's friends claimed to possess, Lizzie had to admit the card reader had clearly seen her future. *Is this the danger the tarot foretold, or should I be on the alert for something more?*

As she mentally retraced her steps yesterday, she recalled meeting Kevin Wraith on the path that led to the end of the promontory—only a few minutes before she'd lost her footing and tumbled into the sea. At least seventy years of age, Kevin could hardly be called an athletic man. Could he have walked so far away in such a short time that he didn't hear her cries of distress? Lizzie had a powerful voice and a singer's ability to project it. Even so, the ocean's roar might have drowned out her shouts, and Kevin claimed he didn't hear well. But if he *had* heard her shouts, why hadn't Ophelia's husband tried to help?

In addition to danger, Cora's tarot reading had predicted "an illustrious" man in Lizzie's future. Alan Peabody came from one of Boston's prominent and influential families. Their brief correspondence over the past two months had alluded only to casual matters. But even if he'd planned to attend Duncan's festivities, how had he known where to find Lizzie at just the right moment? Was it a coincidence that he happened to be there in the nick of time to rescue her? She liked to think he might have gone looking for her, "headed her way" as he put it, before she slid down the embankment. Perhaps he'd seen her walking toward the end of Duncan's property and decided to follow her. The idea sent a tingling warmth into one of the only places in her body that didn't hurt.

As she mulled over these thoughts, the radio suddenly blared a scratchy, screeching noise as if someone had turned up the volume to its maximum output but without connecting to a good signal. It was so loud Lizzie clapped her hands over her ears.

"Sounds like a banshee screaming," she grumbled as she switched off the box. "The electricity in this place sure is balled up."

The fire had gone out in the room's fireplace. When Inge returned with her breakfast, she'd ask the girl to build it up again. Perching on the stool in front of her vanity mirror, she studied her reflection. Although one cheek was slightly bruised, at least her face had been spared the cuts and abrasions that marked the rest of her body.

Before Lizzie could finish examining all her injuries, she heard a knock on her bedchamber door. "It's open," she said, expecting the housemaid.

Instead, Melody entered, wearing a navy-blue sailor frock that made her look years younger than her nineteen. Her blue eyes were wide and questioning. "I heard screaming."

Lizzie flicked her hand dismissively. "The radio. Sorry it disturbed you. It seems to have a mind of its own. Comes on whenever it feels like it. Must be a short in the wiring. It's quite maddening, really."

"How are you feeling?" Melody asked as she crossed the Oriental rug and plopped down in one of the wingchairs by the fireplace.

"Like Jack Dempsey pummeled me in the ring."

As the singer eased herself into the companion chair, Inge appeared at the open doorway. Lizzie motioned her in. The girl set a serving tray on a table between the two women.

"What have you brought me, Inge?"

"Oatmeal with brown sugar, currants, and cream. I hope that's all right."

"Ab-so-lute-ly. Would you be good enough to get the fire going again?" Lizzie asked.

"Certainly, ma'am." The girl knelt before the hearth and poked at the coals with an iron rod, then used a hand-held bellows to blow on them. She placed another log on the grate. In a matter of moments, tiny flames peeked out from the ashes and lapped at the wood. "Shall I run your bath now?"

"I can do it," Melody said.

"Thank you, Inge. I guess that's all then," Lizzie said as she poured herself a cup of coffee.

She offered a cup to Melody, but her friend shook her head. The flutist twisted a lock of blond hair around her finger, then toyed with her amethyst necklace, obviously worried.

"What's the matter, Mel?"

"You could've drowned. That other lady died. This place is full of strange noises and happenings, and odd people. I'm afraid, Lizzie."

Lizzie winced as she reached to grasp Melody's hand. Trying to sound reassuring, she said, "I know. It is strange. But nothing out of the ordinary caused me to slide down that embankment into the ocean. I lost my footing, plain and simple. I shouldn't have tried to climb around on those rocks in the first place. I don't know what foolishness came over me. Just careless, I guess."

"How long will we have to stay here?"

"I don't know," Lizzie said, aware that today should have ended their stay at Halcyon Castle.

If everything had gone according to plan, they would've been driving back to New York today in Sidney's breezer with a thick packet of cash for their week's work. *If a woman hadn't died here from an illegal narcotic and if we weren't under suspicion of murder.* Understandably, Melody wanted to go home to her nice, comfortable, middle-class family in New Jersey, where her life was simple and safe. Where wizards and ghosts and murderers lurked only in books.

Trying to sound optimistic, Lizzie said, "I expect we'll be hearing from Sergeant O'Quinn soon. I'm sure the police will let us know when they have more information. They can't keep us locked up here forever."

While Melody watched, Lizzie plunged her spoon into the bowl of oatmeal the maid had delivered. Precious orange slices lay in a fan-like pattern on a separate dish.

"Want some?"

The blonde shook her head. "I ate hours ago. It's nearly lunchtime, you know."

Lizzie didn't know, but she didn't care. After her ordeal yesterday, she intended to take it easy today. A relaxing bath after she finished eating. A bit of reading. And, if she felt up to it, she might sing a song or two tonight.

"Sidney's worried about you too," Melody added as she smoothed the pleated skirt of her sailor dress.

"Sidney worries a lot, in case you haven't noticed."

"That's because he cares about you."

"I know, and he's a dear. I'll catch up with him later on and let him know I'm copacetic."

"Are we going to keep on performing for as long as we're here?"

"Our contract's up, so we can refuse to perform." Lizzie paused to munch a tangy orange slice before continuing. "We don't really want to do that, though, do we? I mean, we love playing. And what else do we have to do until the police let us go home? Let's try to see this as an opportunity to hone our skills and practice new material. I've rather enjoyed performing the classical pieces this week. Bit of a challenge for us. You've been swell playing Vivaldi and Mozart."

Melody nodded and rubbed her amethyst necklace again. "You're right."

"When I talk with Sid later today, I'll ask him to renegotiate our contract with Duncan. Given that we're now performing above and beyond our original agreement, we should be compensated for our work. I don't know about you, but I'd welcome some extra dough." *And extra time to get to know Alan Peabody better.*

Across the room, the erratic radio burst into grating noise again, startling both women. Melody jumped and spun around to stare at the beast in its wooden case.

"Cripes," Lizzie said. She pushed herself up from her chair and strode painfully across the room. After twisting the off button to no avail, she jerked the electric cord from the wall outlet. "There, that should silence you, impertinent appliance." Then she hobbled back to her chair and finished her breakfast.

* * *

After her bath, she felt a little better. A welcome blaze now warmed the bedchamber, and Lizzie settled herself in one of the room's wing chairs. She opened a journal she'd borrowed from Duncan's library and started reading about something called cross correspondences. Supposedly an Englishman named Frederic W.H. Myers, who died in 1901, communicated from the spirit realm for years with mediums who lived in different parts of the world. Myers fed each of them obscure clues that meant nothing individually, but when put together, formed the solution to an elaborate puzzle.

A knock on her bedroom door interrupted her reading. "It's open," she said.

Cora entered, dressed in a handsome two-piece outfit with a checkered middy blouse and straight skirt that stopped mid-calf. "I hope I'm not bothering you."

"Not a bit," Lizzie said, setting the journal aside. She motioned for Cora to sit in the companion wingchair. "Shall I ring for tea?"

"Oh no, thanks. I just wanted to see how you're feeling."

"I admit I've felt better, but it could've been a lot worse if Alan Peabody hadn't dragged me out of the drink."

"Johnny on the spot, that one," Cora said, and Lizzie thought she noticed a hint of sarcasm or perhaps envy in the other woman's voice.

For a moment, she wondered if Cora might fancy Alan. Recalling the glamorous debutantes Lizzie had seen in his company at the Winslows' party in August, she couldn't imagine him being interested in this rather plain spinster from Salem, regardless of her notable family and financial position. But then again, one never knew the heart's ways. She couldn't imagine Alan being interested in her either, a mere showgirl, yet he'd demonstrated what seemed like genuine concern for her well-being.

"I'm glad you were able to join us last night, even if you couldn't stay for the readings," Cora said.

"I wish I'd been well enough to stay. Was it interesting?"

Cora turned her gaze toward the fireplace. Her left thumb busily rubbed the arm of her chair. "That's partly why I wanted to see you. After the ritual, we gathered downstairs in the parlor for a séance. Ophelia went into a trance, with Kevin guiding her. He invited Natalie to speak through his wife."

"Did she?"

"Did she ever. First, Nat accused everyone of misunderstanding her and insisted she'd never tried to trick anybody, that it was all lies and nonsense. She was very angry. Then she claimed she'd never used heroin or any other drugs, that she'd been murdered in her sleep. 'Tell the police,' she said. When Kevin asked who'd killed her, Natalie said repeatedly 'Friend or foe? Friend or foe?' in a sing-song voice like a child might use."

Lizzie shifted in her chair, trying to find a comfortable position. "Hmm. That's curious."

"Then Natalie—speaking through Ophelia—said, 'Danger lurks behind the scenes, behind what seems real. Search at your own risk.' Again, that's a pretty general statement. But I know you've been asking a lot of questions, and when you nearly drowned after I saw danger in your card reading, well, I felt I had to tell you this."

"Thanks, I appreciate it," Lizzie said. "Is there anything else?"

"Yes. At the end of the séance, Natalie said, 'If these walls could talk,' and then Ophelia began shaking her head. I thought she looked very sad. 'Revenge isn't the answer,' she said."

"That's all?"

Cora nodded and turned her attention back to the crackling fire. She brushed an imaginary bit of lint from her skirt, then smoothed her already neatly styled hair.

Lizzie contemplated what the card reader had said, but still felt she was no closer to the truth than she'd been half an hour ago. All this psychic mumbo-jumbo had raised more questions than it answered. Still, the words "search at your own risk" put her on alert. Right before she fell into the ocean, she'd been poking her nose into the business of the motorboat with the green cabin and the possibility that Roger Young—maybe even Duncan—was involved in alcohol trafficking. Was Natalie Talbot's spirit warning her away from further snooping?

"Cora, I can't help wondering about something. Can we just speculate for a moment?"

"Okay."

"Let's say hypothetically Ophelia is connected with Natalie's death. I don't mean to suggest she is, but could she fake what supposedly comes through her during a séance to cast doubt on someone else and away from her?"

"Yes, that's possible. It could all be an act. That's one of the complaints skeptics frequently raise against mediums and psychics." She shrugged. "Who knows what's true?"

"Well, what do you think?" Lizzie prodded.

Cora fiddled with one of her rings. "I don't know what to think anymore."

Chapter Nineteen

"Magic is believing in yourself. If you can do that, you make anything happen."

— *Johann Wolfgang von Goethe*

After Cora left, the Irish maid brought Lizzie a single pink rose in a crystal vase and a thick, creamy envelope on which her name had been written in an elegant hand. She opened it and withdrew one of Alan Peabody's calling cards, along with a folded sheet of paper on which he'd written the words: "I hope you slept well. If you feel up to it, would you join me in the Art Nouveau parlor for tea this afternoon at 4:00?"

She grabbed a pen and scrawled beneath his graceful script: "I'd be delighted, thank you."

As she handed the envelope back to the maid and slipped her a coin, Lizzie felt her face flush. She still couldn't believe this handsome, wealthy scion of Boston society had shown interest in her, a high school dropout from the Bronx. Unsuccessfully, she tried to tamp down the fantasies that galloped in her mind like racehorses out of the starting gate. *It's only a passing amusement,* she told herself. *He hasn't anything else to do with his time here. Enjoy it while you can.*

A knock on her door jarred her from her daydreams. "It's open," she said.

The heavy wooden door creaked on its hinges as Sidney entered. For a moment, he stood just inside the room, leaving the door open, a nod to propriety. He glanced awkwardly around the room, uncertain whether he should come in or remain where he was. He looked so uncomfortable Lizzie almost laughed. They'd been friends and business partners for seven years, ever since they'd met at a nightspot in Greenwich Village where he played piano, and she waited tables. All this time, he'd been like an older brother to her. His preference for men blocked the possibility of anything more between them. Why was he behaving so strangely now?

"Melody said you're worried about me," she said, motioning him in. "Come in and shut the door. You're letting out the heat."

He crossed the carpet and sat in the empty wingchair in front of the fireplace. "I *am* worried about you, Bearcat. I must admit I was surprised to see you upstairs last night—and on the arm of Alan Peabody, no less. I thought you'd be tucked away in your bed, recuperating. You didn't even let me know you'd be present or that you'd recovered from your trauma."

"But you're ever so glad I'm alive and well, aren't you?"

"Yes, yes, of course, I am." He fitted a cigarette into his silver holder and lit it with a monogrammed lighter. "You look well enough, Lizzie, but I know what a good actress you are."

"Truth be told, I feel better than I thought possible given the circumstances. I hurt from my toenails to my eyebrows, but at least I escaped getting pneumonia." She rapped her knuckles on the wooden table between their chairs for luck.

"You almost *drowned.*"

"And if it hadn't been for Alan, I probably would have."

He took a drag on his cigarette and then exhaled a long, smoky sigh. "When are you going to give up this sleuthing business?"

"I don't know what you're talking about," she lied. "Really, Sid, you're so suspicious. I was taking a walk and slipped on some loose pebbles. It was an accident. Could've happened to anyone."

"Hmph," he muttered, unconvinced.

"In fact, I feel so much better I think I might sing a song or two tonight."

"Aren't you rushing things? I mean, I'd love to have you sing with us tonight, but—"

She cut him off with a wave of her hand. "What do you plan to play?"

"I guess that depends on whether you'll be joining us."

"I'll be there for as long as my voice and energy hold out," she said. "Okay, let's do some of my favorite Gershwin tunes. 'Oh, Lady Be Good!' and 'The Man I Love' and 'Somebody Loves Me.' When I begin to fade, I'll step down, and Bert can come in on his trumpet with 'Everybody Loves My Baby.' Then you can sing 'Sweet Georgia Brown.' It doesn't matter that we've played these songs for this audience before. They're great songs, and they'll lift the dreariness that's still hanging around here since Mrs. Talbot died."

Sidney nodded as she ticked off the night's agenda. "It might work at that."

"What else are you fretting about? Spill."

He glanced at the pink rose on her bedside table and blew a few smoke rings at the ceiling before answering. "Who sent the rose, as if I didn't know?"

"Do I detect a note of jealousy?" she teased.

"Don't be a dumb Dora. You seem quite smitten with him."

She picked up the journal she'd begun reading before Cora's visit. "There's an interesting article in here about a dead guy who communicated with a bunch of people around the world. It says—"

"Good dodge, Bearcat, but you don't fool me."

"I'm talking about spirits, like the ones Duncan's friends believe in."

"And I'm talking about a lothario who'll break your heart and ruin your career."

"Since when did a broken heart ruin a musician's career? All the great blues songs are about love gone wrong."

Sidney laid his hand gently on her bruised arm. "I don't want you to get hurt."

"Neither do I." She patted his hand affectionately. "I appreciate your concern, but I'm not a child. I'm well aware that Alan has no serious intentions toward me. I'm just glad I have someone to amuse me while we're cooped up in this spooky old castle."

"That's something else I wanted to talk to you about. I think we should try to escape. That Irish copper could keep us imprisoned here 'til we rot. Maybe he'll even throw us in the hoosegow."

"Jeepers creepers, Sid. How can we manage to get away? Now that Natalie's funeral is over, O'Quinn's not going to let us travel about freely. I think you may have been right. We should've made our escape then, when we had the chance."

"We have to figure out how to open the gate."

"And then sneak out all our luggage in the dark of night, load up the auto, and drive off without anyone noticing?"

Sidney shrugged. "We could simply tell Duncan we're leaving. What can he do? Refuse to let us go? Telephone Sergeant O'Quinn and squeal on us?"

"He could refuse to pay us," Lizzie said. "I'm not keen on going home broke. We took this engagement for the money, remember? Double our usual fee."

He took a last puff on his cigarette, then ground it out in a crystal ashtray. "I'll come up with a plan. First, I'm going to find a way to open that blasted gate."

After Sidney left, she went back to reading the journal piece about Frederic W.H. Myers. According to the article, a British organization called the Society for Psychical Research, which only six months ago had established an American branch in Boston, claimed his communications showed "life" didn't end with the death of the body. Before she could finish, however, another knock interrupted her.

I'm sure popular today. "It's open," she said.

The door swung in, and Bert stood there, grinning at her shyly. "I wanted to see how you're doing."

"Oh, hi. C'mon in."

Instead of entering, however, he remained in the doorway, nervously shifting his weight from one foot to the other. A rosy blush tinged his big ears.

Lizzie laughed at his awkwardness. "I can't believe you've never been in a lady's boudoir before."

"Well, maybe a time or two," he admitted, and the blush spread to his cheeks.

"Bert, you're letting the heat out into the hallway. Either come in and say your piece or shut the door and go on your way."

He took a step inside and closed the door behind him, but continued grasping the doorknob. "I'm glad you didn't drown."

"Me too."

"I wish I'd been out fishing yesterday. Kevin—Mr. Wraith—said it was too cold. If I'd been there, I could've caught you before you fell in the ocean."

Lizzie felt touched by his concern and admission of guilt. "I'm sure you would've rescued me if you'd been there. But as you can see, I'm just ducky." *If you don't count the bruises and scrapes all over my body.* "I even plan to sing tonight."

"Gee, that's swell."

"Thanks for stopping by, Bert. You're a good egg. No regrets, okay?"

Bert smiled his crooked smile. "See you tonight, then."

* * *

Lizzie spent an inordinate amount of time preparing for her afternoon tea with Alan Peabody. Choosing the perfect frock turned out to be more of a challenge than she'd anticipated. He was accustomed to escorting Boston debutantes, whose exquisite wardrobes made her own stylish outfits look tawdry by comparison. Then there was the added problem of trying to look smart without seeming too eager to impress. After changing three times, she finally settled on a form-fitting afternoon frock of red crepe with long sleeves, a layered calf-length skirt, and a high neck that hid her bruises. She draped a string of pearls around her neck and checked her stockings to make sure the seams were straight before slipping on her favorite T-strap heels. After wrapping her cashmere shawl around her shoulders, she gazed at her reflection in the vanity mirror one last time. Already the bruise on her cheek had started to fade. With a bit of rouge, it seemed more like a blush than an injury.

She rode the elevator down to the first floor. As she gingerly made her way along the castle's stone-paved central hall, she heard animated voices coming from the parlor. Stopping just short of the entryway, she leaned against the wall and listened.

"Natalie didn't give a damn about anyone but herself and getting what she wanted," said a woman's voice that Lizzie quickly identified as Ophelia's.

"That's a strong statement, don't you think?" a man answered. Jonathon Matthews, if she didn't miss her guess.

"Maybe, but true. I've known her since before you and Sabine were born."

Another woman's voice, which Lizzie recognized as Cora's, said impatiently, "Would you please bid Ophelia?"

"Two hearts," the medium answered.

"She was my aunt Frances's best friend," Sabine said.

"And look how she treated your aunt," Ophelia reminded the young woman. "With friends like that, who needs enemies?"

"Two spades," Cora said.

"That was a long time ago," Sabine said.

"Maybe so, but some wounds never heal."

"Three diamonds," Jonathon bid.

Sabine passed. "This all makes me very sad. I had such high expectations for this week, celebrating my father's birthday with his friends. I never thought…"

"Sometimes I wish I could pick Gregory's brain," Ophelia said. "He marries a woman who ran off with her best friend's beau. Then they come back here, and she cuckolds Greg with a low-life bootlegger. What was he thinking? He should've known he couldn't trust her."

"And Natalie wasn't even a looker," Jonathon said. "I say, Ophelia, weren't you just a trifle envious of the old girl? Hobnobbing with all those notorious occultists in England? And now that Nat's dead, I suspect your own business will pick up. Your major competition has been conveniently eliminated. Then there's your long-time association with the victim. Your close proximity to her during her final hours—could give you a bit of caché. Reporters will be beating down your door for interviews. Good publicity, eh? Frankly, I'm surprised they haven't managed to sneak in here already to get a story."

"Pass," said Ophelia.

"I don't want to talk about this anymore," Sabine said. "Can we just play?"

Not wanting to let them know she'd eavesdropped on their conversation, Lizzie waited outside the parlor for several minutes until they'd become involved in their bridge game before she walked by and continued down the hallway.

When she entered the Art Nouveau parlor where Alan waited, he stood and held out both hands. He'd dressed in a beautifully cut charcoal-gray afternoon suit that, despite its attempt at understatement, merely highlighted his fiery hair and handsome features. Lizzie caught her breath and felt her heart skip a few beats as she stepped toward him, placing her battered hands in his.

"Thank you for joining me," he said. "How do you feel?"

"Surprisingly well, thanks to you."

She allowed him to guide her to a rose-colored velvet settee. He sat beside her, still holding her bruised right hand gently.

As if on cue, the freckled serving girl appeared, bearing a tea tray laden with a selection of finger sandwiches cut into triangles, fresh strawberries, salted nuts, pickled vegetables, and small cakes laced with currants. She arranged the various dishes on an oval mahogany coffee table, along with a steaming pot of what smelled like Earl Grey.

"May I bring you anything else?" the girl asked.

Lizzie turned to Alan. "I wonder if we might enjoy a bit of sherry with our tea? For its medicinal effects."

"Certainly," he answered and asked the servant to fulfill Lizzie's request.

After the girl left, Alan said, "I'm happy to see you looking so well today."

"All due to you. You saved my life. How can I ever thank you?"

"The old myths say a person rescued is obliged to her savior for all eternity."

When she frowned in confusion, he laughed, and the golden flecks in his dark eyes sparkled. "I'm just grateful that you're all right."

Lizzie laughed too. "And thank you ever so much for the lovely rose. It brightened my morning." Not for the first time, she wondered where he'd managed to find it. Today was November 1, well past the season for growing roses in Gloucester, Massachusetts.

"You're welcome. I'm glad you liked it."

The serving girl returned carrying a crystal decanter and two glasses. She set them on the table, then poured tea into gold-rimmed porcelain cups.

"Thank you, that will be all for now," Alan dismissed the girl. He filled the glasses with sherry and handed one to Lizzie. Touching his to hers, he said, "To your health."

She sipped the sweet wine, ignoring the cooling tea. "If you don't mind my asking, I'm curious how you came to know Duncan."

"My father knew his father, and my grandfather knew his grandfather. But because Duncan's a lot older than I am, we didn't associate until recently." He leaned toward the tea tray and picked up a Delft china plate. "May I serve you something to eat?"

"Yes, please," she said. "So, what brought you together now? I hope I don't appear rude, but this seems like an odd group to socialize with."

"Duncan and I are Masons, as were our forebears," he answered and handed the plate to her. "Quite a number of U.S. presidents have been Masons too—George Washington, James Monroe, Andrew Jackson, Polk, Buchanan, and Taft, to name a few. Plus, plenty of other famous fellows including Paul Revere, Benjamin Franklin, and John Hancock."

"Not our Mr. Coolidge?"

"Not to my knowledge. Haven't seen him hanging around the Lodge lately," he said with a smile. "Do you know anything about Masons?"

Lizzie had read about the Freemasons in one of Duncan's books, but knew very little. "Only that they're a secret brotherhood."

"A very old one. We trace our history back to the medieval stonemasons who built some of Europe's great cathedrals. We believe in a supreme being and the soul's immortality." He paused to refill their glasses, then continued. "In addition to our mystical practices, we support many educational and charitable causes."

"But what's your connection to this bunch of Spiritualists? And people like Cora and Helen and that old wizard Thaddeus Blake?"

He forked a strawberry and held it out to her. The plump red fruit reminded her of a heart.

Where did Duncan get strawberries in November? she asked herself as she opened her mouth and let Alan feed her. The simple act seemed both intimate and casual, as if they'd known each other for ages and could therefore engage in such familiarities.

"Some magical organizations are rooted in the traditions of Freemasonry," Alan continued. "Perhaps you've heard of the Golden Dawn?"

"Cora's tarot cards."

"Yes, the creators of that deck, Arthur Edward Waite and Pamela Colman Smith, were members." Alan reached for a sandwich half the size of a playing card. "Also, some famous—and infamous—English folks."

"Like Aleister Crowley?"

"Ah, so you know about him. Quite the attention grabber, that one. You wouldn't call them Spiritualists, but some of what Duncan's friends practice have connections to that group."

Lizzie flashed back to what she'd overheard Duncan's son-in-law Jonathon say to Ophelia about Natalie Talbot "hobnobbing with all those notorious occultists in England." Were these the people he meant?

She ate a cucumber and cream cheese sandwich, flavored with fresh dill, then another strawberry, and finally a currant cake with sweet butter and jam. Although she was hungry, having missed lunch, and would have liked more, she didn't want to appear gluttonous.

"Was last night's Samhain ritual part of Freemasonry?"

"No, it's rooted in an even older tradition that predates Christianity. If you decide to dig deeper into what you've seen here, you'll find interweavings and overlaps, as well as influences from the Druids, ancient Egypt, and elsewhere."

"Perhaps we might discuss it someday?" Lizzie suggested.

"I'd be happy to, though I'm no expert. Thaddeus Blake knows much more than I do. You may want to visit his bookshop when you get back to New York."

When they'd finished eating, Alan asked, "Remember what I said about the Freemasons and the craftsmen who built Europe's cathedrals?"

Lizzie nodded.

"Come with me, I want to show you something."

He stood and held out his hand. She took it and let him help her rise. Gently grasping her bruised arm, he led her down the flagstone hallway to the sanctuary where Duncan's pipe organ held pride of place. The last of the day's sunlight shone through the circular stained-glass rose window in the chapel's sea-facing wall. Brilliant reds, blues, and golds flooded the space.

"The most famous rose windows are in Chartres Cathedral in France, built in the twelfth and thirteenth centuries," Alan said. "This is a simplified copy of the South Rose."

"It's beautiful."

"It's more than beautiful. The artisans who created Chartres's windows wove stories into the designs. Remember, at that time, most people were illiterate, and this was a way to teach the Gospel to the masses. But what few people understood then or now, except maybe the alchemists, is that the light shining through the colored glass had healing properties too."

"How is that possible?"

"It may have had something to do with the metals used in making the different colored glass. Or, it might relate to something the yogis in India call the chakras, the body's energy centers that correspond to the rainbow's colors. In earlier times, glassmaking was a big secret. Nobody knows the truth, not even today."

"If I stand in the colored light, will it heal my aches and pains?" Lizzie asked.

"Why not give it a try? You've got nothing to lose and everything to gain."

He placed his fingertips under her chin and tilted her face upward until her eyes met his. Then he brushed his lips lightly against hers and led her into the rainbow of light.

Chapter Twenty

"I want to be with those who know secret things."

— Rainer Maria Rilke

She'd sung better than she'd expected to, but the effort had taken its toll. After locking her bedchamber door, Lizzie unclasped her ermine stole and tossed it over the back of one of the wingchairs. She slid out of her evening gown and hung it in the wardrobe, then wrapped herself in her Chinese silk bathrobe. Thoughts of Alan Peabody swirled in her mind, but she was too tired to bring any of them into focus.

A black form on her bed caught her eye. It looked like a fur muff. Stepping closer, she recognized it as a cat—Thaddeus Blake's black cat Bast. The animal regarded her with wide, golden eyes. Cautiously, Lizzie approached the bed. She liked cats, admired their grace and independence, but remembered how this one had hissed at her and swiped at Cora. She didn't want to frighten it away or cause it to lash out at her.

"How did you get in here, Bast?" she asked. *One of the chambermaids must have come in to rebuild the fire while I was upstairs singing, and the cat snuck in,* she supposed. "The old wizard must be worried about you. I'd better let him know you're visiting me so he can come fetch you."

She inched closer and pulled the velvet cord that hung beside the bed to summon a housemaid. Bast stood up and arched her back.

Lizzie laughed. "Don't you look like the perfect witch's companion."

The cat glared at her, then jumped from the bed, streaked across the carpet, and slid under the wardrobe.

"Don't be afraid, Bast. I never meant to harm you."

If she hadn't been so sore and stiff, she might have knelt down to look under the wardrobe, commune with the cat, and perhaps cajole Bast out of her hiding place. Instead, she sat on the edge of the bed. Only a few minutes passed before she heard a knock on her door. Lizzie eased herself up, crossed the room, and invited the Irish housemaid inside.

"You rang for me, ma'am?"

"Yes. Mr. Blake's cat has found her way into my bedroom. I expect he'll be missing her. Would you take a message to him, letting him know she's here, safe and sound, and he can come collect her?"

"Yes, ma'am."

Lizzie jotted a note to Thaddeus Blake and handed it to the servant. After the girl left, she changed into a pair of woolen trousers, a sweater, thick cotton stockings, and low-heeled shoes as quickly as she could, given her injuries. Then she sat in one of the wingchairs by the fireplace and waited for the old wizard. She rested her head against the chair's high back. Just as she started to doze off, a loud knock roused her.

"Come in," she called.

The Irish maid opened the door, and the white-bearded magician stepped inside.

Lizzie rose to greet him and gave the girl a coin. "Thank you, that will be all for now."

"My apologies for this bother, Miss Crane," Thaddeus said. "Where is Bast?"

His eyes darted about the room, searching for the elusive cat. He hadn't brought his leafy staff with him, Lizzie observed, and he appeared to get around quite well without its support. For a man of his advanced years, he seemed surprisingly nimble.

"She's hiding under the wardrobe. I'm afraid I must have spooked her."

Thaddeus bent down and peered under the wardrobe. "I don't see her. Could she have crawled up into the cabinet?"

Lizzie opened the doors, but saw nothing inside other than her clothing. "Oh dear, where could she be? She couldn't have gotten out of this room. The door's been closed all the while."

Thaddeus stood on one side of the wardrobe, fingering his beard as he contemplated the situation. Lizzie, noticing the heavy piece of furniture sat out from the wall a few inches, peeked behind it, but it was too dark to see anything. She grabbed a candle in a brass holder from the mantelpiece, lit it, and held the flame near the back of the cabinet. Just behind it she saw a push-button switch. She pressed it. To her amazement, the wardrobe slowly swung away from the wall with a groan, revealing an opening large enough for a person to crawl through.

"What the dickens?"

"Bast must have gone exploring," Thaddeus said.

Lizzie studied the old man's face and sensed him contemplating whether to follow his cat through the hole in the wall or simply wait for her to return in her own time. However, Lizzie longed to see where that secret opening led. Perhaps it would explain the strange voices and noises she'd heard through the walls this week.

"We have to find her," she said. The excitement of the discovery pumped adrenalin into her system. The exhaustion she'd felt earlier faded.

Thaddeus motioned her to lead the way. "After you, Miss Crane."

For a moment, she hesitated as she recalled Cora's warning—Natalie Talbot's, actually, speaking through Ophelia. "Search at your own risk." Yet Lizzie's curiosity and the hope of gaining answers to the questions that had perplexed her since her arrival at Halcyon Castle won out over her fears. Besides, she couldn't bear to think of Bast lost and scared, maybe trapped somewhere in the spooky castle, unable to find her way back.

She climbed through the opening, and Thaddeus Blake followed.

* * *

A musty smell greeted her as she entered the dark passageway. Once through the narrow opening, they could stand upright. She held the candle aloft.

The flame threw weak light into a hallway about three feet wide and six feet high. No windows or other sources of illumination brightened the bleak space. *This must be where the voices came from,* she realized, *but whose voices? And why would anyone want to poke around in this dank, dismal place?*

Lizzie looked to the left, then to the right, trying to decide which way to go. To her left, she saw a wooden ramp that inclined toward the third floor of the castle. To her right, the hallway ran behind the second floor's guest bedrooms. As she inched in that direction, she spotted another hole cut in the wall, a hole much like the one that led into her own bedchamber.

"It's blocked off," she said, tapping on a wooden panel. Perhaps another wardrobe, like the one in her room, covered the opening and prevented access.

Guiding the candle's light along the edge of the cutout, she found a button. She pressed it, and the wooden barrier slowly shifted aside. They stood at the threshold, looking into the bedchamber where Natalie Talbot spent her last night on earth.

"The button must activate a pulley that moves the cabinet," the elderly wizard said as he followed Lizzie into the room. "Is this where our controversial friend passed?"

"Yes. I was the first person on the scene, well, after the housemaid who found her, that is."

"And what was your take on the situation?"

"I beg your pardon?"

"What did you experience when you saw Natalie's body lying in the bed? What sensations came to you when you first entered this room?"

His questions surprised her, and she struggled to remember what emotions she'd felt that awful morning. Horror, naturally. Fear. Urgency. A desire to flee. Repulsion. As she followed the thread of those reactions, however, she discovered more: a reminder of her colleague Henry Ives's death, plus anxiety about her own demise and the loss of people close to her. Finally, she recalled a peculiar scent that hung in the room, a stuffy decaying smell like that of old clothing, old books, things that were never exposed to fresh air or the light of day. She remembered the faded photograph she'd found there later of a man and woman on horseback. The photograph Gregory Talbot demanded she hand over to him. She'd had a feeling of being stuck in the past, caught in the dust and shadows of a bygone era like an insect trapped in amber.

"Hold onto those thoughts," Thaddeus said as he motioned her toward the opening in the bedchamber wall. "Let us see what other mysteries these walls hold."

His words reminded her of what Natalie had communicated through Ophelia: "If these walls could talk." Lizzie's heart stepped up its pace as she anticipated the discovery that lay ahead.

Carrying the candle in its brass holder, she led the old wizard back through the hole into the dark passageway. With the fingers on her other hand, she felt her way along the stone wall until she came to wooden stairs that led down to the basement. She glanced back at Thaddeus, and he nodded. Cautiously, she descended step by step, her palm pressed against the wall in the absence of a railing. The wall grew colder and damper as she plunged deeper into the castle's bowels.

At the end of the stairway, another hallway turned at a 90-degree angle. They passed an airless room where double-decker bunk beds with lumpy straw mattresses lined three of the walls. Several straight-backed chairs, a wooden table that held a chipped pitcher and bowl, and a chamber pot completed the furnishings. *Who had inhabited this bleak space?* Lizzie wondered. Then she remembered that Duncan's grandfather, Quentin Fox, who built Halcyon, had been an abolitionist and a member of the Underground Railroad. *This must be where he hid runaway slaves,* she realized.

Farther on, they came to another room. Tentatively, Lizzie opened the unlocked door. Inside she saw crates of bottles, hundreds of them, stacked along the walls. She held her candle aloft, slowly sweeping its light from one end of the chamber to the other.

"Holy moly."

"It appears our good friend Duncan has plenty of 'spirits' in his corner," Thaddeus said.

Lizzie chuckled at his play on words. "What do you make of all this?"

The old man shrugged. "I make nothing of it. I expect our friend knows what he's doing."

She spotted another door on the opposite side of the storage room and walked toward it. A metal lock hung on the latch, but it wasn't fastened, and Lizzie pushed the heavy oak door open. As it swung inward, she found herself in the underground larder where two days ago, she'd inadvertently come upon the castle's cold storage warehouse. Where she'd watched Roger Young unloading cargo from the mysterious motorboat. Illicit cargo, as it seemed.

"Let's go back," she said, having seen enough.

They retraced their steps through the two storerooms and closed the doors behind them. In the hallway outside, waiting for them, sat Bast.

"Ah, there you are, my lovely. You've led us on quite a hunt," Thaddeus said. He scooped up the curious black cat and placed her on his shoulder. "She found us, not the other way around."

Although Lizzie's bruised legs cried out as she climbed the stairs back up to the castle's second story, she could barely contain her excitement at having discovered Halcyon's secret. The eerie voices that had troubled her and Melody since their arrival at Halcyon Castle must have belonged to men moving about in the passageways behind the castle's walls. Men—including Roger Young and Duncan Fox—engaged in the illegal business of smuggling alcohol. Not ghosts or demons or other spirits. Now, Lizzie knew what the walls knew.

The opening in her bedroom wall allowed her to hear those voices, even though Duncan's other guests couldn't. But she still didn't understand why her bedroom and Natalie Talbot's had hidden access to those clandestine spaces.

Chapter Twenty-One

"I am longing to be with you, and by the sea, where we can talk together freely and build our castles in the air."

— Bram Stoker, Dracula

When Lizzie pulled aside the heavy drapes that covered the windows of her bedchamber, she saw that the sun had already climbed high in the sky, and the day had progressed without her. After her late-night exploration, she'd feared she wouldn't be able to sleep, knowing that someone else might know of the secret opening into her room. Perhaps the person who killed Natalie Talbot. However, the events of the day had exhausted her, and she'd fallen quickly into a deep, dreamless slumber.

The morning sunlight illuminated two envelopes lying on the floor, where they'd been slipped under the bedroom door. Clutching her Chinese silk robe around her aching body, she scooped them up and carried them to her dressing table.

She recognized Alan Peabody's distinctive script and the thick, richly textured paper that she'd come to identify with him. She slit open the envelope and read his brief note: "Please say you'll join me for lunch in the sculpture garden at one o'clock." Flipping over the sheet of paper, she scrawled on the backside: "Yes. I look forward to it." Although she suspected sophisticated and educated ladies penned more eloquent letters to their suitors, she hadn't the skill or the patience to follow decorum. She didn't even know what that might entail. *Better not try to pretend I'm more than I am,* she decided. I'd *only fall flat on my face.*

The second note was more perplexing. It came from Duncan Fox and hinted at her late-night rambling through the castle's secret byways: "Thaddeus says you're interested in Halcyon's history. Would you like a private tour of the castle?" Again, she turned the note over and wrote on its back: "Yes, thank you. When?"

She pulled the velvet cord beside her bed to summon a chambermaid, then eased into one of her bedroom's comfortable wingchairs to think. How much did Thaddeus Blake tell Duncan about their trip through the hidden passages? And why? Until now, Duncan had seemed the epitome of congeniality, but he must know that she'd trespassed into his private and dangerous territory.

Before she had time to explore the possible ramifications of her sojourn, a knock on the door roused her. She opened it to admit Inge, bearing a tray of delicious-looking pastries and a pot of coffee.

"Good morning, ma'am," the fair-haired housemaid said.

"Ah, Inge, thank you. This is just what I needed."

While the girl set down the tray, Lizzie fetched a coin from her purse and handed it to Inge, along with the two letters. "Would you be kind enough to deliver these?"

"Yes, ma'am. Will there be anything else?"

"The night of my accident, you sprinkled herbs in my bathwater. Might you have more of those herbs on hand?"

"Yes, ma'am. Lavender, chamomile, mullein, and hyssop. Shall I bring you some?"

"Would you? I'd be ever so grateful," Lizzie said.

"Yes, ma'am."

Lizzie handed the girl another coin. "Thank you, Inge. Oh, and by the way, might you happen to have any herbs to enhance, um, romance?"

"A love potion, you mean?" The young servant smiled mischievously. "Leave it to me."

* * *

"The room where you're staying was once my parents' bedchamber," Duncan told Lizzie as they walked through the hidden passageway that ran behind the walls of the castle's second-floor guest rooms. "I was conceived here."

When they approached the opening to the room where Natalie Talbot died, he said, "This was my aunt's bedroom. She never married, but lived here with us until her death. I found her quite delightful. She was a poet, a literate lady who spoke several languages, and an avid abolitionist."

"Why did secret openings lead from these two rooms?" Lizzie asked.

"To give my parents and aunt access to the hidden passageways, to avoid being observed by the castle's staff as they helped slaves escape. As you may have guessed, runaways came to Halcyon by boat. My family sheltered them here until they could take their next step toward freedom."

"Where does the ramp go?"

"To the third floor," he said. "There's an opening in my library."

"Don't tell me. Touch a button, and a bookcase swings aside to reveal a secret room?"

"Yes," Duncan admitted. "It seems I'm a cliché."

"A charming one," Lizzie said. "I'd love to have a revolving bookcase in my home, but in my dinky Greenwich Village apartment, it would dump me out onto the fire escape."

They rode the elevator down to the first floor, and Duncan showed her through the various rooms filled with treasures and artifacts gathered from the four corners of the earth. Each object had a story, which he gladly shared.

"My parents and grandparents were collectors, like Isabella Stewart Gardner," he said. "She was the artist John Singer Sargent's patron. Have you been to Mrs. Gardner's museum in Boston? It's much more extensive than this. Full of all sorts of intriguing delights. She died last year, but her will stipulates that her home remain open to the public."

"Not yet," Lizzie said and made a mental note to learn more about the museum and the woman behind it.

Next, they came to the sanctuary where Duncan's pipe organ resided. The sun shining through the rose window cast a patchwork of colors over the vast space. To Lizzie, it seemed as if fairies danced in the aisles, tossing garlands of light every which way. She wondered if standing in that rainbow, as Alan Peabody had suggested, might indeed have aided her healing.

"I enjoyed listening to you play the organ," she said. "Sidney says it's ever so difficult to play."

Her host beamed. His eyes lit up, and his cheeks flushed with pride. "Yes, it's an amazingly complex and awe-inspiring instrument. I've been studying it for forty years, but I'm still a novice." He mounted the steps to the platform on which the organ sat and lovingly ran his fingertips over its ivory keys. "In the ninth century, churches in Europe began adopting pipe organs after Charlemagne had one installed in his chapel at Aachen. This one was built in Austria and shipped here in 1880."

"I hope to hear you perform again while I'm here."

"Of course, Lizzie dear. It would be my pleasure to play for you, anytime you wish. You need only say the word."

"Thank you, I will." Her gaze drifted up to the bank of pipes arrayed on a balcony above the organ. "There's a door behind the pipes. Where does it lead?"

"To the organ's mechanism. Nothing to do with the secret passageways in the walls." He smiled and looked up at the balcony. "I doubt the slaves who passed through here were thinking much about organ music."

At last, they descended to the deepest level of the castle, where Lizzie had seen the green-cabined motorboat unloading crates of contraband. The elevator's door opened, and they stepped out onto the wooden platform. Today the slip was empty. Seawater lapped at the pilings that supported the dock. The smell of brine hung heavy in the damp, enclosed space. Trying not to appear obvious about it, she glanced down the dock and noticed the door to the storage room was closed. *Does he know Thaddeus and I found this secret place last night?*

"Here's where small fishing boats entered to collect the slaves," Duncan explained in what she thought of as his tour guide voice. "Some of those people continued on to Canada. Others were relocated throughout New

England."

"Your relatives were very brave."

"Yes, yes, they were. Many people were. But I can't help wondering, would we have been so noble if we'd been an agrarian lot, like the southerners who needed slaves to work the crops? New England didn't have large-scale plantations, so slave labor wasn't as essential to us, although some people here did keep slaves. It's harder to follow the righteous road when doing so interferes with your livelihood." He clapped his hands together once, then said, "Well, my dear, that's the end of our little tour. Unless you'd like to continue outdoors?"

Seizing her chance, Lizzie asked, "Could we? If you have time, that is. I must admit, I've taken quite a fancy to the magnificent entry gate with the dragons on it. And the moat and the bridge. They're straight out of a fairy tale."

He waved her back to the elevator. "Let's fetch our coats. There's a nip in the air even though the sun's shining brightly. Wouldn't want you to catch cold now, after all you've been through."

"Swell. Thank you, Duncan."

At the second floor, he stopped the lift and let her out. "I'll meet you downstairs by the front door in a few minutes."

Maybe I can get him to show me how the gate operates, she thought as she pulled on a dove-gray wool coat. She wrapped a red cashmere scarf around her head and tied it at her neck. After grabbing a pair of kidskin gloves, she took the elevator downstairs, where Duncan awaited her.

He opened the front door with its pattern of old nails and held her arm as they stepped down to the granite-paved parking area. A biting wind blew in off the ocean, and she was glad she'd bundled up.

"You realize, of course, this castle is a reproduction," Duncan said as they approached the moat.

Lizzie laughed. "Yes, Duncan, I know nobody lived here in the Gothic period, except the Indians, that is."

"I didn't mean to sound condescending." He smiled back at her, his gray hair blowing about his head like smoke. "A real Gothic castle would have had a drawbridge connected to the castle wall, which could be lowered across a moat to allow access or cranked up to prevent invaders from entering. This one is just for show. It doesn't move, although I suppose it could be burned in the event of an attack."

She leaned over to observe the foaming water rolling in with the rising tide. "No alligators in the moat?"

"You might find some fierce bluefish in late summer, but alligators aren't common in these parts. They prefer warmer climes."

Their footsteps thumped on the wooden planks as they crossed the bridge. Duncan held her arm until they were safely on the other side, as if he feared she might topple into the icy water. Again. They continued walking along the promontory's winding driveway, etched into a thin neck of granite where sumac and juniper clung tenaciously to scraps of sandy soil between the rocks.

As they approached the entry gate, Duncan asked, "Are you familiar with the work of Hector Guimard?"

"No, sorry to say I've never heard of him."

"He designed the entrances to the Paris Metro. My parents met him on one of their trips abroad and convinced him to design this gate for Halcyon."

Lizzie ran her gloved hands over the intricate patterns wrought in iron: vines, flowers, and finally, the two magnificent winged dragons. "How does it open?"

"Elves open it," he said.

"Elves?"

He laughed at his own joke. "Actually, it relies on an ancient method devised by a brilliant Egyptian inventor named Heron. Quite simple, really. A system of ropes and pulleys connect it to very large buckets, which fill with water when the tide comes in. They float on the surface, easing the tension and allowing the gate to swing closed. When the tide goes out again, the buckets sink back to the low-tide line. The weight of the water as they descend pulls the gate open."

"The gate opens and closes every day according to the tides?"

Duncan nodded. "Yes, just like Halcyon's swimming pool fills and empties every day with the tides."

All we have to do is wait for low tide to escape, Lizzie thought excitedly. She tried to remember if she'd seen the dragon gate open and close periodically during her stay at Halcyon Castle, but drew a blank. She'd been so focused on what happened inside the castle, she'd missed the gate's twice-daily openings.

"Of course, it can be overridden electronically," Duncan said. "Still, it's quite ingenious what this man invented nearly two thousand years ago. Heron even designed the first coin-operated vending machine to dispense holy water."

"You're not serious."

"Indeed I am. That invention brought the early Church a bundle of money."

The wind whipped at Lizzie's scarf, and she tucked it back into her coat. "What's the significance of the dragons?"

"The Chinese consider them good luck. In mythology, they represent primordial power, as well as courage and wisdom. I like to think of them as guardians."

"Have they done their job?" she asked, thinking about the red dragon embroidered on the back of her silk bathrobe. Was it guarding her during this tenuous time?

"Yes, until last week," Duncan said, a note of sadness in his voice. "Alas, they didn't protect Natalie."

Lizzie saw an opening and grabbed it. "The policeman Sergeant O'Quinn implied she was murdered—and by someone in your household. What do you make of that?"

"Dear Lizzie, I don't know what to make of it. I'm confounded and distraught. Every time I try to examine the matter seriously, I feel such unhappiness that I recoil—even though I know I should delve deeper and try to bring some sort of resolution to the mystery of her passing. After all, I was her friend for many years, as well as her host. I invited her here, and here she met her death. That gives me some responsibility for what happened to Natalie. I'm afraid I've failed her."

Then there's the matter of you and her lover being engaged in an illegal and profitable business venture, Lizzie thought. *Does it relate to her murder?*

Duncan took her arm again. "I'm growing chilled. Come, let's go back inside, shall we?"

"Thank you for this entertaining and educational tour, Duncan. I've enjoyed it ever so much."

"You're quite welcome. It's been my pleasure. I rarely have a chance to share the secrets of my home with people who value them."

Chapter Twenty-Two

"He looked at her the way all women want to be looked at by a man."

— *F. Scott Fitzgerald, The Great Gatsby*

She barely had time to change clothes and freshen her makeup before meeting Alan in the sculpture garden. Again, she struggled with choosing the right outfit for their luncheon: sophisticated and sexy, but subtly so. Fashionable, but not flashy. Finally, she settled on a figure-flattering royal blue wool frock with a petal skirt. Thankfully styles were moving away from the tubular forms popular last year and now embraced more feminine lines. Designs that accented Lizzie's womanly curves. She slipped a topaz necklace over her head—its egg-sized bauble fell into the hollow between her full breasts—then grabbed a silk shawl with a peacock woven on it.

Although the sculpture garden wasn't heated, three walls of windows sheltered it from the wind. Some of them could be opened on salubrious days. The stone wall where the courtyard joined the castle retained solar warmth, so that even in the depth of winter, the conservatory was usually cozy enough on sunny days.

Statues of mythical gods and goddesses, along with an assortment of nubile nymphs, angels, and winsome animals populated the enclosed space. A half-nude female poured water onto a pot of deep-red chrysanthemums. A male, also scantily clad, bent over a sundial. Here and there stone cherubs peeked out from banks of ivy, and mature angels spread their wings as if providing shelter to those below. Around them grew plants of all sorts, including many tropical species that Lizzie was surprised could survive here, even with the protection offered by the walls of glass.

With her peacock shawl draped over her arm and her face glowing with the anticipation a woman wears when she's eager to meet her suitor, Lizzie crossed the garden. Alan sat in an ironwork chair beneath a Ficus tree, his right ankle crossed over his left knee. He wore a double-breasted afternoon suit of russet tweed, casual but exquisitely cut, that echoed his red hair. As she approached, he stood and extended his hands.

"Thank you for agreeing to join me for lunch," he said, closing his fingers over hers.

"Thank you for inviting me."

He held a chair for her to sit at a round, glass-topped table. "How are you feeling?"

"Surprisingly well."

"Well enough to sing tonight, I hope?"

"Ab-so-lute-ly."

He motioned to a serving girl who brought bowls of steaming fish chowder and a basket of crusty French bread still warm from the oven. For a while, they ate in companionable silence, enjoying the honey-colored sunshine that spilled through the conservatory windows. Lizzie draped her silk shawl over the back of her chair; she didn't need it after all in this comfortably warm environment.

As soon as they'd finished, the servant returned with a platter of sliced lamb, pale pink, juicy, and sprinkled with chopped mint. A separate plate held mashed orange acorn squash and green peas with pearl onions.

"How pretty," Lizzie exclaimed as the girl arranged colorful portions on a gold-edged plate and set it in front of her.

The girl prepared a plate for Alan, too, and refilled their teacups. "May I be of further service to you now, sir?"

Gracefully, he dismissed her. "Thank you, no. You've been most efficient."

For several moments, he sat watching Lizzie eat. He sipped his tea, biding his time.

Finally, he said, "Lizzie, I have some things I'd like to talk to you about, if you're willing."

She laid down her silverware. "Certainly."

"First, I'm glad we've gotten to spend this time together. Although I wanted to celebrate Duncan's birthday, the real reason I came to Halcyon was to see you again."

"I'm ever so glad you did. I might not be alive now if you hadn't shown up just in the nick of time."

"That was good fortune," he said. "After meeting you at the Winslows' home, I had every intention of visiting you in New York. But my work has been all-consuming lately, and I haven't been able to take time off. I know that's a poor excuse, yet it's the truth."

"What kind of work do you do?"

"I'm in the financial business," he said, without elaborating. "And tomorrow morning I must return to it. I've already stayed on here a day longer than I'd planned."

Lizzie's heart sank. Trying to keep her disappointment from showing on her face, she said, "I'm sorry to hear that. I've enjoyed your company."

"If I can get away, I'll try to come back Saturday evening. If you're still here, that is."

"I don't know how long I'll be here, that depends on Sergeant O'Quinn. You're lucky. You can come and go as you please, because you weren't here when Mrs. Talbot died. You're not under suspicion like the rest of us."

"Say, how about I hide you in the trunk of my car and steal you away?" Alan said with a wink.

"Smashing idea. I'm game."

"Of course, then the cops would surely think you're guilty and nab me for aiding and abetting. We'd both end up in jail." He reached into his jacket pocket and pulled out a black satin pouch. "I have a gift for you."

"It's heavy. Let me guess. A bag full of doubloons?"

He laughed, and the gold flecks in his brown eyes sparkled. "Open it and see."

Loosening the drawstring, she reached in and pulled a book from the pouch. Ornate bands of etched silver decorated the spine and corners of its leather cover. Both its front and back were richly carved and studded with deep blue gemstones. *Lapis lazuli, if I don't miss my guess.* Carefully she opened it and gazed at the intricate frontispiece, colorfully illustrated and edged with gilt.

"It's beautiful," she said, running her fingers over the elaborate binding.

"Are you familiar with Rumi?"

Lizzie shook her head.

"A Persian Sufi poet who lived in the thirteenth century, but his work has only been available in English for about forty years. This one is called *The Masnavi*. I hope you'll find it inspiring."

"What a wonderful present." She clutched it to her chest, awed and delighted. None of her suitors had ever given her a book, and she'd never seen one as exquisite as this. Surely it belonged in a museum. "Thank you, Alan. I shall treasure it and the great poet's words. When I see you next, perhaps we may discuss Mr. Rumi?"

"Certainly." He reached across the table for her hand and lifted it to his lips. "I'm glad you like it. I'll be eager to hear what you think after you've read it."

* * *

Lizzie knew she was late. As she'd suspected, Sidney was pacing impatiently in front of the ballroom's stage when she emerged from the elevator.

"How nice that our diva has decided to honor us with her presence."

Ignoring him, she approached the stage.

"You look very pretty," Melody said, eying Lizzie's stylish blue afternoon frock.

Usually, the singer would have shown up for practice wearing trousers and a thick sweater. Only in the evenings, for performances, did she don glamorous gowns or flapper dresses that revealed a bit more skin than some people might consider proper.

"Let me guess why you're all dolled up."

"Can it, Sid," she cut him off.

She wished she could tell him about her luncheon with Alan Peabody. About the magnificent book of Rumi's poetry. About the Samhain ritual and all the rest of it. Sidney had been her best friend for seven years, but friends were all they'd ever be. She knew he wanted her to be happy, yet he couldn't make her happy in the way she longed for as a woman. Instead, he'd grumbled, discounted, or criticized her for getting involved with Alan. If she hadn't known better, she'd have thought Sid was jealous. *Maybe I need a new best friend I can confide in. This is all too discombobulating for me to grapple with alone.*

* * *

The Irish housemaid brought tea to Lizzie's bedroom, where she and Melody sat in front of the fireplace. After serving lapsang souchong and blueberry scones to the two musicians, the girl asked, "Will there be anything else, ma'am?"

"No, thank you. We're quite copacetic," Lizzie said.

Melody spooned sugar into her tea and stirred it three times for good luck. "How did your lunch with Alan go?"

"Splendid. I'm quite in awe of him, actually. He gave me a lovely book of poetry by an ancient Persian fella named Rumi."

Lizzie set her tea aside and fetched the jeweled book from her bedside table. She handed it to her friend. Melody ran her fingertips over the lapis lazuli studs on the book's cover, the silver trim on its spine, its gilded pages.

"This is beautiful. Lizzie. He must really care about you to give you such a lovely present."

"Or he's hoping to win not only my heart, but other parts of my body as well."

Melody blushed, and Lizzie realized she'd shocked her younger and more naïve friend.

"That's rather uncharitable of you, don't you think? All things considered."

"You're right, Mel. Alan's been nothing but helpful, kind, and generous to me." Lizzie sipped her tea, examining her feelings. Although she longed for his touch, his kiss, his intimate embrace, she knew many people considered female entertainers little better than prostitutes. She couldn't bear to think he might put her in that class. "I guess I'm trying not to let myself hope for anything more. He's a Boston blueblood, and I'm the daughter of poor Irish immigrants from the Bronx. What are my chances with someone like Alan?"

"Zero, if you think like that." Melody buttered a scone, then took a bite.

"What do you suggest?"

"Didn't he say he came here this weekend, not only to celebrate Duncan's birthday but to see you?"

Lizzie shrugged. "Pretty words."

"He could've stayed in Boston and found plenty of other ways to amuse himself."

"True," Lizzie admitted.

"My suggestion is, make the best of it. Enjoy your time with him. Maybe it won't go anywhere. Maybe he'll jilt you. Maybe you'll discover he's not the knight in shining armor you'd hoped for. But how will you know if you don't give it a shot?"

"Sidney thinks Alan will break my heart."

"You know what Margaret Kennedy says, 'it's better to break one's heart than to do nothing with it.' I guess that's a chance you'll have to take. If you don't, you'll regret it forever."

Chapter Twenty-Three

"Being deeply loved by someone gives you strength, while loving someone deeply gives you courage."

— Lao Tzu

Surprised and pleased that she'd managed to make it through the entire evening's performance, Lizzie bowed to her audience and stepped down from the stage. She'd taken only a few steps before Alan reached her and grasped her arm. *Perhaps knowing he was in the audience gave me the extra energy I needed*, she thought. In any case, she gladly accepted his support and let him steer her to a chair. Several of Duncan's guests complimented her performance. Others asked about her health.

Duncan approached her, an orange ascot blazing at his throat in bright contrast to his proper dark suit. His unruly hair stuck out in all directions. "Dear lady, thank you for entertaining us so eloquently this evening. How are you feeling?"

"Well enough, thank you."

"I see our friend Alan is taking good care of you."

"He is, indeed, for which I'm very grateful."

"Then I'll bid you adieu and see you on the morrow."

Alan held out his hand to their host. "I must leave before dawn, so I'll say farewell now. Thank you for your hospitality, Duncan."

"So soon?" Duncan peered over his spectacles at Alan. "Ah, well, I expect you have important matters to attend to in Boston. Perhaps you'll honor us again with your presence, if not to visit your old chum, then to call upon the lovely Lizzie Crane while she still abides here, though against her will, I dare say."

"Duncan, you've been a most generous and congenial host," Lizzie said. "You're not to blame for these unfortunate circumstances."

Alan smiled and slid his arm around Lizzie's waist. "If Fate, and the financial world will it, I'll return to visit you both this weekend."

Duncan clapped him on the shoulder. "Good man. Fare thee well, then."

"And you."

"Sleep tight, Duncan," Lizzie said.

Her host's guests began ambling down the stairway or squeezed themselves into the lift, chatting animatedly. Onstage, Melody and Bert finished packing up their instruments. From the corner of her eye, Lizzie caught what she interpreted as a look of pique from Sidney as he glanced at her on his way to the elevator. She knew he meant to protect her, but wished he could just relax and let her enjoy the brief time she had with Alan. As Sid stepped into the lift, she blew him a kiss. He turned away.

Alan bent toward her and asked, "Would you care to go downstairs for a nightcap?"

"Ab-so-lute-ly," Lizzie said, leaning more heavily on his arm than perhaps was necessary.

After the other guests had descended, he pressed the call button to summon the elevator back to the castle's ballroom. He held the door open for her. She stepped in and he followed her, shut the door, and pressed the down button.

"Do you know how the color of your dress emphasizes your beauty?"

To her chagrin, the low-cut, emerald-green silk gown she'd worn tonight showed more of her bruises than she would have liked. "You don't think it's too revealing?"

"Hardly." He laughed and let his gaze sweep leisurely over her figure. "I suspect most men would agree it's not revealing enough, except maybe your friend Sidney. What's with him anyway?"

"He sees himself as my big brother, which entails safeguarding me from men he thinks might have 'improper' designs on me."

"What do you think?"

"I think I'm old enough to make my own decisions."

The lift rumbled down two stories, then bumped to a stop. Alan opened the door and helped her out. He guided her down the castle's central hallway to the billiard room where several of Duncan's guests had already gathered.

Ophelia and Kevin Wraith sat at a table for two near the bar. They looked up as Lizzie and Alan entered. It took the medium an awkward moment to compose her face into something resembling an agreeable expression and respond to Lizzie's hello. Kevin didn't even bother. He stared down at the table as if trying to read something meaningful in its woodgrain.

Jonathon and Sabine Matthews, Helen Simms, and Roger Young stood around the billiard table, cues in hand, engaged in what appeared to be an animated game. As Lizzie and Alan entered, Jonathan hailed them.

"Bar's open," he said. "I'm about to demolish my opponents. You're welcome to take me on in the next game if you dare."

Alan waved him off amiably, then ducked behind the bar. He pulled out a bottle of Lagavulin and held it aloft for Lizzie to see. "Will this do?"

"Ab-so-lute-ly."

He'd barely finished pouring the golden scotch into two tumblers when Cora Delaney, dressed in a stunning violet gown with her mink draped over her shoulders, strolled into the room with Thaddeus Blake, in his coarse monk's robe, at her side. Lizzie noticed the old wizard's curious cat Bast wasn't perched on his shoulder, and that the tarot reader's hand rested on the magician's left arm. In his right hand, he grasped the gnarled staff that inexplicably sprouted green leaves and seemed to glide along at his side like a companion, rather than a stick of wood.

"Good show tonight," Thaddeus said to Lizzie as he insinuated himself into the group.

Has he told Cora and the others about our exploration last night through the secret passageways behind the castle's walls? Lizzie hoped not.

After all, one of these people may have accessed the hidden door into

Natalie Talbot's bedroom and killed her. Cora, whose mother had hanged herself because of what Natalie told her, and whose father took heroin for tuberculosis? Ophelia and Kevin, who felt threatened by Natalie's success and would benefit if their competitor were eliminated? Natalie's husband and her lover, fighting over a woman who'd shamed them both?

Jonathon called a pocket and sunk the 8-ball, ending the game. He pumped his fist in the air and crowed, "Yahoo! Who's brave enough to take on Sabine and me next?"

Helen swatted him playfully on his backside with her cue as she made her way to the bar. Roger Young shrugged and followed her.

Thaddeus stepped forward. "Cora and I will."

"Care to wager a bet?" Jonathon asked.

"As you wish," the old magician said.

Jonathon nodded at Thaddeus's strange walking stick. "No fair using your stave. Only regular cues allowed here."

Alan leaned toward Lizzie, close enough that she could smell the warm, spicy scent of his skin. "Do you want to witness this contest, or shall we find a quieter place to talk?"

"Let's get out of here."

He escorted her down the hallway with its Dickensesque gas-lit lamps and somber family portraits into the dining hall. "There's a small, private breakfast room through that door," he pointed. "It's right beside the kitchen, so it may be warmer there than it is in here."

Lizzie wondered why she'd never noticed the secluded room before, but she let him guide her into it. As he'd said, the intimate space, tucked into one of the castle's turrets away from the main dining room, was pleasantly warm. A round table and four chairs sat in the center of the room. Above them hung a chandelier, much smaller and simpler than those she'd seen in other parts of the castle. Tall, peaked windows overlooked the ocean. A pale-gold moon, two days past full, shone in the indigo sky.

"How lovely," Lizzie said.

Alan clinked his glass to hers. "You're lovely."

For a few moments, they stood silently sipping their scotch, gazing out at the tranquil scene beyond the castle. In the distance, the moon's light glistened on the ocean. Lizzie contemplated the King of Wands in the tarot reading Cora had done for her. *Are you my king, Alan?*

As if intercepting her thoughts, he took her drink from her hand and set their glasses on the table. Gently, he placed his hands on her shoulders, then turned her to face him. He kissed her lightly, then more deeply. When he took her in his arms and pulled her against him, she felt his arousal. His lips trailed kisses along her throat, to her shoulder, then across her bare collarbones and down the V of her gown's revealing neckline. Whispering her name, he slid his hands over her hips and pressed her more tightly to him. Lizzie felt a familiar heat start in her belly and melt downward, lodging in her core. Erotic images flashed in her mind.

Reluctantly, she pulled away. "I desire you, Alan, but we barely know each other. What would you think of me afterward?"

"I'd think I was the luckiest man on earth to have known intimacy with such a beautiful, talented, and intelligent woman."

Laying her cheek against his chest, she said, "I'd like you to know me in more than the biblical sense."

"I'd like that too."

"Then perhaps you might be willing to continue this when we meet again?"

He sighed, then ran his hands slowly down her bare arms. He kissed her forehead. "As you wish."

"As I think best, at least for now."

He held her close and kissed her again, but this time with less passion and more tenderness. Finally, he stepped away and retrieved their glasses from the table. He handed Lizzie's to her. "I'll think of nothing but you until we meet again."

"Maybe you should think a tiny bit about financial matters too. Otherwise, Boston might tumble into a huge mess."

He chuckled, but without mirth. "Not only Boston."

They turned back to the arched windows and watched the moon shining on the black water while they finished their scotch. Alan kept one arm around her waist, and she leaned against him comfortably.

"I promise I'll try to come back on the weekend, Lizzie. If something should change, if the police release you, will you please notify me?"

"I will."

What a dilemma. I'd dearly love to go home, but then I might not see Alan again for a long time, maybe never. And I'd dearly love to sleep with him, but then he might think me easy and lose interest in me.

"Do you still have my calling card?" he asked.

"Of course. And by the time I see you again, I will have finished reading the beautiful book of poetry you gave me. Then we can discuss Mr. Rumi."

"Among other things," he said, caressing her cheek with the backs of his fingers. "Now, I expect you're probably tired. It's past one o'clock, and I must be up and away in a few hours. I'll see you to your bedchamber, well, to the door at least unless you change your mind on the way."

They rode the elevator to the second floor and said goodnight. They shared one last long, delicious kiss, then Lizzie unlocked her bedroom door and stepped inside. She took off her evening gown and hung it in the wardrobe, washed off her face paint, and brushed her teeth. As she climbed into her big, comfortable bed to spend the rest of the night alone, she scolded herself, "What a fool you are, Lizzie Crane."

Chapter Twenty-Four

"What fun it had been, having an admirer even for that little while. No wonder people liked admirers. They seemed, in some strange way, to make one come alive."

— Elizabeth von Arnim, The Enchanted April

Lizzie woke to a weak, gray light sifting through a gap in the drapes of her bedchamber. She knew Alan had departed hours ago and was back in Boston by now. Even if she hadn't known in advance, if he hadn't said a passionate goodbye last night, she still would've felt his absence in her very bones. *I should have taken him into my bed when I had the opportunity instead of abiding by ridiculous, outdated mores,* she thought. *Will I ever have another chance?*

Reluctantly, she threw aside her bed's puffy down comforter and stepped onto the cold wooden floor. Her body still ached as she pushed herself up, but the pain had lessened. Again, her thoughts circled back to Alan and how he'd rescued her. *If it weren't for him, I wouldn't even be alive now.*

Tentatively, she opened the door into the bathroom she shared with Melody, not wanting to intrude if her fellow musician was there indisposed, but found it empty. She turned on the tap and let hot water flow into the deep, porcelain tub. After dropping a handful of Epsom salts and the dried herbs Inge had given her into the steaming water, she wrapped her dark hair in a Turkish towel and climbed into the womblike vat. Already, the bruises that quilted her body were fading from purple to bilious green.

I must find a way to escape from here, she thought as she immersed herself in the hot bathwater. *All I have to do is pay attention to the tides that open the dragon gate—and get Sid and the others to skedaddle with me. I can't remain a prisoner at Halcyon forever. The police will solve Natalie Talbot's murder in their own time, with or without us. And if Alan is serious about seeing me again, he can come to New York, where I'll welcome him with open arms.* In the soothing water's embrace, the answers to those conundrums seemed simple. Yet as she toweled off and dressed to face the day, the doubts and worries flooded in once again.

Downstairs in the dining hall, she spotted Sidney finishing a cigarette and a cup of coffee. He looked up and narrowed his eyes, then flicked ash into a crystal receptacle. Lizzie took a seat across the table from him and signaled a serving girl for coffee.

"Please bring me two eggs scrambled with toast and bacon," she said as the maid filled her cup.

After the girl was out of earshot, Sidney asked, "Did you sleep with him?"

"What do you care if I did or didn't?"

"Boston Brahmin sweeps showgirl off her feet," he mocked a newspaper headline. "Successful musical revue dissolves after losing its diva."

"Don't you think you're being a bit melodramatic?"

"We can't afford to lose you, Lizzie."

She rolled her eyes and took a sip of coffee. "You should know by now I'm not keen on marriage. And I'm not stupid enough to get knocked up."

He ground out his cigarette and lit another. "He won't marry you anyway. He's a rich and powerful man who can have all the women he wants—women younger, wealthier, and more esteemed than you. You're just a bit of crumpet on the smorgasbord."

His words stung, and she snapped back. "Thanks very much, Sid. What a pretty picture you've painted of me."

"It's the truth, Lizzie, no matter how much it hurts. Better you face it now than later."

"Are you worried about me or about The Troubadours' future?"

"Both. They're inseparable. Without you, The Troubadours don't exist." He reached for her hand, and his handsome face showed genuine concern. "Ah, Lizzie, truly, I don't want you to get hurt. And I can't bear to imagine The Troubadours disbanding. We've worked so hard and come so far."

The maid brought Lizzie's breakfast and topped off their coffee cups. "Will there be anything else, ma'am?"

"No, thank you."

She bit into a slice of bacon while Sidney puffed his cigarette and sipped his coffee, watching her eat. Periodically, he fiddled with his tie or ran a hand over the top of his head where his dark hair was thinning.

"Jeepers creepers, Sid. Will you stop fussing like a mother superior? If you must know, I didn't sleep with him, but I wish I had. And if I get another chance, I will. Now let's talk about something else. Like how to escape from here. I think we should come up with a plan, then tell Melody and Bert right before we're ready to break out. That way, Mel won't have time to worry, and Bert will be less likely to slip up and spill the beans."

Sid seemed only slightly relieved by her admission. "Okay, Madame Houdini. What've you got in mind?"

Lizzie slathered her toast with butter and jam as she explained what Duncan had told her about the gate's mechanism. "This morning, I'm going to take a closer look at the dragon gate's operation. Duncan said the weight-of-water method can be overridden electrically, but I want to see if the old system might still function independently."

"Good idea."

"But there's still the money issue. We've done our bit and more. Frankly, I think we're due hazard pay, but that's probably too much to ask."

"Duncan's agreed to pay us per diem for as long as we're stuck here," Sidney said.

"Do you think you could convince him to tally up now, considering we've fulfilled our original agreement?"

"I'll give it a shot."

* * *

After Sidney left, Lizzie carried her cup of coffee into the breakfast room, where she'd kissed Alan last night. She peered out one of the tall, narrow turret windows at the ocean below and remembered his touch, his scent, how he tasted. The way his body felt against hers. *Don't get all goofy over him,* she cautioned herself. *You may never see him again, and you have other things to concentrate on now.*

As she turned to leave, her gaze fell on a sideboard that held a collection of framed photographs. Last night, in the dark, she hadn't noticed them. Stepping closer, she spotted soldiers in Union uniforms, women in Victorian garb, children in white dresses and buttoned shoes. A bearded man seated at the pipe organ. Two men standing on the deck of a sailing sloop. A man and woman beside a Model T Ford. Family portraits.

One pictured two young women on horseback, sidesaddle, wearing old-fashioned riding habits. Lizzie picked it up for a closer look. Although she couldn't recall the details of the photograph she'd found in Natalie Talbot's room after her death, this one seemed similar. Except the other photo showed a man and a woman, whereas this pictured two young ladies sitting on their mounts. One woman wore eyeglasses.

"May I help you, ma'am?"

Lizzie looked up, startled out of her thoughts, and saw Duncan's cook Febe standing at the kitchen door. "Oh, hello. I was merely admiring these delightful old photographs." She tilted the picture of the two equestrians so Febe could see it. "Who are these young ladies?"

The Italian cook wiped her hands on her apron and squinted at the faded photograph. She nodded and tapped it with her fingertip, leaving a spot of flour on the glass. "Miss Frances. And Miss Natalie. Long ago. Before the accident."

"What happened?" Lizzie pressed.

"Miss Natalie's horse ran in front of Miss Frances's. The horse tripped. It fell on her. Miss Frances was hurt very much."

Lizzie returned the photograph to the sideboard. Her thoughts flashed back to Yvonne's automatic writing and the message from Natalie: *I didn't mean to hurt you.*

"How sad."

"Mr. Duncan has cared for his sister all these years. A good man."

"Yes," Lizzie said, her mind spinning. "Thank you, Febe."

* * *

In deference to the morning chill, Lizzie buttoned a woolen jacket over her sweater. She rolled heavy cotton stockings up to her knees, secured them beneath gray flannel knickers, and slipped into what the English would call "sensible shoes."

She strolled along the path to the rocky promontory, puffing out small white clouds of smoke with each breath. Neither Kevin Wraith nor Bert cast their lines out into the sea today. As she passed the saltwater pool, she mentally shifted around pieces of the puzzle and watched them form a disturbing picture. Who had a stronger reason for taking revenge than the person Natalie Talbot crippled, before stealing the wounded woman's beau? Contemplating the Agatha Christie novels Lizzie loved, she ticked off *motive.*

She recalled the ramp in the hidden hallway that led up to Duncan and Frances Fox's private quarters on the castle's third floor. She remembered the sound of wheels rolling through the secret passageway beyond her bedchamber walls at night. She thought about encountering Duncan's sister in her wheelchair—in his library, where a trick door led behind the walls. Secret passageways ran to other secret doors, including one into the room where Natalie Talbot spent her last night. *Opportunity,* Lizzie said to herself.

Taking a seat on her favorite rock overlooking the ocean, Lizzie contemplated the last piece: *Means.* Her mind flashed back to a conversation between Kevin and Cora. Was it really less than a week ago? It seemed like she'd been sequestered here at Halcyon Castle forever.

Until recently, physicians routinely treated patients with heroin for all sorts of ailments. Surely a compassionate doctor would have prescribed the drug for a woman who suffered as much pain as Frances Fox did. But the Heroin Act outlawed its possession now, even for medicinal purposes. That meant people who needed it had to purchase the drug on the black market. Which brought Lizzie back to the business between Duncan and Roger. *If Roger can procure illegal alcohol, surely he can get his hands on illegal drugs.*

The lobster boat she'd grown accustomed to watching from this promontory motored into view, and its captain began checking his traps. Sunlight sparkled on the blue-green water. Even though a nip still hung in the morning air, the day promised to be mild. A damp breeze blew in off the sea, ruffling her dark hair. With some effort, Lizzie pushed herself up from the rock and shoved her hands into her pockets.

A good man who'd cared for his sister all these years, Febe had said of Duncan. Had he procured heroin from Roger to relieve Frances Fox's pain? Then another, more disturbing, thought surfaced in her mind. Had Duncan killed Natalie to avenge his sister?

Chapter Twenty-Five

"He looked around him wildly, as if the past were lurking here in the shadow of his house, just out of reach of his hand."

— *F. Scott Fitzgerald, The Great Gatsby*

She found Duncan in his study, seated behind his huge oak desk strewn with books and paperwork. He stood when she knocked on the open door and motioned her in.

"*Entrez-vous*, Lizzie dear. I'm glad to see you looking so well. Please, have a seat. To what do I owe this pleasure?"

She sat in one of his delicate Gothic armchairs and studied her genial host with his fly-away gray hair, tatty brown sweater, and childlike smile. "I doubt you'll consider it a pleasure once you've heard me out."

"Goodness me, this sounds serious."

"I'm afraid it is."

"Very well, then." He sat back in his leather desk chair and steepled his hands in front of his chest. "What's on your mind?"

Although she'd rehearsed what she'd planned to say, when it came right down to confronting him, the words caught in her throat. She coughed and turned away to gaze out a window for a moment before coming to the point. "It's about Natalie Talbot," she said finally.

"Yes?"

"I think I know who killed her."

"Ah." Duncan tapped his fingertips together in a staccato rhythm, and his eyebrows lifted like bushy gray caterpillars crawling up his forehead. "Have you shared your thoughts with the police?"

Lizzie shook her head. "No, I wanted to talk to you first."

His shoulders relaxed, and the caterpillar eyebrows settled back into a more-or-less straight line. "What do you think you've discovered, Lizzie?"

She crossed her legs, then uncrossed them again nervously. "May I ask a question?"

"Of course."

"Does your sister, given her injuries, take heroin for relief from her pain?"

He paused a moment before answering. "You realize that doctors are no longer allowed to prescribe heroin for pain, don't you?"

"Yes, but I also know that thousands of people in this country are suffering horribly from all sorts of injuries and illnesses, including your sister."

"What are you implying, Lizzie?"

"I know about Natalie Talbot's role in your sister's horseback riding injury. And I know that after the incident, Natalie ran off to England with the man both she and your sister fancied. That combination must have been devastating for your sister." She fixed her gaze on Duncan's dark eyes and thought she saw them narrow behind his spectacles.

Slowly, he nodded. "Yes, it was."

In a low voice, Lizzie asked, "Is it possible Frances killed Natalie?"

Duncan stopped tapping his fingertips together and sat quietly. He stared up at the wall above Lizzie's head. He breathed slowly and deeply, deliberately inhaling and exhaling as if following steps in an exercise routine. When he finally looked back at Lizzie, his eyes were cold and flat.

"I don't know how you could suggest such a thing, Lizzie, but I'm afraid I must ask you to leave now."

I've made things worse, Lizzie thought as she rose from her chair. *Not only have I offended our host, but if I'm right, I've tipped my hand and left myself open to risk.*

Duncan stood, took her elbow, and steered her down the hallway to the elevator in the ballroom. He pressed a button on the display panel beside the elevator door. For several moments, Lizzie waited for the lift to rise, rumbling noisily through the shaft, but heard nothing.

"Is it stuck?" she asked.

"No, it's locked."

"Why?"

"A safety feature. It prevents the elevator from moving. No one can gain access unless I allow it. Until I release the lift, it remains immobile in the basement," he said with a menacing grin. "Think of it as a modern-day drawbridge."

Duncan opened the door that would have led into the elevator had it been there, revealing a dark, empty shaft. Cold, damp, salty air whooshed up from the sea far below. Clutching her elbow tighter, he tugged her toward the opening. "Too bad Alan Peabody showed up to rescue you the last time you took a tumble. Well, he won't intervene now."

She kicked him in the shin and yanked her arm free.

"Ow," he yelled and lunged at her.

Lizzie slammed the heel of her hand under his jaw. His head snapped back, and she punched him in the Adam's apple. Choking, Duncan stumbled dizzily toward the elevator shaft. Like a fledgling bird trying to fly, he flapped his arms in panic as he tripped over the edge.

His thick woolen sweater snagged on the door's metal hinge. There he hung, four stories above the secret, underground loading dock, and boat slip. He kicked his feet frantically, desperately seeking a purchase.

Lizzie dashed into the hallway and called for help. "Sidney! Bert! Jonathon! Kevin! Mrs. Beane! Come quickly!" her powerful voice echoed down the stairway. "Duncan's in trouble!"

A creaking sound and the rumble of wheels caused her to spin around. Frances Fox, in her rattan wheelchair, rolled toward Lizzie. She held her arms outstretched to push the singer down the flight of stone steps. Just before the crippled woman reached her, however, Lizzie jumped aside.

Still breathing hard, Lizzie said, "I know what happened. Duncan got the heroin for you, didn't he?"

"Duncan took care of me," Frances said. "He's not a criminal."

"And you killed Natalie."

"I've waited twenty-four years to get my revenge."

Below, Lizzie heard scuffling feet and confused voices. "Up here," she called. "Hurry, Duncan needs help!"

As if confirming her plea, Duncan shouted from the elevator shaft, "Help!"

The castle owner's relatives and guests hurried up the stairs as Lizzie turned back to Frances. "Your brother tried to kill me."

"He was protecting me."

Sidney reached them first. "Lizzie, what's going on? Are you okay?"

"Yes, but Duncan's in danger."

Jonathon bounded up the stairs behind Sidney, taking them two at a time. "Where's Duncan?" Then spotting the crippled woman, he asked, "Aunt Frances, what's going on?"

Lizzie interrupted. "Duncan's trapped in the elevator shaft."

She led them to the lift and pointed at their angry, terrified host, who hung there helplessly. His ragged sweater served as his only lifeline.

"Get me out of here!" he demanded. His arms grasped at air, his legs scissored above the abyss.

"Stop squirming," Jonathon said as he assessed Duncan's situation. "You're hanging by a thread, literally. You don't want that sweater to unravel."

Mrs. Beane rushed toward them and stood gaping at the scene. Sabine followed.

"Get a rope," Jonathon told the house matron.

"Why can't you just grab him and pull him up?" Sabine's voice trembled, and her hands flitted about like frightened birds. She reached for Duncan, then stepped back in horror, realizing she could do nothing to rescue her father.

In a calm, steady voice, Sidney tried to assure the young woman. "He might slip out of our grasp or pull one of us down with him. Stand back, now, and let us reel him in."

Mrs. Beane, having assessed her employer's predicament, unfastened a length of heavy braided cord used to tie back a pair of the ballroom's drapes. She handed it to Jonathon.

"Wrap it around your waist, Duncan," Jonathon said as he tossed one end of the rope to his father-in-law. "When you're secure, we'll haul you in."

As Duncan knotted the drapery cord around his ample belly, a faint thumping caused Lizzie to turn around. Thaddeus Blake, leaning on his staff, entered the room. The others parted to let the esteemed elder pass.

"Quite a precarious position you're in, my friend," the old wizard said as he studied the man hanging by his sweater in the elevator shaft.

"Help me, Thaddeus!" Duncan cried.

With a bemused smile, the old magician stepped to the edge of the opening and pointed his leafy stave at Duncan. Duncan stared up at him, his face blanched with fear and desperation.

"Grab it," Thaddeus said.

Jonathon held onto Thaddeus. Sidney and Bert grasped the drapery cord.

"One, two, three," Jonathon said, and the four men pulled in unison.

Duncan's sweater ripped away from the hinge. A moment later, his body flopped like a mackerel onto the floor.

"Mrs. Beane," Lizzie said. "Please telephone the police."

* * *

Sergeant O'Quinn and another policeman, the middle-aged man with the ruddy face and bulbous nose Lizzie had seen rummaging about in Natalie Talbot's bedchamber the morning after the woman's death, corralled Duncan's family and houseguests in the castle's ballroom. All except Roger Young, whom Lizzie suspected had absconded ahead of the police, perhaps escaping on the green-cabined motorboat. They mingled awkwardly, avoiding each other's eyes, uncertain how to behave toward one another now.

The Troubadours took refuge on the stage, the place where they felt most comfortable. Bert tried to calm Melody, who now feared human menaces more than ghosts or vampires. He hugged her to his chest as she dabbed at her eyes and blew her nose on an embroidered handkerchief.

"Lizzie almost died, and now Duncan..." the flutist sobbed on Bert's shoulder. "I hate this place. I want to go home."

Lizzie sat next to them and stroked her colleague's blond curls. She wished she could bring Melody a glass of sherry to settle her nerves. "I'm okay, Mel. Duncan's okay. Everything's okay. We'll be leaving soon."

The big Irish cop with the long red scar on his face crossed the ballroom and approached Lizzie, his boots hammering on the wooden floor. He'd already questioned Duncan and Frances Fox, and handed them over to his fellow officer to keep an eye on them. Now it was her turn.

"Come with me, Miss Crane," O'Quinn said. He motioned for her to follow him into Duncan's library. "We can talk privately in here."

Lizzie sat in a chair in the alcove where she'd spent contented hours perusing her host's books. Where she'd first learned about Natalie and Gregory Talbot's questionable practices as mediums. The policeman remained standing.

"Miss Crane, Mr. Fox claims you tried to kill him by pushing him down the elevator shaft. He says he only survived because his sweater got hung up on a hinge."

"That's a lie! *He* tried to push *me* down the shaft."

"Miss Fox confirms his statement."

"Well, she would, wouldn't she? He's her brother. Besides, she murdered Natalie Talbot."

O'Quinn raised an eyebrow. "What makes you think that, Miss Crane?"

"She told me herself. Just before she tried to push me down the stairs."

Again, the sergeant gave her a dubious look. "The lady's in a wheelchair. How could she push you down the stairs?"

"Obviously, she didn't succeed. But she rolled her chair at me and tried to knock me off-balance so I'd fall."

Sergeant O'Quinn clasped his hands behind his back and paced across the alcove, then back again. Lizzie watched him, panic rising in her chest. She hadn't counted on the possibility that Duncan and his sister would turn the scenario around and frame her as the culprit. The Fox family had long-standing and respectable ties in this area. Lizzie was not only an outsider, but a showgirl from a poor family. A showgirl who'd been implicated just two months before in another murder case.

"Sergeant, Mrs. Talbot died from an overdose of heroin, as you know. Miss Fox takes heroin for pain resulting from an injury she suffered because of an equestrian accident caused by Mrs. Talbot. I believe that if you search her quarters, you'll find the drug in her possession."

"You seem quite sure of this, Miss Crane. Only a week ago, you denied knowing anything about heroin, and now you're an expert on its medicinal uses?"

"I've learned a great deal during the past week, Sergeant," Lizzie said. "I've also learned that Duncan Fox has been trafficking in alcohol and probably heroin. He has a secret storeroom located beneath this castle. Motorboats periodically deliver contraband there."

"How do you know about this alleged activity?"

"I've seen it. I've been in Duncan's storeroom and watched boats deliver crates of booze there." She considered telling him that Thaddeus Blake had accompanied her on her exploration, but nixed the idea. What if the old magician sided with Duncan instead of her?

"I can't investigate these areas you claim exist without a search warrant," O'Quinn said.

"How long will that take?"

"It depends."

"Sergeant, if you don't act immediately, Frances Fox will hide her drugs. Duncan and Roger Young will move their stock. You'll find nothing to base your case on."

O'Quinn seemed to consider her points. "All right, I'll telephone headquarters and ask them to draw up a warrant right away. In the meantime, we'll make sure no one has an opportunity to destroy evidence. By the way, who is this Roger Young?"

"I guess you'd call him Duncan's business associate or partner in crime. He was also Natalie Talbot's lover. By now, he's probably sailed off into the sunset and left Halcyon Castle in the dust."

Chapter Twenty-Six

"Truth is so often disconcerting."

— *Rafael Sabatini, Scaramouche*

Sabine sat beside her father at the oak trestle table, holding his hand and talking to him quietly. Her husband Jonathon tried to calm Frances Fox, who scowled at everyone in the ballroom as if she hoped looks could, indeed, kill.

Cora, Helen, Yvonne, and the Wraiths hadn't rushed upstairs in response to Lizzie's cry for help, nor had Gregory Talbot. However, Sergeant O'Quinn had ordered them all into the ballroom, along with the others. So far, no one had been able to locate Roger Young.

"Are we going to jail?" Melody asked, her blue eyes wide with fear.

"Poor little bunny, of course not," Lizzie said. "You haven't done anything wrong. I bet you never even stole a Tootsie Roll from the corner candy store."

"No, I wouldn't. But Lizzie...?"

"Yeah, I swiped a couple Tootsie Rolls in my day." Lizzie put her arm around her friend's shoulders. "Relax, Mel. This is just police procedure. The good news is, none of us is guilty of wrongdoing, and that means we'll be going home soon."

Sidney eyed her askance. "Bearcat, I still don't understand why Duncan was hanging in the elevator shaft or what you had to do with it. Do I want to know?"

"But you and Bert helped rescue him, didn't you, Sid?" Melody asked.

"They did. They're heroes," Lizzie said. "It's a long story. I'll explain everything during our drive back to New York."

* * *

Sergeant O'Quinn had insisted the elevator remain untouched. That meant the serving staff had to carry heavy trays of food upstairs from the kitchen to the third-floor ballroom to feed Halcyon's guests. By the time a courier arrived via motorcycle, bearing the warrant necessary to launch a search of the castle, the sun had dipped low in the sky, and tendrils of brilliant orange stretched across the steely-blue expanse.

"Keep an eye on them. Don't let anyone leave," O'Quinn told his fellow policeman. He motioned to Lizzie. "You, come with me."

Following his orders, Lizzie showed him to Frances Fox's quarters, which adjoined the library, but the door was locked. With a frown on his scarred face, O'Quinn went back to the ballroom, leaving Lizzie standing in the hallway until he returned jingling Duncan's set of keys.

Frances's apartment consisted of a posh bedchamber, a comfortable sitting room, and a bath outfitted with railings to aid her movement and provide support as she tended to her personal hygiene. Hepplewhite settees and chairs upholstered in ivory silk adorned the rooms, along with graceful mahogany chests and tables. No carpets on the floors, however, Lizzie noticed. They might have hampered her wheelchair's movement.

"Don't come in," O'Quinn said, pulling on a pair of gloves.

While Lizzie remained in the doorway, the policeman opened drawers and cabinets. He poked around in Frances's jewel chest, secretary, and wardrobe. He looked under chair cushions and behind window curtains. He disappeared into the bathroom, and she could hear him rummaging about for a time, but he emerged empty-handed and blank-faced. Just when she feared he might not find any reason to incriminate the murderer, Lizzie spied something that seemed out of place amid the chamber's feminine décor.

A humidor. So far as Lizzie knew, Frances Fox didn't smoke, and the room didn't smell of cigars.

"Sergeant, would you mind taking a peek in that humidor?" she asked.

She pointed to a marble-topped table on which a mahogany box sat. O'Quinn lifted its lid and reached in. After withdrawing a collection of Cuban cigars, he extracted a beaded purse. Carefully, he shook out the contents. From the expression on his face, Lizzie knew he'd found what he was searching for.

Digging deeper, he retrieved a pair of tortoiseshell eyeglasses. He held them up for Lizzie to see. "Do you recognize these?"

"I can't be sure, but they look like the ones Natalie Talbot wore. You could ask her husband to identify them."

"Thank you, Miss Crane. Now, let's see what else we can discover."

They took the stairs down to the second floor, where Lizzie guided him toward her bedchamber. As she unlocked the door, the policeman raised an eyebrow. One corner of his mouth twitched as he followed her in. She wondered how many ladies' bedrooms he'd visited and decided *not many*.

"We have to go through the walls to get there," she said.

He chuckled. "Walk through the walls, Miss Crane? You mean like ghosts?"

"Duncan's grandfather built a secret passageway behind the walls to hide runaway slaves. He was involved in the Underground Railroad. I believe Duncan, Roger Young, and maybe others used this passageway to move through the castle when they didn't want to be seen by guests and servants—or perhaps to escape if the police ever raided the place."

She crossed to the wardrobe and pressed a button behind it. Slowly the heavy cabinet swung away from the wall, revealing the opening Lizzie and Thaddeus Blake had climbed through when they went hunting for his wandering cat. "Do you have a flashlight, Sergeant?"

O'Quinn reached under his coat, unhooked a torch from his belt, and snapped it on. Then he ducked through the opening and followed her into the musty passage.

"That ramp," she said, pointing to her left, "leads up to the castle's third floor. You'll find another opening like this one behind a bookcase in Duncan's library. That's how Frances Fox got down here to kill Natalie without anyone seeing her."

"Let me guess. There's another opening into the room where Mrs. Talbot died."

"Bingo."

They made their way along the hidden hallway until they reached the secret entrance to the murder scene. The bedroom beside Lizzie's own. She located the button on the wall and pressed it. The wardrobe eased away, revealing the bedchamber where Frances Fox had ushered her old friend and foe into her final sleep. For the first time, Lizzie wondered if Natalie Talbot had been aware of Frances Fox's entrance into her bedroom in such a peculiar fashion. Had she known Frances meant her harm? If so, what last words had the two women spoken after all these years? Or was Natalie already sound asleep when Frances administered the lethal dose of heroin that sent her into the next dimension?

The big cop stepped inside, leaving Lizzie waiting outside. He made a circuit of the room, observing every detail. *It's as if he has a camera in his head, snapping pictures,* she thought. She remembered the photograph she'd found here the morning Natalie Talbot's body was discovered, and regretted having handed it over to Gregory. It might have been useful to Sergeant O'Quinn's investigation.

After ambling about in the room for several minutes, he seemed satisfied, although Lizzie couldn't see that he'd engaged in any further examination or collected any additional information.

"All right, Miss Crane, lead on," O'Quinn said as he climbed back through the opening behind the wardrobe.

The air in the passageway grew increasingly cold and damp as they descended the narrow flight of stairs. Moisture sheened the walls, and the briny scent of the sea tickled Lizzie's nostrils. They passed the bleak cubicle where long ago Quentin Fox had hidden runaway slaves, then rounded a corner and followed another flight of stairs down to the castle's basement.

Lizzie stopped at the heavy wooden door that led into Duncan's secret storeroom. "Here," she said.

Stepping aside, she let the policeman pick the lock and open the door. As he shone his flashlight into the crowded space, he let out a low whistle. Floor-to-ceiling racks and crates full of bottles stretched before them, exactly as she remembered. Dozens of casks occupied one end of the room. Lizzie led him through the adjoining larder, where ordinary foodstuffs were stored, and out onto the loading dock. Waves lapped against the pilings as the tide rolled in. With mixed emotions, she said, "This is where I saw the boat enter and unload its cargo."

O'Quinn strode back and forth, from one end of the dock to the other, his boots echoing on the wooden boards. For a few moments, he stared out at the opening to the tunnel as if waiting for a boat to motor in with a hold full of contraband. Then he examined the elevator that Duncan had locked in a holding position here in the castle's nether regions.

Lizzie closed her eyes and regretted how things had shaken down. She thought about the wounded woman who'd suffered so long and so deeply that she'd taken her former friend's life in revenge. The compassionate brother who'd sought to ease her pain, even though it meant breaking the law. The peculiar, triangular relationship between Natalie, Greg, and Roger.

Furthermore, Lizzie felt like a hypocrite. For years she'd skirted Prohibition's laws, imbibing with delight whenever she got the chance. Legislation hadn't stemmed people's desire for drink, but it had certainly increased crime and violence. The recent ban on heroin seemed equally misguided. So many people—including the elderly soldiers horribly wounded in the War Between the States and others like Frances Fox—relied on the drug doctors had prescribed for fifty years. Now, these same people risked criminal charges for trying to relieve their suffering.

Sergeant O'Quinn, apparently satisfied that he'd seen what he needed to see, tramped back down the dock where Lizzie stood waiting. "Do you know how to unlock the elevator?" he asked.

"No, we'll have to go back the way we came."

As they retraced their steps through the castle's hidden passageway, Lizzie lamented the situation into which she'd tumbled, like Alice falling down the rabbit hole. This engagement at Halcyon, an engagement for which she'd held such high hopes, had turned into a convoluted mess. *Why did you and your sister thrust me into this position, Duncan? You even tried to kill me. I never wanted to hurt either of you. All I've ever wanted was to make people happy.*

* * *

By the time Lizzie and Sergeant O'Quinn returned to the ballroom, servants had laid out foodstuffs the length of the antique oak banquet table. A few guests sat at the table, savoring their meal. Others had carried plates to more discreet areas of the spacious hall and ate from their laps. No wine was being passed around the table this evening, Lizzie noted. She glanced at her colleagues seated on the stage and cringed when she met Sidney's anxious stare.

As Sergeant O'Quinn approached Gregory Talbot, Lizzie dropped back a few paces, uncertain whether the policeman had released her. She studied Greg's face as the Irish cop held out the spectacles he'd found in Frances Fox's apartment.

"Do you recognize these glasses?" O'Quinn asked.

The widower nodded. "They belonged to my wife."

Greg reached for the glasses, but the cop hung onto them. "Evidence," Lizzie heard him say.

Sergeant O'Quinn drew himself up and puffed out his chest to appear even more formidable than he was as he addressed Duncan. "Mr. Fox, I'm arresting you for suspicion of trafficking in an illegal substance, to whit but not limited to, alcohol."

Duncan stiffened and turned to glare at Lizzie. She dropped her eyes sadly, wishing she could explain and hear his side of the story.

"Miss Fox," O'Quinn continued, "I'm arresting you for possession of an illegal substance, to whit heroin, and also for suspicion of the murder of Natalie Talbot."

A collective gasp swept through the ballroom as Duncan's guests considered the charges laid against their longtime friends. For several moments, they all fell silent before beginning to mutter among themselves. Lizzie quietly retreated a few steps at a time until the ballroom's shadows engulfed her, and she could watch the others' reactions without attracting attention to herself.

"I insist on contacting my lawyer," Duncan said angrily.

"Go ahead," O'Quinn said. "Do you have a telephone in your study? I'll accompany you there while you make the call."

Lizzie turned her attention briefly to the spread of food on the banquet table, but felt too dispirited to eat. *How sad this all is.* She tried to imagine Frances Fox, in her wheelchair, locked in prison for the rest of her life. She tried to envision Duncan Fox, with his playful manner and enthusiastic nature, rotting away in a cramped moldy cell for having abetted his sister. Surrounded by brutal and ruthless thugs who might slit his throat as easily as an envelope.

Although she'd had no role in Natalie Talbot's murder, and had only defended herself against Duncan and his sister's attacks, Lizzie couldn't help feeling partly responsible for the futures they now faced. Sidney was right. She shouldn't have nosed around in things that didn't involve her. She was an entertainer, not a detective. She'd been hired to bring these people pleasure, not to uncover their crimes. Viewed in that light, she'd failed miserably.

Chapter Twenty-Seven

"The city seen from the Queensboro Bridge is always the city seen for the first time, in its first wild promise of all the mystery and the beauty in the world."

— F. Scott Fitzgerald, The Great Gatsby

Despite Sergeant O'Quinn's commanding demeanor, Lizzie figured he must have reservations about the charges he'd levied against Duncan and Frances Fox, as well as how he would deal with the pair now that he'd charged them. This situation bore no similarity to the barroom brawls, robberies, and other common complaints he usually handled. He hadn't room in Gloucester's jail for a crippled woman, and what could he do with a rich bootlegger from a respectable family whose attorney would likely spring the man tomorrow? Watching the big cop smoke one cigarette after the other, she sensed his uneasiness and decided to take advantage of it.

"Sergeant O'Quinn," she said, "I wonder if I might have a moment of your time?"

He nodded and motioned her to the far end of the ballroom, away from the others.

"Sergeant, now that you've arrested Mr. and Miss Fox, and my friends and I are no longer suspects in Mrs. Talbot's death, would you be kind enough to allow us to leave this troubled place and return to our home?"

"New York, is it?"

Lizzie nodded. "Truthfully, sir, I'm afraid to remain here another night. It's been frightening enough this past week, cooped up with all these peculiar people. But now that Mr. and Miss Fox know I've exposed their secrets, well, I fear they may try to silence me."

O'Quinn rubbed his thumb along his facial scar and frowned.

"Please permit us to leave. After all, we're no longer under suspicion. We're no threat to anyone."

The policeman butted a cigarette off the ash of the one he'd just finished. His discomfort and uncertainty lay plain upon his ruddy face.

Time for a little theatrics, she decided. She leaned toward O'Quinn and spoke in a low voice, as if entrusting him with a confidence. She cast her eyes from side to side in an anxious manner like a hunted animal, studying each of Duncan's guests in turn. "Sergeant, I fear for my life if I'm forced to stay here another night with these people. You saw the opening into my bedchamber, which can't be locked. Mrs. Talbot died because she crossed Miss Fox. Do you wish me to be the next victim?"

When he didn't answer, she clasped her hands together in a gesture that seemed to both plead and promise. Her smoky eyes glistened with barely restrained tears. "Will you at least allow us to quit Halcyon Castle to a place nearby that no one except you knows about? Where we can be assured a modicum of safety?"

O'Quinn's broad shoulders sagged as he considered her request. "If I allow you to leave, you must remain available to assist me in this investigation as necessary. You must testify in a trial, should a trial come about."

"Agreed."

"You cannot change your address without letting the Gloucester Police Department know your whereabouts. You may not leave the country or attempt to hide from the law until this matter is resolved."

"I understand."

With an air of dismissal, the policeman said, "Go home, Miss Crane. But don't think for a moment that I'm unaware of your actions or that you can escape me. I'll know what you're doing and wherever you are at all times."

Relief washed over her. Whether he was bluffing or serious didn't matter. All she cared about now was going home. "Yes, sir, and thank you, sir."

* * *

"We're leaving. Pack up as fast as you can," Lizzie told her colleagues.

"The mulligan copper went for it, eh?" Sidney said.

"He has nothing to hold us on anymore. But we've got to get out of here quick, before he has second thoughts."

Fixing her eyes first on Melody, then Bert, Lizzie filled them in and gave them instructions. She noticed Melody's countenance brightening; a weight had been lifted from her shoulders. The flutist touched her amethyst pendant, fingering her good luck charm. Bert grinned and whistled through his gapped front teeth in anticipation of heading back to New York.

"Let's meet in the parking area in half an hour. I'll arrange to have the servants carry our luggage downstairs and stow it in Sid's auto." Lizzie shooed them with a wave of her hands. "Okay, go now."

After Melody and Bert had scurried off to pack, Sidney stared hard at his longtime friend. "I'm not sure I want to know, but how did you figure out who killed Mrs. Talbot?"

"It's a long story, and right now, we have other things to attend to," she said. "By the way, you did get Duncan to pay up, didn't you?"

"Yep. He wrote a check for payment in full."

"Let's hope it doesn't bounce. Okay, meet you at the breezer in half an hour. We're homeward bound."

* * *

At half-past eight, they arrived in Salem, twenty miles south of Gloucester, and pulled up in front of the new Hawthorn Hotel. The handsome brick structure next to Salem Common seemed like a sheltering fortress to Lizzie. She felt a rush of relief as a porter fetched their suitcases from Sidney's

Buick, stacked them on a trolley, and rolled them into the posh lobby.

"I've never spent the night in a hotel before," Bert said.

Melody spun around like a little girl, taking in every detail of the hotel's décor. "This is so pretty. I could stay here forever."

Lizzie smiled at her colleagues' childlike pleasure. *No more strange voices in the walls. No more ghosts or bats or other eerie occurrences.* Eerie occurrences she'd never figure out. She wished she could dismiss the horrors of the past week as easily as her friends did. But of course, they hadn't seen Natalie Talbot's lifeless body or been attacked by their host, or nearly pushed down a flight of stairs by his vengeful sister.

After checking them in, Sidney handed Lizzie a key for the room she and Melody would share and motioned to the porter. The man, dressed in a uniform that reminded her of an organ grinder's outfit, conveyed their bags to the elevator and held the door for them. Lizzie's thoughts spun back to her near-death encounter with Duncan. Her mind whirred, and her stomach churned.

"I'll take the stairs," she said.

* * *

They breakfasted in the hotel's sunny restaurant, with its white linen tablecloths and vases of fresh flowers on the tables. Melody babbled on and on about how happy she was to be going home, how she looked forward to seeing her parents and her new beau. Sid and Bert talked about the clubs they planned to play when they got back to Manhattan. Lizzie ate in virtual silence, only speaking when someone asked her a question. No one mentioned the murder, Halcyon Castle, or what had transpired there. Sooner or later, Lizzie knew she'd have to explain things to her friends, but right now, they all seemed eager to put the nightmare behind them and get back to their normal lives.

When Sidney called for the check, Lizzie excused herself and went to the lobby. A young man in a dark blue uniform smiled at her from the reception desk.

"May I send a telegram from here?" she asked him.

"Yes, miss." He handed her a form on which to write her message.

She pulled Alan Peabody's calling card from her purse and printed the address on the form. Then she wrote: "Dear Alan. I'll arrive in NYC tonight. Duncan and sister arrested. Much to tell. Hope to see you soon. Fondly, Lizzie." She handed the message to the clerk, along with the fee.

As she returned to the restaurant and her friends, memories of the red-haired man flashed in her mind. Less than thirty-six hours had passed since their nighttime tryst in the castle's breakfast room, yet it seemed like weeks, so much had happened since then. Perhaps, for him, however, real time still existed. Was his attraction to her more than a passing fancy? Would he respond to her telegram? Visit her in New York, as he'd promised? Alas, at a distance, she couldn't exercise her erotic power, which, she admitted reluctantly, was the only coin she had. Men, especially rich ones, held the high cards in life and love.

* * *

"It's all so sad," Melody said after Lizzie had finished telling her friends the story of Frances Fox's injury and betrayal by her childhood friend.

"Yes, it is," Lizzie agreed. "One can't condone murder, and yet it's easy to understand why she did it."

"What will happen to them now?" Bert asked.

Sidney flicked ash out the breezer's window as they motored south through Connecticut. "They'll be chained in a dungeon someplace dark and dank, where rats will bite them at night and demons torment them by day. The coppers will purloin all Duncan's booze and divide it up among themselves. The magnificent pipe organ will be silenced forever. Ghosts and vampires will take over the castle."

Lizzie slapped him lightly on the arm. "Enough, Sid. Don't go scaring them further." She turned to Melody and Bert in the backseat of the Buick. "That's all baloney, in case you didn't realize Sid was joshing you. Most likely, Duncan will post bail and go free today, or tomorrow at the latest. In the meantime, unless Sergeant O'Quinn puts a man on guard in the castle's underground storeroom, Roger Young will move the liquor elsewhere, if he hasn't already."

"What about Miss Fox?" Melody asked.

"Hard to say. If she's found guilty, she could go to prison or even be executed, but a jury might take pity on her. Maybe she'll be placed in an asylum." Even though Lizzie wasn't a religious person, the words *may God have mercy on her soul* echoed in her mind.

* * *

Night had settled over Manhattan by the time Sidney parked his Buick in front of Lizzie's apartment building in the Village. He escorted her into the lobby, where she located the janitor, and tipped him to take her luggage up to the third floor.

"Say, miss, they's a bunch o' posies come fer ya. Got 'em downstairs. Want I should fetch 'em up here?"

"Ab-so-lute-ly."

She expected Sidney to make a wisecrack or roll his eyes when the man returned bearing a bouquet of coral-pink roses and deep blue irises. Instead, he kissed her on the cheek. "Night-ski."

"Sleep tight-ski."

After the janitor had finished shuttling her belongings into her apartment, Lizzie locked the door and read the card attached to the flowers: "I'm coming to New York Friday on business. Please say you'll honor me with your presence at dinner. Alan."

She put the flowers in a vase of water and set them on her nightstand, where she could smell their fragrance throughout the night. Despite the exhausting trip home and the calamitous events at Halcyon Castle, she couldn't stop smiling. As she washed and readied herself for bed, the old saying about clouds with silver linings kept running through her mind. Tomorrow she'd telephone Alan to thank him for the flowers and accept his invitation. Tomorrow she'd shop for a stunning new outfit to wear to dinner.

Once again, she pondered the tarot reading Cora had done for her. Cora had warned of deception and danger, but she'd also predicted "an illustrious man in your future." Maybe there really was something to this strange stuff after all. Lizzie added a third item to her list of things to do tomorrow: visit Thaddeus Blake's store and buy a deck of tarot cards.

A Note from the Author

This is a work of fiction, though it contains real places and events that did happen. Except in the case of historic fact, any resemblance to actual persons, living or dead, is purely coincidental. When such people or situations are presented, it is in a fictional context. Halcyon Castle, for example, was inspired by Hammond Castle in Gloucester, Massachusetts, and includes some features similar to those in John Hammond's residence, such as the pipe organ. Hammond Castle did not exist at the time this story takes place, however, and no resemblance is intended between Mr. Hammond and the characters in this novel. Myopia Hunt Club and Gloucester's Unitarian Universalist Church, which also play roles in this book, are real and still exist, but the actions I describe as having occurred there are the products of my imagination.

I have endeavored to convey events, people, products, technology, music, literature, social norms, fashion, and other details accurately, in keeping with the period. I hope you'll find this information intriguing and that it will enrich your enjoyment of the story. And I hope you'll have fun reading about this colorful decade in our history.

Acknowledgements

First and foremost, I wish to acknowledge my fellow authors and friends, Kate Flora and Susan Oleksiw, who cofounded Level Best Books with me way back in 2003 to provide a venue where New England's many talented crime writers could share their work. Over the years, LBB's subsequent owners have taken the company to new heights, winning all the important awards in the mystery/thriller field and delighting readers not only in New England, but worldwide. I am especially grateful to Level Best's current team—Verena Rose, Shawn Reilly Simmons, and Harriette Sackler—for giving me a chance to reach readers who love historical mysteries.

I want to thank all of you who took the time to read early drafts of this book and who offered much-needed guidance, insight, and encouragement: Kate Flora and Susan Oleksiw, naturally, and also Paula Munier. Your editorial expertise was crucial in polishing this rough stone and making it shine. Thanks, too, to my writing group Mary Lee Gowland, Robert Swoboda, Des and Lenore White, Betsy Fields, Daryl Herring, David McCormick, Dave Kaczynski, and Donna Boy Dermody for catching my mistakes. I'm also grateful to my Level Besties for their support. Finally, I'm indebted to Debbie Sessions of Vintage Dancer for providing me with an in-depth course in 1920s fashion.

About the Author

Skye Alexander is the author of more than forty fiction and nonfiction books. Her stories have been published in anthologies internationally and her work has been translated into more than a dozen languages. In 2003, she cofounded Level Best Books with fellow authors Kate Flora and Susan Oleksiw. *What the Walls Know* is the second in her Lizzie Crane mystery series. Skye is also an astrologer and tarot reader, and has trained as a medium. She's best known for her many metaphysical books including *Magickal Astrology* and *The Modern Witchcraft Book of Tarot*.

AUTHOR WEBSITE:
 www.skyealexander.com

Also by Skye Alexander

Never Try to Catch a Falling Knife

What the Walls Know

The Goddess of Shipwrecked Sailors

Running in the Shadows

www.ingramcontent.com/pod-product-compliance
Lightning Source LLC
Chambersburg PA
CBHW020624110726
47899CB00002B/647